WRITING STEAMPUNK

Beth Daniels
aka Beth Henderson, J.B. Dane

First Edition   3 Media Press

WRITING STEAMPUNK

WRITING STEAMPUNK
© Beth Daniels 2011
First Edition

ISBN 978-1-257-3605-6

All rights reserved. No part of this publication may be reproduced, stored in a retrieval system (other than an e-book reader when in electronic format), or transmitted, in any form or by any means, without prior permission of the author.

Contact the author through 3 Media Press, P. O. Box 262, Englewood, Ohio 45322-0262 or via e-mail at Beth@RomanceAndMystery.com

Author's website: www.RomanceAndMystery.com

This title is available in trade paperback and also in electronic formats at Lulu.com, Amazon.com and BarnesAndNoble.com.

Introduction

Polish those brass goggles up, grab your parasols or your sword canes and carpetbags, and get ready to board the airship. Our dirigible is equipped with a lovely parlour complete with steam powered automaton waiters to serve tea or spirits, but do open the window should you feel the need to indulge in cigars, pipes, or hookas. Those of you with paranormal leanings, please refrain from considering the other guests as possible snacks.

It's time to board our vessel into the past, or into a parallel universe or alternative dimension or perhaps, even into the future!

Steampunk tales can take you any of these places.

Where we will not be venturing is into a discussion of the Steampunk society here in the modern age. There are numerous websites that will key you into what's going on in the...well, pseudo *real* world of Steampunk.

This book will also not tell you HOW to write a novel or short story. There are plenty of tomes available on these subjects. In fact, this topic is too plebian for us. Yes, you do need to know how to put together a plot, build characters, have them perform and fascinate, but again, other books will tell you how to do that.

What this book does is deal with writing Steampunk themed fiction. There are a lot of elements to cover, consider, and even pick and choose from.

Why are we sidestepping the Steampunk as a society idea though? Well, because not everyone who enjoys *reading* Steampunk is interested in living Steampunk. Many simply find that what they have been enjoying in fantasy books, at the movies, and on television actually has a name: Steampunk.

I have attempted to put this together in a way that will appeal to both Plotters and Pantsers (organic writers), so at times it may feel frivolous and too freeform to some and at other times a bit stodgy to others. It's a difficult fence to straddle, but the goal is to give launching pads for Steampunk ideas to writers of any preplanning organizational style.

There is a recipe for writing this style of story, and that is what we are about to spring into doing – stir up a batch of Steampunk magic.

In fact, let's get started on the journey of creation right now!

WRITING STEAMPUNK

TABLE OF CONTENTS

Chapter One
What Steampunk Is
Chapter Two
Making Your Choices
Chapter Three
Where to Begin
Chapter Four
Dazzling the Readers
Chapter Five
World Building
Chapter Six
Human and Mechanical Characters
Chapter Seven
Non-Human, Non-Mechanical Characters
and Magical Elements
Chapter Eight
Research Aids:
Wardrobes and Coinage
Chapter Nine
Research Aids: Weapons
Chapter Ten
Research Aids: Slang
Chapter Eleven
Research Aids: Entertainment
Chapter Twelve
The Markets

Appendix I
The 19th Century: What's Happening
Appendix II
19th Century Technology
Appendix III
Early 20th Century: What's Happening
Appendix IV
Early 20th Century Technology
Appendix V
The Competition

Acknowledgements and Author Bio

CHAPTER ONE
What Steampunk Is

Steampunk is a hybrid, a blending of many bits and pieces of other genres to create a new genre.

Well, subgenre, actually.

Steampunk falls under the major genre heading of Fantasy.

Because it frequently takes place in a pseudo past it also falls under the umbrella of historical fiction.

I said "pseudo past," right? That means Steampunk writers alter – sometimes mutate or mutilate --- history to fit their own purposes. Therefore it falls under the Fantasy subdivision of Alternative History.

We aren't going to stop there though.

Does it have a strong romantic theme? It can, which tucks it, sometimes, in the Romance field.

How about Action-Adventure? Absolutely! The majority of Steampunk tales incorporate just that! Thrills, chills, excitement!

Mystery? Suspense? Yep, put it in.

Horror or magic? Why not?

Science and invention and exploration? Yes, yes, and yes.

Steampunk can be dark; it can be silly.

It is the early science fiction of Jules Verne, H. G. Wells, and others, recreated and embellished by modern writers.

Steampunk can have any of the following:

Victorian/Edwardian Setting
In other words, the island nations of Great Britain (encompassing Ireland, Scotland, Wales, the Isle of Wight, etc.). Usually set partially within London, or totally within London, though there is nothing wrong with plunking it all down in Dublin or Edinburgh or Cardiff. This can actually be any time period during the Industrial Revolution which, while it began in the 18th century, we will put at 1800 on through and including the 1920s, perhaps even the 1930s.

American West
Frequently post Civil War era, but it can be set earlier. Settlement west of the Mississippi was limited prior to the 1850s when the various mining

rushes *really* began populating California, Nevada, Arizona, Colorado, Montana, Idaho, and Utah in particular. That doesn't mean you can't alter things. Go into the cities: Denver and San Francisco are the best bets as there aren't many large cities out this way until the 20th century – not even in Texas! Whether in the outlands or the infant cities, American West settings are usually known as Weird West Steampunk.

American East
Head East, thou diligent Steampunk scribbler! Any large city east of the Mississippi or on the Mississippi is a candidate for a Steampunk setting as well: New York, Boston, Philadelphia, Chicago, Pittsburg, Cincinnati, Cleveland, and those river cities of St. Louis and New Orleans can all offer fodder for your tale. In fact, any locale that has something worth mining for a story, like manufacturing or shipping, is fair game, not just these I've mentioned.

Go Elsewhere
Go where no Steampunk writer – or few of them – have gone and see what you can dream up using other locations in the world. Australia had gold rushes and was very much like the American West; the Orient was just opening to the West and looking very mysterious; and as Steampunk tales can go exploring, there's jungles and mountains and ice caps for the dauntless to seek out.

Go REALLY Elsewhere
An alternative universe or parallel world where steam power is still the preferred mode of energy and/or Victorian ideals or elements are prevalent is also an option – build the entire world to your specifications.

Head into the Future!
A future where Victorian ideals or elements are still the mode, of course – it's been done at least once, so why not do it again?

Stick with the 19th century Sci-Fi Classics
Take a leaf from the history of the 20th or 21st century and journey to the depths of the ocean, to the Moon or to Mars, only do it in the 19th century – Jules Verne and H.G. Wells took us there but it can be done again in your own inimitable way.

And if none of these appeal to you?
Just because these are the most common settings that HAVE been used, and are therefore familiar to readers, doesn't mean they are the only

ones that can be used. You can dream up any type of setting.

We'll go into each of these a bit more later on, but for now we're moving on. Why? Well, there's still a bit more *grounding* in the genre...er, subgenre...to do before we can get steam up. Think of this as shoveling those first chunks of coal in the boiler.

The true charm of Steampunk for a writer is that there are few things set in granite, or even in diamond. Steampunk is flexible, even if the iron of a steam engine isn't.

Rules of the Road

Obviously there do have to be *some* rules or guidelines to ensure that your tale be considered Steampunk. Based on what is currently available to readers, here's what these "rules" are:

1) As Steampunk stories are remakes, updates, reconfiguring, inspired by the first science fiction stories ever written, they need to be, in essence, Victorian. It doesn't matter where in the world or universe or alternative universe or parallel dimension they take place, the feel, the setting, is one with the Victorian world.

2) The story involves steam driven machines, clockwork mechanics, doing things that similar devices were incapable of actually doing in the time period. For Verne and Wells this was science fiction. For the 21st century writer of Steampunk, this is Alternative History.

3) The storyline uses elements of magic or that appear to be magic (such as conjuring, slight-of-hand, magician's tricks).

4) Because Steampunk is Alternative History, if set on Earth or involving the citizens of Earth, historical figures can appear or be mentioned. Queen Victoria herself has figured in a number of stories, though she might not recognize the portrait painted by a Steampunker's pen.

5) Paranormal creatures and the fae can become featured performers in your piece. Bram Stoker's *Dracula* was a Victorian release and Wilhelm and Jakob Grimm collected all those peasant tales and combined them in a book of fairytales

during the 19th century. Categories here range from vampires and were-creatures to faeries, pixies, trolls, dwarfs (the magical variety), banshees, etc. So can creatures of spirit such as ghosts, gods, demons, djinn, imps, devils and angels.

6) Science is very much a part of the Victorian era, and thus beings created by science are welcomed in Steampunk tales. These can be robots, cyborgs, people with mechanical limbs, creatures built from spare biological parts (Mary Shelley's *Frankenstein* is a Regency tale rather than a Victorian one, but it is still within the time of the Industrial Revolution, and considered a reaction to the creations of the Industrial Age). You can also breed your own biological creature or being. Or make your hero disappear (Wells' *Invisible Man*) after downing a bit of formula.

7) Mystery, suspense, danger, and frequently a ticking-clock feature (i.e. as there is a time limit in which to accomplish something by) can be part of Steampunk story. Not only was the science fiction genre created in the closing years of the 19th century, the mid to late part of the era gave birth to the mystery novel, the detective, with Edgar Allan Poe, Wilkie Collins, and Arthur Conan Doyle leading the way.

8) Time travel has been a fictional trope for a long time but it really kicked into popularity when science fiction was born. H.G. Wells's hero in *The Time Machine* went forward to a world that appeared nearly pre-historic, but authors in both fantasy and romance have been tossing characters back into the past for a couple of decades now. The trick is to make the process by which the traveling is done believable…and Steampunkishly creative for your audience.

9) Beings created via magic are another trope used in Steampunk. Golems, homunculi, and zombies are among these.

10) Practitioners of magic, though these do not need to be wizards, witches, sorcerers or shamen. They can be humans with a found or stolen conjuring book.

WRITING STEAMPUNK

If there is any guideline <u>that cannot, should not</u>, be broken it is this two-parter:

**The story must reflect
the world of early science fiction tales in some way**

and

**It must include *a being* either mechanically,
biologically, or magically constructed,
or with a paranormal, fae or spirit nature,
or a person turned into a monster via a mysterious disease.**

CHAPTER TWO
Making Your Choices

Deciding what elements to include in your storyline can be time consuming – but if you don't make a few decisions at the start, knowing what sort of world you need to build to set your characters in – well, it will be very tough going.

One of the first decisions to make is…

The First Decision
WHO IS YOUR AUDIENCE?

The answer is not readers who enjoy Steampunk. I mean, that goes without saying, right? No, we're talking about the age group.

There is Steampunk for adults and there is Steampunk for young adults, and middle grade readers. While all these stories will have similar elements, they won't have them appear in quite the same way.

For instance, you can offer the children's and YA audience some pretty scary situations, but you cannot – or shouldn't if you want parents to let your book through their door – go overboard with the dark slant to the horror or into detail on any sexual elements. For adults the gates are totally open for the most part. There are many niches within Steampunk that your story can slip into.

Naturally, this is why choosing the age of your target readership is the first thing to decide.

It also guides your hand in choosing your reading matter, the research materials needed. Well, let's call it what it is to us – fodder.

Yep, fodder. It helps to know what has already been written for your chosen audience before you start plotting out your own Steampunk adventure. There is a list of published Steampunk titles in Appendix V to give a leg up but right now we'll move on to making your first choice:

Adult audience or 12- to 16-year-olds or younger?

WRITING STEAMPUNK

The Second Decision
WHAT IS YOUR SETTING?

Let's move on to the setting for your story.

No doubt you already have a preference based on the sort of things you enjoy reading or have written in the past, only without a Steampunk kick. This time we're going to focus on the setting.

First, the "soil". The choices are:

England

Scotland

Wales

Ireland

The continent of Europe

The continent of Asia

The subcontinent of India

Africa

South America

An island in the Caribbean,
the Atlantic, Pacific, Indian Ocean
or other large body of water

Australia

Mexico

Canada

The Eastern United States

The Western United States

WRITING STEAMPUNK

The Moon

Mars

An Alternative Universe

A Parallel Universe

A Distant Earth-like Planet

A Space Craft

The Center of the Earth

Beneath an Ocean on Earth

Quite a few choices here, aren't there? Pick up to three locales, though one or two is the usual. I'm offering options here.

The **Second** choice in regards to setting is from among these possibilities:

The Early Industrial Age
(1750 to 1800)

The Mechanical Industrial Age
(1800 to 1850)

The Scientific Industrial Age
(1850 to 1900)

The Modern Industrial Age
(1900 to 1930 or slightly beyond)

The Future
(which is wide open to interpretation)

Much shorter list until you realize that it might be handy to pick a particular decade, or more specifically, an exact year.
That choice will take a bit more heavy duty pre-quill wielding thought though, so for the nonce, settle on one of the listed possibilities. Chances are you know enough history to guesstimate what could be possible

mechanically or scientifically within fifty years. If not, see Appendixes I, II, III, and IV for an overview of the decades and some dates for real inventions.

The Third Decision
WHAT IS YOUR FOCUS?

By focus I mean, are you planning on having an evil mastermind plot to take over the world? Are you going to change the course of history in a war? Are your characters going to be involved in a social revolt? Will they be scouring the jungles, the mountains, the deserts, or the depths of the oceans (or an off planet location) for fabled riches, a lost tribe, extinct creatures, or just out of curiosity because "it is there"? Will they be fiendish scientists doing horrific experiments on people or other living things? Will they be fighting demon forces with fantastic man-made devices, using magic to corrupt or save? Falling in love with their animatronic creations or…well, just what did you have in mind for them?

Scribble something down for an answer. Either use one of the generalities above, or if you already have a glimmer of an idea, jot that down. If you need further help consider these simplified ideas for a focus:

Action-Adventure

Spy Thriller

Medical Thriller/Horror

Supernatural Battles

Political Maneuvering

Murder Mystery

Industrial Theft

Caper

Mystic/Magical Threats
and/or Rewards

Detection

WRITING STEAMPUNK

Criminal Mastermind

Science Run Amuck

Romance

Immigration

Incarceration

Exploration

The Search for Knowledge

Comedy, Slapstick

Comedy of Manners

Utopian Society

Dystopian Society

Apocalypic

By the way, the world doesn't have to end by the close of an apocalyptic tale, it merely has to have a lot of the place be majorly in need of rebuilding – from buildings to social structure.

If none of these categories seem to apply, create your own for this choice – but make a choice.

The Fourth Choice
CONSIDER YOUR CAST

Again we have some categories that you might want to choose from.

The Inventor

The 19th century took the inventions of the late 18th century and hurled toward the future with them. Clockwork movements are an icon in the Steampunk world. They make it possible to do more than simply tell time. They run machines, they can run mechanical men, too. The man with a spanner in his hand and an oil smear across his nose is king here and he can do wondrous things. Babbage created what is considered the first computer in the 1830s, and that's real history, not altered or made up. There are lady inventors, too – real ones!

The Diplomat
The world she was a changing what with revolutions and the larger nations thinking they were helping less fortunate parts of the world by taking over and reaping the benefits of turning the natural resources of an unraped environment into profit for the governing body back home. Expansionism, colonization and Empire – all catch phrase words that kept diplomats busy throughout the world.

The Explorer
Why does one climb the once unclimbable mountain? Because it is there! Some explorers think this way. It's why they head off up the Amazon River, or into the Himalayas, or the jungles of the Congo, or to the Moon or Mars. For others it's the promise of Fortune and Glory. Let's find King Solomon's mine or the source of the Nile or that guy that went missing. Only one of these things happened in fiction, the other two are historical fact.

The Explorer-Diplomat
Strange category, huh? But many diplomats were also explorers and many explorers were diplomats. In fact, some of the best ones to harvest from historical fact were educated lady explorers who had to be diplomats considering they ended up meeting people who kept their women folk under their thumb in many cases.

The Scientist
Where the inventor tinkers with mechanics, the scientist plays with biology and chemistry and other naturally occurring phenomena like electricity. A number of discoveries were made in the 19th century, from Darwin's theory on the evolution of species to aspirin.

The Scientist-Inventor
This category seemed required for those fellows who played with electricity and created things to use it: Edison and Tesla. Now, I'm not saying that ALL of the creations that came out of their labs rated inclusion under *science* but there is no splitting the two categories where electric current and the mastery of it is concerned.

The Industrialist

These are the guys who build the factories that cause the pollution that ruins the health of workers and citizens alike in the cities. Most of them are of the middle class, because the 19th century truly saw the rise of the middle class to a position of power. In earlier centuries these people were looked down on by the aristocrats but with incomes falling among the peerage, the well dowered (when it came to pounds sterling or American dollars) daughters of the industrial giants began to look downright ravishing. It may be a cliché now, but I'll bet the industrialist father who manipulated a titled prospect to the altar was once very real.

The Merchant
These can be the folks on the street, the merchant prince who owns a fleet of ships, the banker/investor who funds various ventures in the hope of profit, the East India Company, the madam at the bordello, the used clothing merchant, the cobbler, the seamstress, the tea merchant. If they are selling wares of any sort in exchange for coin, they're a merchant.

The Royals
Naturally we have Victoria and her horde of children, the beloved Albert, and assorted relatives in Britain and across Europe who may or may not make an appearance. Vicky herself has appeared in a couple Steampunk tales. As royals usually have a hand, if not both hands, in running their realms, no matter where you run into them in the world, they are most definitely a class unto themselves.

The Religious
These are the Church of England and other various protestant groups, the Catholics, the Jews, Muslim, Hindu and other belief systems of the various peoples of the Far East, India, Africa, and the multitude of religions practiced by indigenous tribes in both of the Americas, Australia, and the islands of the Pacific. It also includes any ancient religions you care to revive, revisit, reinvent, or borrow from. There are always priests, ministers, monks, priestesses, nuns, and other employment opportunities to be had by characters dreaming of changing the world…or running it.

The Reformers and Missionaries
What with Papa and husbands (purchased or not) busy running factories or at the beck and call of the government, wives and daughters of the wealthy middle class needed something to occupy their time. As the middle class, unlike the peers, tended toward more of a religious bent, these ladies took to charities. Yes, there were gentlemen of the same mind, but there had to be since *ladies* could visit and suggest things but a

gentleman was needed to order things done. Orphans, prostitutes, unwed mothers, and anyone of non-Christian belief were all in desperate need of saving. Actually, laws did begin coming into being that limited the hours in a work day for children and adults as well as begin outlawing child labor for the very young. Missionaries can be self serving at one end of the scales and innocently incompetent but earnest at the other. These can also be people who found places like Hull House in Chicago or sit on the boards of orphanages. They could also be the newspaper people like Nellie Bly who exposed conditions in a series of articles.

The Socialites

This category covers those sweet young things being married off to gain a title in the family, or to refinance the family. It's also the mothers, the brothers, the uncles, the aunts, the second cousins twice removed. Socialites drink tea, gossip, shop, have their dressmakers visit them, engage in modest (or not so modest) betting when playing whisk or, later on, bridge. They are seen at balls, at the theatre, at spectacles, and may even be presented at court. They are the apparent social butterflies but they can also be forces to reckon with if matriarchs or strong minded misses. They can also be the moneyed and carefree and self-centered sons of these families, feckless characters spending the family fortune for their own enjoyment, which frequently involves horse racing, betting and gambling, dallying with actresses or bored young society matrons, etc.

The Servants

Upstairs, downstairs, in the kitchen, in the stable, on the home farm, these are the people who tend to be treated as though they were invisible. They see all, hear all, and sometimes get blamed for any item that goes missing or for being available and either overpowered or agreeable to bedding the master or the young master. They are indispensible when it comes to having shaving water ready, a gown pressed, curls crimped, boots polished, the table set, the plates filled, the floors gleaming, and the house running like it was on well oiled clockwork gears. They are also the first fodder fed to the proverbial cannon. You know the unnamed ensign who is the first to die when the crew steps out of the ship? His ancestors belong to this group.

The Spiritualists

These folks may be the ones running the table at the séance, contacting the spirits, or pretending to contact the spirits, but they could also be the ones who believe that the spirits can be contacted through the medium falling into a trance. Peering into crystal balls is 20th century stuff, but the spiritual movement was all the go in Britain and the United States, and no doubt on the Continent as well. Both Brits and Yanks being such gung-ho world travelers, they would have brought the fad with them wherever they went.

Members of the Royal Society
The Royal Society of London for Improving Natural Knowledge was the place to go for lectures on science, recent archaeological finds, and just about any other notion to catch the eye of one of their members. It wasn't easy to become a member, but to be one meant you were someone in the know when it came to matters requiring education and study, in promoting the Empire, and jolly well lording it over those weren't members. You didn't actually need to be an explorer to belong, but if you were an explorer looking for financial backing for an expedition, this was the place to go. Until they changed the membership rules, that is. Then it was scientists only.

The Military
As with any other century, the 19th had its full quota of wars. The British saw action against Napoleon and the U.S. early on, had continuing squabbles in India during the Raj (including a munity of the native troops), in the Crimea against Russia, in Afghanistan, in China, in Africa against the Zulu and the Boers, and possibly a few other places that haven't come to mind. The Americans went up against the British a second time (War of 1812), pirates in the Barbary states of the Mediterranean, the Mexicans (both over Texas in the 1830s and in the Mexican War of the 1840s), the native tribes in Florida, Ohio and Indiana, on West to the Plains and the Southwest and the Northwest, with the Spanish (in Cuba), and with each other. If you pick a different country, you'll have a list of engagements that are likely to include one or more of these.

The Military gives us enlisted men, officers, and various branches, such as the Army, the Navy, and the Politicals (the British military men who integrated themselves into the native culture and acted as spies, messengers, and whatever else was needed). We have infantry, cavalry, munitions, bands, surgeons, commissaries, camp followers, scavengers, raiders, engineers, scouts, and mercenaries. Let's not forget the deserters, too.

The Spies
Following the Military as it does, one tends to think MI5 and military intelligence, but we covered them with the British Politicals above. No

here is where we have spies who aren't attached to a particular unit, the sort who live in a foreign city and pretend to be someone they aren't. This also covers industrial spies who go undercover in a rival firm's factory to steal the secrets to their success then possibly destroy any data left behind. Spies can be Victorian versions of Jason Bourne, James Bond, or whoever you please.

The Urchins

Be they the innocent unfortunates like Oliver Twist or the street-wise pickpockets who work alone or run a gang of kids, teaching them the art of the undetected lift of a wallet, purse, or fine linen handkerchief, the urchins of London, New York, Chicago and any other major city with overpopulated slum neighborhoods are a cast to be reckoned with.

The Thieves and Pirates

One could think of these as those grown up urchins, I suppose, but they aren't always escapees from the stews. Sometimes they still live in the stews and do basic breaking and entering, just like always. Sometimes they upgrade to become master thieves themselves rather than part of a gang. If you don't have to work for Professor Moriarty, why do so? The days of the highwayman had faded but in its place came train robbery, both in the New World and the Old World.

Pirates in the Steampunk world can be upon the Seven seas, but they can also be in the skies above. Wherever there is a ship of any sort that can float next to another for boarding purposes, piracy beckons. While it's impossible with air planes, it's very possible with balloons and their cousin the dirigible.

The Resurrectionists

When a scientist needs something but the law doesn't want him to have that particular item, say a human brain, a spleen, a heart, where's he gonna go? To his friendly neighborhood Resurrectionist, of course! Their motto is "see new grave, see opportunity for cash." Whether they are selling the dead to a mad or merely curious scientist or to a medical man, these are the guys you gotta see.

The Entertainers

While there were a few actors and actresses and playwrights whose names were known to the public, who had "fans" in the previous century, the 19th century was the first to have far, far more…and to see these famous folk take to the road. With transportation so much more comfortable and fast once steam came into use, the beckoning call of going on tour was answered by many. There were the scandalous ladies who showed their legs (in tights) while performing acrobatics; famous singers and actors and actresses who headlined plays, doing one-night stands before enthusiastic crowds. There were authors who went on the lecture circuit (Dickens and Twain among them). And there were the variety acts: acrobats, magicians, illusionists, escape artists, circus perfomers.

Away from the theatres were the entertainments that required a larger arena: the circus with its menagerie of exotic animals, trick riders; and later in the century, the Wild West Shows with staged Indian attacks on settlers, holdups of stagecoaches, and fancy exhibitions of rifle and pistol target shooting.

As the 19th century closes down and the 20th begins, silent motion pictures begin to make their appearance, giving audiences a whole new venue to ooh and aah over – and a new group of actors and actresses (females of this period would have used the gender differentiated term rather than be termed "actors") to titillate the public's inquiring minds.

The Socialists

The 19th century gave us Karl Marx and his friend Engles arguing for the rights of the workers. Considering conditions and wages in the factories were terrible, a lot of ears perked up in the Old World. Marx had been run out of his homeland, finding sanctuary in England, but that didn't stop the growth of his ideas in Europe. Most of the fruit was born in the 20th century, but there were plenty of rabble rousers talking socialism in the 19th. And the Irish weren't happy about conditions either – but they hadn't been for years, wanting to shrug free of British rule. The potato famine didn't help much and immigration to America and Australia whittled away at the population numbers there. So social unrest is definitely something a Steampunk character could be involved in.

The Immigrants

While there were indeed citizens from the Imperial outposts arriving to set up shop in Britain, the majority of immigrants were bound out on the next ship, headed for bigger territories: the United States, Canada, Australia. Yes, a few went elsewhere, but the majority hit the ports of these three countries with wide eyes and even wider dreams. In the US, early immigrantes arrived from Britain, Germany. Many of the French, Dutch and Spanish were still here from when it had been their territory. By the mid 19th century the Irish were arriving on the East Coast and the Chinese on the West Coast, neither much liked by the populace. By the turn of the century, the flow came from the Mediterranean countries: Italy,

Greece, the Balkans. In Canada the French had never left, simply moved further north, and they would have experienced their own wave of immigrants. In Australia the first large influx of Europeans had been prisoners from English gaols, but when gold was discovered, anyone with a pick, a pan, and the fever was likely to show up.

The one thing all immigrants have in common is their desire to find a better life than could be had in their mother countries. Some planned to stay; some planned to make their fortune and go home. Few got that chance.

The Writers

Be they newspaper reporters, the novelists, dime novelists, or explorers writing up reports of their travels or linguists translating ancient texts for publication, writers can be those on the move, poking their nose into various situations, or living vicariously through their pens. There are a host of real life writers to use as models, from Nellie Bly to Charles Dickens and Mark Twain, to Ned Buntline, to Sir Richard Burton.

The Crushers

Or, in other words, the cops. After 1748, in England it was the Bow Street Runners who tracked miscreants down until Sir Robert Peel reorganized things in 1829, creating The Metropolitan Police Force. Peel reformed the criminal law system as well, tossing out a number of hanging offenses, and started paying gaolers. The Met began with 1000 constables and worked out of 4 Whitehall Place, a building that just happened to have a rear door that became the public entrance on the street behind. The address was 7 Great Scotland Yard. The public began calling the London constables Bobbies (in Ireland they were Peelers) after Sir Robert, and the force itself Scotland Yard, but to the criminal element they were The Crushers.

And interesting tidbit is that both Boston and New York City reconfigured their own police forces in the mid 1900s using Sir Robert's organizational set up as their model. In case you were curious, Interpol doesn't come into being until 1923.

Lawyers and Barristers

If you can afford them, need advice, a patent, or simply need an intelligent subject to experiment on, these are the guys. You can find them anywhere in the British Empire, though more specifically in London, and in America and other "new world" locations from cities to small towns.

The Aviators

WRITING STEAMPUNK

The first fellows to get closer to the stars without climbing a mountain were balloonists. Balloons began being used for aerial reconnaissance in wars, but the airship beloved of the Steampunk enthusiast made its first appearance at the Grand Expedition in 1851, with the first steam powered dirigible being flown the next year. The Golden Age of Airships began in July 1900 with the arrival of the Zeppelin LZ1 though. While there are a lot of dirigibles in the air over London in Steampunk books, it's wishful thinking.

But that's what Steampunk fiction is all about – wish fulfillment.

The Paranormals, the Fae and Spirit World Characters

Steampunk is a lot like urban fantasy – if the "urban" part is the 19th century city. Therefore it is quite common to find vampires, werewolves, and beings from the world of the fae represented in Steampunk. The spirit world can contribute to the cast as well with ghosts, demons, angels, djinn, and unemployed gods. Any of them can be major characters, the heroes or the villains, or merely part of the problem.

The Monsters

There are frequently monsters in Steampunk. Be they of the paranormal or legendary variety, made with nuts, bolts, and generators, or biologicals, here there be – in fact here there **must** be -- monsters. Build them yourself or invite them in with a summoning. Just put one in…somewhere.

The Fifth Choice
THE TECHNOLOGY

The Industrial Age actually beings in the 18th century, but for Steampunk purposes, writers tend to concentrate more on the years of Victoria's and Edward's reign (say 1830s to 1919), and this covers more technological development than one writer could ever use in a lifetime. Okay, maybe not quite that long but close!

The First Industrial Age concentrates on mechanical things, thus clockworks, the first computer (the Babbage engine), and the railroad fall into it. For simplicity purposes, say everything that was invented, created, patented and improved on prior to 1850.

That includes photography and the revolver (as opposed to its parent, the pistol), two items that have a large impact on invention and historical events in the later part of the century and into the 20th. The sewing machine and the typewriter are dreamed up, produced, patented, and improved upon. Factories – factories as we know them today as large manufacturing plants – were raised into existence to turn out goods to sell around the world, particularly to British subjects who were off converting as much of the world as they could into the British Empire.

The Second Industrial Age had its share of inventions as well, but science was its main focus. Or another way to look at it is, this was the era when we couldn't SEE how things worked as had been possible previously with those clockwork gears. Now things might as well have been working via magic, though it was science that gave us the telephone, the telegraph, the electric light bulb, 3-D pictures, moving pictures (as in flix, not those portraits in the Harry Potter books), phonographs, hot air balloons, and lots, lots more. The sort of things that today we take for granted. There were still mechanical things being created for it's easy to see how a bicycle works or a player piano. Even the engines built to run on petrol, that new comer to the field of power, had workings that were easily understood, and horseless carriages were in use in the 1890s.

And these things are merely a handful or so of what really DID come out of inventor's workshops. Think about what you could invent on paper by borrowing a few things from the 20th century or the 21st! Steampunk is about inventing your own pseudo world and filling it with pseudo devices.

So what are you going to need? Something to terrify, force, control, subdue an opposing force, be it at home or away? Something to make things run more smoothly, more economically, more swiftly, in a more organized fashion in the work place or government?

Is it related to transportation? If so, what is the terrain it must cover? Civilized countryside, untamed mountains, long stretches of desert? Should it cross the oceans riding the waves or cruising beneath them? Shall it conquer the skies for jaunts from country to country, or are you aiming for the Moon or perhaps Mars? Will you need to penetrate thickly grown jungles or journey toward the center of the Earth, or merely a bit beneath it (the Underground opens in London in the late 1800s, by the way).

There is a list of some of the inventions and when they were first produced in Appendixes III and IV, but for now, make your choices in regards to what you might need a contraption to do in your Steampunk tale. I'll repeat them:

> Something mechanical to terrify
> force, control, subdue
> an opposing force
>
> Something to make

WRITING STEAMPUNK

things run more smoothly,
more economically, more swiftly,
in a more organized fashion
in business or home

Something related to
land transportation

Something related to
travel in the skies

Something related to
travel underwater

Something to travel
through time
or into other dimensions

Some alien devise

Choices all made? They can be changed if need be, but they give you a starting point when it comes to research.

Yep, you heard right – Research. Why? Because you have some more questions to answer!

A FEW QUESTIONS MORE

IF you are going to stick with a Victorian setting, which means the story will take place somewhere within Vicky's reign, you'll need to decide exactly when and sort out some history, even if you'll be warping it to your own needs later.

IF you are going to set your story earlier than Victoria but still within the 19th century, and thus the Industrial Age, again you need to decide when and where.

IF you are going to use either of the above but NOT set the story in England, or not have all of the story roll forth in England (neither *Jonathan Strange and Mr. Norrell* or Gail Carriger's 3rd Parasol Protectorate tale stay within the bounds of the island kingdom), you need to know where else it will journey to.

IF you are going to use an American setting, be it in the American West, one of the Eastern cities, such as NYC or Boston, or lake cities such as Chicago or Cleveland, or a Pacific coast locale such as suitably foggy

WRITING STEAMPUNK

San Francisco, again you need to pick and point to a date.

IF you will be using machinery, is it going to be based on what was available, will you upgrade it, or will you create it from scratch? If so, what is it and what is it supposed to do? If the answer is "take over the world" it better be a doozy.

IF there will be automatons or golems or homunculi or similar constructs of gears and/or flesh and/or magic, who has them, how will they be used, and how were they constructed?

IF there is a strong romance in the tale, is the couple totally human, partly human, one human and one paranormal creature, or two paranormal creatures or the same or different geneses, or aliens or a combination with an alien? And when both aren't human, is it even possible for them to mate...not to mention how often will they be doing so and to what degree do you intend to give your reader a graphic image? (There are those erotic Steampunk tales, after all.)

IF there is a "take over the world" theme...the bad guys, obviously (though a real twist would be for the good guys to do it)...how are they going to do it and why and what will they gain, other than the whole world, that is?

IF there is magic involved, who is slinging it? The good guys, the bad guys, or both the good and the bad guys, and to what ends? And what type?

IF your setting is in a different dimension or on a different world or in the future, what Victorian and steam elements will be represented and how and why and all that jazz did they get there or not evolve past it or...well, whatever.

IF you are going to use any Darwinian elements what are they and how will they be used? Are they more DNA constructs as in *Leviathan* or something out of Mieville's tales or something silly like a giant newt that looks like Queen Victoria as Di Filippo delivered?

IF any famous historical personages will be waltzing through your tale, are they there for name dropping purposes or to set a particular stage or are they involved in the storyline, and if so, in what way and who are they? I'm thinking along the lines of Edison, Tesla, Marconi, Einstein, Freud, Marx (and not Groucho and his kin), etc.

IF time travel is involved, how will it be accomplished and can you devise a logical reason why it works?

IF space travel is involved (yes, in Victorian set Steampunk), when and how is it being done and is it manned or not manned?

IF exploration is involved is it into undiscovered territory such as areas of Africa, South America, Southeast Asia, the Himalayas, or to the center of the Earth?

IF hunting is involved, is the beast in question a yeti or one of its cousins, another legendary creature or a mythical one, such as a unicorn, dragon, gargoyle, phoenix, or something else?

IF mythology is involved, what civilization does it belong to and is it something known or unknown?

IF treasure is involved, is it something like *King Solomon's Mines*, King Tut's Tomb, or something similar?

Will you need to know much about or reconstruct or build from scratch anything related to transportation (yes, we have airships), communication over distance (Transatlantic Line, anyone?), entertainment, science, medicine, etc.? If so, what is it, do you have something to model it on, or do you need to dream it up from scratch?

These are just SOME of the questions that need sorting out and follow through on with research.

The most important reason you need to answer these questions then find research related to them is this:

**YOU CAN'T TWIST HISTORY
TO YOUR OWN DEVICES
UNTIL YOU KNOW
WHAT THERE IS TO TWIST**

CHAPTER THREE
WHERE TO BEGIN

Because a Steampunk story is built with machines in mind, you'd think that it's where we begin our research.

Not so. What we really need next is a year to tie things to.

Why? Although we are altering history to suit our needs, we still need to know what the one corner of history was like that we'll be using. Tying in specific things that DON'T change helps stabilize the world we're creating. In fact, the more things that stay the same, the less you'll need to build from scratch.

Choosing a year in which to set your story is a time saver.

It can also supply some inspiration.

For the sake of illustration, let's pick a year. How about 1839.

I'm starting with *The Timetables of History: A Horizontal Linkage of People and Events* by Bernard Grun. It has columns dealing with History and Politics, Literature and the Theater, Religion and Philosophy, the Visual Arts, Music, Science and Technology, and Daily Life. Since I'm not dealing with modern history, an old copy of this works just as well as a brand new edition.

As an example, *Timetables* tells me that in 1839 the First Opium War broke out between Britain and China, Edgar Allan Poe's "The Fall of the House of Usher" was published, John Lloyd Stephens discovered and examined the antiquities of the ancient Maya in Central America, Mendelssohn conducted Schubert's Symphony in C major, Charles Goodyear discovered the process of "vulcanization" making the commercial use of rubber possible, the metallic element lanthanum and the ozone were both discovered, the theory of cell-growth was formulated, the first electric clock was built, Abner Doubleday laid out the first baseball field and conducted the first baseball game ever played, the first bicycle was constructed, Cunard got in the shipping business, the First Grand National (that's a horse race) was run at Aintree, England, Prussia restricted juvenile labor to a maximum of 10 hours a day and W.H. Fox Talbot claimed that he obtained successes with his photographic experiments before Daguerre and communicates the results to the Royal Society.

WRITING STEAMPUNK

There's some fodder here, but I want more options, so I'm heading for *The Illustrated History of the 19th Century*. This supplies a month-by-month and year-by-year list of events, discoveries, etc. to work with…and supplies pictures, both drawings, paintings, daguerreotypes, and photographs. The benefit here is that I now know that the Opium War broke out November 10th. I also learned that Poe headed to Philadelphia to edit *Burton's Gentleman's Magazine*, that the first commercial production of an artificial fertilizer was applied to a turnip crop with "spectacular results," that Charles Darwin's *Beagle* Diaries were published (and no they weren't about the antics of his dogs), an English photographer was the first to successfully reduce the size of a paper document on film thus inventing the concept of storing information on microfilm, an abortion law was passed in the UK making it a three year prison worthy offense, two ships headed out in an effort to reach the Magnetic South Pole (the Ross Sea is named after James Clark Ross, the leader of the expedition), the British were also at war in Afghanistan, and the American West was opened for settlement and further exploration.

If I decided to set my Steampunk tale in 1839 I've already got a lot of things that are worthy of inclusion here. A bit of further, more detailed or in-depth research for things I want to freeze in their historical place and a half-cup of imagination could give me quite a bit to work with here.

How's this for off the top of my head: Our hero has just watched or participated in the very first baseball game ever played, but he needs to be en route to England for undisclosed reasons (he could be a spy! Either governmental or industrial…I like industrial for my purposes here). Tucking either the magazine in which "The Fall of the House of Usher" was published, or the current copy of *Burton's Gentleman's Magazine* under his arm, he manages to get passage on a ship partially owned by a fellow named Cunard who has big dreams. They fall into a discussion of Darwin's finds whilst aboard the sailing ship, *The Beagle*, and Cunard mentions the war in Afghanistan and how he's heard relations in China will soon disrupt the Opium Trade, damn shame, not that he agrees with that sort of thing. Our hero says he's tempted to find adventure in the Western Territories, shake a few Sioux or Blackfoot hands, but he's heard there are some rather mysterious gold items being unearthed in the South American jungles, some lost civilization or some such. Upon docking in Liverpool, our hero really gets down to business. Seems there is some deranged genius who intends to hold the world for ransom – if he doesn't get oodles and oodles of cash (the technical term for it, of course) he's going to destroy the ozone and suck all the oxygen from the atmosphere. And the plans for the machine he has built to do the evil deed are stored on a series of photographic cells (those infant microfiche thingies).

However, to complicate things the hero has to attend the Grand National and it is there he discovers someone else is out to get our evil genius, a girl out for revenge because the villain forced her sister to get an abortion or perform one and now she's on trial and will soon be headed to prison for three years and what with her sad health – consumption, you know – she'll never survive the ordeal!

Hey, have we got a possible story going here, or what? And all we've done is work with really basic information from sources that gave us just the highlights.

But wait! I left some of the data out! We never made it to the South Pole, though isn't it one of those spots where the ozone went holey in modern times? Could that early bicycle be used to create/generate electricity for the electric clock that could set off the destructo machine? Mendelssohn didn't get to conduct the orchestra, Goodyear's rubber didn't get used...but maybe it could be in the ozone eater? And if Mendelssohn instigates a really BIG crescendo...? What the heck is lanthanum and could it be used to destroy the world in our scenario? Perhaps when mixed with the fertilizer that grew that awesome turnip? Or is one of those turnips just the right size to jam the giant steam powered Destructo the Ozone Eater machine? And how could all of this be related to the theory of cell growth? Hmm, there should be a way. Our evil genius is probably ticked off that children in Prussia, where he grew up, now work shorter hours than he ever did, and Fox Talbot is lying about his own experiments predating Daguerre's because HE (our evil genius, not Fox Talbot) was the one who hired Daguerre to front his own success when it comes to the photographic process.

Ah, research! What a bountiful field of ideas just waiting to be plucked, shucked, processed, and regurgitated in story form.

I wouldn't actually recommend writing your story based on these tidbits, of course. You need to know a bit more about just a few things and then invent like crazy around them. Tempting though, isn't it? Particularly if you have a weird sense of humor? Afraid I do. But back to business!

What things like the *Timetable* and *Illustrated History* do is give names of things, of people, to go in search of. Your first stop can most certainly be Wikipedia, but move on from there...find actual books, be they paper or electronic, and get a good grounding in the things that will be most in evidence in your story.

I actually just opened the *Timetable* blindly and got 1839 but it supplied some really awesome Steampunk themes. Lost civilizations in the jungles of South America, Africa, Siam, India, the Himalayas, were popular situations milked by H. Rider Haggard, Arthur Conan Doyle, Edgar Rice Burroughs and either H.G. Wells or/and Jules Verne. The trip to the South Pole fits in here, too, as could the Afghan war or the Opium War.

We also have the concept of cell growth, the discovery of the ozone and that lanthanum (which I will really have to look up because it intrigues me now), and the reports Darwin wrote of the odd creatures discovered during his journey aboard *The Beagle*.

And if an electric clock has been invented in 1839, what else could conceivably be created using electricity by an evil genius. Just because Thomas Edison and Nikola Tesla put electricity on the map…and in the houses and down the city streets…doesn't mean we can't lift some of their work free from the close of the 19th century and relocate it to 1839. In fact, it's what Steampunk does.

And the evil genius *has* to want to take over the world, or rule a particular part of civilization – at least in this wildly spun scenario. Wouldn't you say the wealthy and colony rich British Empire was a good target? Taking over the government after destroying or having gotten control over government officials has been a rather constant theme in much of the Steampunk I've read. But that's because it is a reoccurring theme in science fiction and Steampunk is a remake of the first science fiction stories, the ones spun by those founding fathers Jules Verne and H.G. Wells. That doesn't mean you're required to use this theme. It's simply a common one because it frequently reflects what's going on in the world – someone is always trying to take over something somewhere, teach another country or society a lesson for simply existing, or gain a financial hold for selfish purposes, aren't they?

So how to begin your search for creative fodder.

1) Find a year and discover all the marvels and disasters and wars and discoveries, inventions, and mores particular to that year. Sure you can have a story arc that is longer than a single year, but that's a long time to cover. Best to keep it within a single year, and even better to within a few months, weeks, or days.

2) Go deep. Find out even more about these titillating possibilities by working your way from lesser, more basic sources, up to more detailed ones. Pick and choose what you want to use, what will give you the flavor, the adventure, the mouth-dropping awe necessary. You do want readers (particularly readers who are writers) to say, "Damn, why didn't I think of that?"

3) Now that you know what you have to work with, what else might you need to round out your particular Steampunk

WRITING STEAMPUNK

universe? Are you going to plunk the action down in Dickens' London? If so, just reading Dickens will give you a nice gloomy feel for Industrial London, or Manchester, or Liverpool, or any other major merchandise or shipping capital. Find a copy of *What Jane Austen Ate and What Charles Dickens Knew*, particularly if you are setting your action in England. Another handy source for London in this period is *Dickens' London*. If you're headed elsewhere in the world, find out what life was like there, in Calcutta, for instance.

4) Know your machines. What is being used, what's up and coming, and what has a twinkle of a future technology within its grasp? Build a bigger, a better, a more dangerous machine.

5) Know your society. For a rather fascinating twist on boxing and transportation to a penal colony read the Steampunk short story "Steampunch" (in the anthology *Extraordinary Engines*). I'm saying no more about the tale – don't want to give the twist away.

6) Know enough of politics in the era that you can twist them to your own devices. But only do so if politics will somehow relate to your story. Cherie Priest's *Dreadnaught* uses the conflict between the American North and South. She has not only stretched the Civil War out, she kept Texas a Republic rather than have it become a state, and gave Texians an interest in finding uses for all that oil oozing out of their ground.

7) Toss in some titles of treatises, novels, serials, songs, performers, plays, sports, and cant (slang) for flavor. It rounds out the "life" in any book to have such things mentioned but in Steampunk there's no reason why you can't have a jukebox in a Dodge City saloon playing Edison cylinders years before they were available. The Jersey Lily would have made the top ten on the Billboard charts, wouldn't she?

Now, stir well and create your scenario. We'll be adding other ingredients very soon.

Here are a few more sources you might access:

Industry, Power & Social Change at

WRITING STEAMPUNK

http://www.vam.ac.uk/collections/
periods_styles/ 19th century/
steam/social_change/index.html

The Power of Steam at Sea at
http://www.vam.ac.uk/collections/
periods_styles/19thcentury/
steam/steam/index.html

The Power of Steam on Land at
http://www.vam.ac.uk/collections/
periods_styles/19thcentury/
steam/land/index/html

Other Forms of Victorian Transport & Communication at
http://www.vam.ac.uk/collections/
periods_styles/19thcentury/steam/
other_transport/index.html

VAM stands for Victoria-Albert Museum, by the way.

- Robert's 19th Century History Blog (there are probably other blogs that would be helpful as well)
- *The Wicked Waltz and Other Scandalous Dances* by Mark A. Knowles.
- *An Alphabetical List of English Words, Occurring in the Literature of the 18th and 19th Centuries.*
- *The Civil War Word Book* (that's the American Civil War)
- *The Writers' Guide to Everyday Life in the 1800s*
- *The Writers' Guide to Everyday Life in the Wild West*
- *American 1908* (Yes, Steampunk does go into the Edwardian Age)
- *The 1811 Dictionary of the Vulgar Tongue*
- *The Dictionary of the Underworld*
- *The Dictionary of Vulgar Tongues*

This is just a sampling and mention of many of them will surface again as we go into research areas more in the coming pages.

CHAPTER FOUR
DAZZLING THE READERS

Once the Industrial Revolution got rolling, the rest of the world – particularly the British Empire – shifted into a higher gear, too. The more creations poured from inventors' workshops, the faster the wheels of progress turned. And once steam power was added, the Victorians appeared to feel Fate had most definitely made them the chosen people.

If you need some guidelines on what was happening in the world or in technology, be it 19th or early 20th century that you have your eye on, check the first four appendixes at the end of the book for simple guidelines. I've used that handy dandy *Timetables of History*, Wikipedia, and About.com to help compile this sampling...and it is only a sampling...of what was happening in the world in the 19th century, but it should be enough to get you started.

Of course, we aren't writing historical novels. We're writing Steampunk novels, and that means some alterations need to be made.

Let's go back to the things I found for 1839, only this time get serious about building a workable Steampunk tale.

If you remember the list from the first chapter, you know we need certain things.

MORE ON THE SETTING

Because Edgar Allan Poe's name comes up frequently in both the *Timetables of History* and *The Illustrated History of the 19th Century*, it is very tempting to use him as a main character. In the majority of Steampunk stories historic personages aren't given the role of hero or heroine, but rather appear as a minor character. However, Mark Hodder has a Steampunk mystery series where the Victorian explorer Sir Richard Burton is hired to be the Crown's sleuth in matters that aren't already covered by one of the various ministry offices. As a historical novelist outside of the Steampunk category, I already know that using a real person ups the time ante in regards to research. Therefore, I'm not giving Poe anything other than a very minor role. He may not even been seen.

I think I'll malign his memory instead. My tweak of history is going to be that Poe prefers to write poetry but he dabbled in short fiction with

"The Fall of the House of Usher" and there is a pushy publisher who wants him to write less poetry and more fiction. Poe's solution in the backstory will have been to hire my main character to be his ghost writer.

That's historical change #1.

Since Poe begins editing *Burton's Gentleman's Magazine* this year, and it is quartered in Philadelphia, that centers my story in Philadelphia or anywhere that my main character can easily reach by leaping on a train.

For further research purposes I now need to know a) what Philadelphia was like in 1839, b) if there was much to offer in the way of rail travel (though I can upgrade it), and c) what story my main character will be writing for Poe at this time, so some quick check of Poe's publishing history will be necessary, but I think he'll write those first detective stories of Poe's.

The answer to "c" can come from Wikipedia, probably as I don't intend to do anything more than possibly read the tale to be written, which I can likely get online as an e-book or at the library.

For "b" Wikipedia will probably be just a start, but there are maps out there showing the rail lines, and a further web search should help me narrow in on them. Historical Archive.com might have some for sale.

Now "a" will depend on how much of the story plays out IN Philadelphia. Again, I can get maps, but finding a link or source for Interlibrary Loan to drag in digital or microfiche copies of the Philadelphia newspapers of 1839 will give me an even better grounding. Newspapers inadvertently give a writer the names of hotels, restaurants, shops, theatres, events, and addresses that come in handy for an authentic touch.

I'm not messing with Philadelphia's layout or history other than how any upgrades to technology I decide to put in place.

RULES OF THE ROAD

The very first Rule of the Road that I gave you was that there needed to be a Victorian feel, an essence of the 19th century to the world the characters move about in. Leaving Philadelphia alone for the most part will do this, as long as I keep certain elements.

I think I'll keep the wardrobes historically accurate and mix in a dystopian touch by having my main character living in what amounts to a ghetto (to be found during my Philadelphia research). This will also allow me to mix in some period cant (slang) for flavor.

The second rule says using steam driven or clockwork mechanisms is necessary. This is another excellent opportunity to upgrade the technology. While the typewriter in reality doesn't begin turning up in offices or on writer's desks until the later half of the century, I'm going to give my hero one. Still, I like the very untypewriter look of the earliest models, so that will stay. But if I have him rubbing shoulders with a mechanic/inventor who is down on his luck and living in the same sad neighborhood, then perhaps a clockwork typewriter can be on my hero's desk. Perhaps it can be made more portable, too. I'm going to forego making it steam powered as he won't have cash to waste on coal to fuel it. A windup mechanism to make the carriage return automatic and give it a paper feed feature, now that is a moderate and doable Steampunk feature.

As I'm already planning to upgrade train travel, figuring in what manner I want to improve it is the only decision there.

I think he should have a quicker way of getting around town though than relying on any horse drawn conveyance, which would also be costly in the long run. The bicycle wasn't around yet, but something similar could be created, possibly with a clockwork "motor" that can be engaged or not. Perhaps he could travel with a parrot and use it as an alarm should anyone attempt to nip off with the bike. Worth a thunk or two, I think.

The third rule mentioned magic or something appearing to be magic. Magic seems very apropos to a Poe tale. Perhaps for a switch, it can be first displayed as a stage magician's trick, an illusion, and then turn out to be magic. Just have to stay away from Tesla type electric shows or it will come off too much like part of *The Prestige*. This does give me a fourth character though, the magician.

The fourth rule has already been seen with an offstage Edgar Allan Poe as a character. Whether to incorporate any paranormal beings will probably have to wait since I don't know what my plot will require yet. However, as I'm fairly attracted to the discovery of ancient Mayan artifacts, a twist on the "curse of the mummy" might be fun, and it would cover the fifth rule. There could be a local professor or museum patron who paid smugglers for one of the artifacts and it is now in Philadelphia with mysterious deaths following. Could be that the magician mentioned earlier has Mayan blood, or is a reincarnation of one of the priests?

My number of characters is growing: hero/ghost writer; Poe (offstage); mechanic/inventor; magician/reincarnated Mayan; professor/museum patron; smuggler; mummy (?).

The sixth rule says I need a created creature, either via mechanics, or biological tampering. Now, I don't ACTUALLY need something for ALL the rules of the Steampunk road, but I'll admit that it is the combination of all of them that draws me to Steampunk. That means, while you might not want a created creature, I do. And I do need a monster.

The mummy could fill this role. But in being an animated corpse, it is a magical security device, after all, and that's a different rule (number nine, in fact). Because I'd like to set this up as the first tale of a possible series, my world building for this first book really should include elements that will return regularly. There is nothing in this sixth rule that says the creature has to be evil or created by the villain.

I'm sorta leaning toward a robotic character and yet...well, it's obviously something to leave percolating in the back of my mind for now, so I'll move on.

Rule the seventh mentions mystery, suspense, danger, and a ticking clock. Yes, yes, yes and most definitely yes are my choices. This needs to be a mystery and an action-adventure tale to suit my tastes. I don't have a plot yet, however, I do have a number of Steampunk elements that one can be worked around or that can be woven into a plot line, so all's well. If it turns out that I can lift elements from a Poe story that my hero will write as Poe's ghost writer, it will fit in well. Simply have to find out what that story is.

The eighth rule brings up the idea of time travel. Although I have other stories that do use this fictional trope, I'm going to pass it up this time.

The ninth rule involves beings created via magic, and that's my Mayan mummy, so it's already covered.

The tenth rule of the road deals with practitioners of magic, and this is also a category I've covered with the stage magician who actually deals in magic rather than tricks of illusion.

We're down to the guidelines that weren't numbered but carried the admonition that they could not and should not be broken: "The story must reflect the world of early science fiction tales in some way" and "it must include a being either mechanically, biologically or magically constructed, or with a paranormal nature, or a person turned into a monster via a mysterious disease."

In this case, if I have the professor (who may or may not have been involved with the removal of the artifact from the cache at the Mayan ruin) sit down with the main character and tell about the expedition (yes, the dreaded flashback), the story will have the "lost world" feel with a touch of King Tut's tomb tossed in. That will work in regards to the early science fiction link.

I am going to read the second admonition to refer to a monster linked to the evil nemesis, in which case the mummy does meet the criteria as it is magically animated.

Now I just have one problem. I think I need to work in a girl somewhere to round out my cast of major and secondary characters. Oh, and dream up a plot.

WRITING STEAMPUNK

My Steampunk elements are in place though. They can be added to, in fact, they should be added to as the story progresses, but for now I have enough elements to integrate for this to qualify as a Steampunk story, a Steampunk world.

TIME TRAVEL

Time Travel isn't featured in Steampunk novels as often as one might think. That doesn't mean it isn't a viable element. But it's a tricky one.

In *The Anubis Gates*, a 20th century English professor travels with a group of wealthy people back in time to London where they are all to listen to a famous poet give a lecture. They travel in a coach with horses (everyone in authentic clothing, of course) driven onto a platform that is then activated and they are transported. Everyone has to be back in the coach and the coach at the right coordinates to be retrieved back from the early 19th to the 1990s, when the story was published.

What I'm getting at is, you need to have a logical method by which to travel. Doctor Who has the Tardis, and we need something, too.

Now it doesn't have to be a machine, though H.G. Wells had his character build one in *The Time Machine*. But it does need to be or sound logical, ergo, we enter the field of science.

Put your tea cups and whiskeys down, extinguish all smoking items (cigars, cigarettes, pipes, hookas), tie any bonnets down securely, settle those bowlers and top hats, and take a firm grip on your chair. We're about to travel…elsewhere.

TIME TRAVEL Part One: Of the Non-Steampunk Variety

You know, every time travel/historical tale out there is an alternative history tale (as is Steampunk). Usually it is a character from the present who is transported – stumbles, is probably more like what happens as it usually isn't planned – to a past era.

Sometimes they change places with someone – often enough with someone on their wedding night if it's a romance.

I've read stories where the modern heroine looked into her grandmother's mirror on a night when the moon was full and POOF they changed places – the uptight, proper woman from the past finding herself in a body that is REALLY foreign to her because it is pregnant and she's never given herself to a man. The heroine, on the other hand, finds herself in a form that has yet to experience passion and a wedding night with a stranger beckoning.

WRITING STEAMPUNK

That wasn't a drastic switch…and they did switch back into their own bodies just as the heroine, in the grandmother's body, was about to die just as the heroine's own form was about to be born. Very confusing, huh?

Another had a heroine in a castle in Europe at night…again the moon helped with the transfer and this time the "poof" popped her into the Middle Ages. She clashed with the hero, the master of the castle, immediately and was banished as a punishment to the kitchens. Except she was a gourmet chef in her own reality and began inventing things like cookies and designing eggbeaters and whisks for the blacksmith to make for her. SHE was definitely tampering with history.

It isn't often that the hero does the time travel…at least not in the books I've picked up – your experience might be different…and travel to the present doesn't happen nearly as often. However, it does in the movie *Kate and Leopold*, where he follows another time traveler (Kate's neighbor and scientist ex-boyfriend) and ends up in modern day New York. But he has to get back to his own time or things he is supposed to do that impact their future won't happen if he doesn't. The only question is whether she'll travel back with him, which means giving up a career and corner office that she's worked hard to achieve.

We're all familiar with the way Christopher Reeve managed to travel back to the turn of the century to court and win the heart of Jane Seymour in *Somewhere in Time* then gets yanked back into his own time just because he found a modern coin in his pocket. It's the kind of storyline where you go through a box of Kleenex at the end.

Another old movie has H.G. Wells chasing Jack the Ripper, who borrowed his time machine (one he used, not merely wrote about…at least in THIS reality), to modern day San Francisco. Well, if you've got the Ripper on the loose, of course you need a setting with fog, right? Naturally the Ripper sets his sights on the heroine and she needs to be rescued. And she goes back to the past with H.G. at the end. The movie is *Time After Time*.

Of course, just evoking H.G. Wells' name should bring to mind the original Time Travel novel he wrote, *The Time Machine* which takes the main character far, far into the future when mankind…well, isn't what it was anymore, and everything resembles the Prehistoric era in many ways.

In a *Star Trek* Classic (with the original Jim Kirk, Spock and the crew) movie, they manage to travel back in time to transport a couple whales back to the future because only whales can answer a message beamed at Earth – and if no whale answers, it's good bye Planet Earth.

Hey, even Superman managed to zip around the Earth enough times to halt the rotation and reverse time to save Lois since he didn't get there in time to prevent her dying. Think that happened in one of the Christopher Reeve Superman films.

What's my point in all of this? Time travel is a fictional trope that has been around for a lot longer than you might think. There are takes in Hindu mythology, Japanese folk tales and the Talmud that deliver "Rip Van Winkle" scenarios, so that idea predates Washington Irving's short story, published in 1819. In 1733 Samuel Maddens wrote "Memoirs of the Twentieth Century" in which an angel delivers political reports about life in the 1990s written by ambassorial staff reporting back to ministers in the 1730s. A story using the same trope as Mark Twain's *A Connecticut Yankee in King Arthur's Court* (1889) was written in Russian in 1836. Some folks consider Charles Dickens' "A Christmas Carol" (1843) to have time travel sequences rather than dream ones. An 1861 French tale has the main character transported back to prehistoric times, and in 1888 H.G. Wells' "The Chronic Argonauts" was a time travel tale that predates his more famous *The Time Machine* (1894-1895 as it was serialized in a magazine during that time).

And if you'd like to read "The Clock That Went Backward", a short time travel story written by Edward Page Mitchell and published in the 1881 *New York Sun*, see if you can get the PDF file to open at **www.horrormasters.com/Text/a2221.pdf** though if you can't simply feed the title into a search engine (which is what I ended up doing) and an html version can be found. The address was like a mile long so I'm not even going to attempt to give it. The search engine will get you there faster.

It's easy to see that the Victorian mind – the Industrial Age mind – looked at the mechanical wonders around them and felt anything was possible – including time travel.

The trick with using Time Travel in a manuscript is coming up with a believable – buyable as believable to your reader – way to actually DO the Time Travel. Wells did the obviously believable way…he built a machine for his character to use. Wasn't it a machine that our hero Sam used in the first episode of *Quantum Leap* that then proceeded to drop him in different bodies in different time periods to do something that the person themselves apparently couldn't do? And Marty McFly uses a car with a flux capacitor to go both backward and forwards in time in the *Back To The Future* trilogy.

Michael Crichton did the same thing with *Timeline* where his histio-archaeologists have their molecules broken down and transported back in time to the same site they are digging at so that they can rescue the head of the dig who traveled a few days earlier to the Middle Ages and was captured by the castle's soldiers and thus was unable to make it back to the departure site in time.

In *Brigadoon* they walk over a bridge on the exact day the enchanted town resurfaces for 24 hours not to appear again for another 100 years. I guess you could say the entire town is traveling through time though they don't interact with the outside – in this case, current – world for none of them can leave the town without endangering the rest of their friends and relatives, although modern visitors can come and go during that 24 hours. No machine though, just cursed. Or perhaps enchanted.

Ah – TIME. In nearly all of the things I've mentioned, there is a ticking clock involved. The return trip timing is set in stone…is unchangeable or sometimes unpredictable.

TIME TRAVEL Part Two: Steampunk

There are a number of different ways to use Time Travel scenarios in Steampunk or other alternative history scenarios. According to a really long article on Wikipedia (that had my brain overheating with ideas while being clueless about a number of things mentioned) these are some of the scenarios you might consider using:

1) "There is a single fixed history, which is self-consistent and unchangeable."

2) "History is flexible and is subject to change [because]…changes to history are easy and can impact the traveler or world of both" – they reference both *Doctor Who* and the *Back To The Future* trilogy – and "…history is change resistant in direct relationship to the importance of the event" – and it has to be a BIG event and they reference *Twilight Zone* and *Doctor Who* episodes as well as the 2002 movie version of *The Time Machine*.

3) "Alternative time lines" with a reference to a number of *Star Trek* episodes in Classic and spin-off versions.

4) There is also the Predestination Paradox that I thought was rather cool though tricky for this is an event in the future (or the character's present possibly) that helps cause an event in the past (well traveling from the future and interacting with people in the past could do this) which ends up causing the event in the future.

Did you manage to follow that?

WRITING STEAMPUNK

It depends on how believable you want your trip to another age to be...and who your audience is. A patly science fiction audience will want more science in the layout while non-science fiction audiences will be quite happy to buy into whatever seemingly believable explanation you give. You know, like that looking in the mirror thing. As Steampunk is fantasy as well as alternative history, one of its relatives is science fiction. And as it mimics the early science fiction tales of Verne and Wells, etc., there's no telling how precise your audience might want the details to be.

Now Stephen Hawking doesn't believe time travel is possible because there are no time traveling tourists visiting us – the dearth of such indicating there are none. Carl Sagan thought these travelers from the future could be among us, simply disguised to blend in – that's usually the scenario used in novels dealing with Time Travel, unless the traveling was done in a hurry or inadvertently (as Marty McFly does and H.G. Wells does in *Time After Time*, and happens again in *Bill and Ted's Excellent Adventure*. Doctor Who rarely changes what he's wearing and his companions might dress for the era now and again, but not always). However, to stick with the big names in physics, Albert Einstein's special and general theories of relativity DO permit the idea of Time Dilation. Thank goodness for that, right? Whatever Time Dilation is.

It, and a number of other things, left me speechless...particularly in regards to explaining what they are, but they all SOUND great. I'm sure a bit more in depth reading on whichever you might pick will clear the fog though.

Here are a few of the names of things that I plucked free from the Wikipedia entry...which was so long and involved I never made it past it to look for other Time Travel info.

- Time Dilation (already mentioned)
- The Theory of Special Relativity – the Twin Paradox in particular, apparently
- Gravitational Time Dilation
- The Theory of General Relativity
- Closed Timelike Curves
- Worldlines
- Gödel Spacetime
- The Tipler Cylinder
- The Alcubierre Drive
- The Novikov Self-Consistency Principle
- The Grandfather Paradox
- Mutable Timelines (*Back To The Future*)
- Ripple Effect

- Time Slips
- Cosmic Slips
- Black Holes
- Gradual and Instantaneous Time Travel (*Bill and Ted's Excellent Adventure* and the 1871 *Through the Looking Glass* and 20th century *Once and Future King* where the White Queen in *Glass* and Merlin in *Once and Future* both live backwards in time)
- The Ontological Paradox (used in *Somewhere in Time* and considered a violation of the second law of thermodynamics by Kelley L. Ross in *Time Travel Paradoxes*)
- Parallel Universes (which you can reference for a number of different alternative fiction titles as well as at least one *Doctor Who* episode, considering that the Tardis can't do dimensional slips – apparently previous Time Lords abused the privilege).

Oddly enough, the laws of physics haven't caught up to writers' imaginations yet. The "laws" allow that time travel may be possible but whether it will be possible to travel BACK in time – well, they are "taking the fifth" on that, clamming up, mum's the word.

None of this even touches on magic, and magic does surface in Steampunk as often as Time Travel does.

Unless you consider the power of Mother Nature to be magical for many time travel tales use lightning storms or the moon on particular nights, as portals in time or dimension.

THE TRICK

The trick to using Time Travel, whether in Steampunk or simply an Alternative History sort of tale, is to make it believable. And you do that with your set up. Explain just enough to have the reader nodding in agreement, make them feel it is possible using the machine or portal or incantation, and you've sold them on the believability of Time Travel in your storyline.

Now all you need to do is figure out if Time Travel belongs in your story and, if so, what kind.

CHAPTER FIVE
WORLD BUILDING

Because Steampunk is Alternative History every element that goes into your story is directly tied or influenced by the things you alter or construct as you build the world of your novel.

Of course there are also Steampunk short stories and novellas, but if you build a complicated world, a novel is really the best place to make use of it. In shorter things you are forced to narrow your sights when it comes to world building. We will spend some time looking at how to minimize things for shorter pieces, but let's go all out first.

So what are we looking at here? Characters, communication, transportation, altered events and the "what ifs" that resulted from them, things that one might take for granted if you lived in this world, too.

For illustration purposes, let's breakdown an already published Steampunk novel: *The Strange Affair of Spring Heeled Jack* by Mark Hodder © 2010. If you haven't read it, this is where I give the "spoilers" warning. I don't think too much is given away though.

What this title has going for it is 1) its fairly new, 2) its easily available from a major publisher, and 3) it has all the elements mentioned above.

CHARACTERS and ALTERED EVENTS

Hodder chose to use historical personages almost entirely. Here is who they are, their role within the story and how he altered their lives.

Sir Richard Francis Burton. Our hero here. Real life soldier, explorer, diplomat, writer, and linguist. He is still all of these in the story. Hodder only derails Burton's life at the point where he is searching for the source of the Nile. Then he hastily gets rid of Burton's fiancé and sets the explorer's feet on a different path as a special agent for the crown in 1861.

Queen Victoria. Hodder takes us back to 1840 when there is an assassination attempt on the queen. In reality, the queen and ***Prince Albert*** weren't injured. In Hodder's relatity Vicky is killed and after a bit of shuffling around behind the scenes, Albert becomes king.

Edward Oxford. Historically, Oxford really existed, really did take a couple of potshots at the royal couple, but he missed. Onlookers overcame him, he was arrested, went on trail for treason, was sent to Bedlam after being judged insane, then years later released. He went to Australia and died there in 1900. That's not how it happens in this story, though. Oxford dies after his shot kills Victoria, and thus…well, read on.

Everything that happens in this story is a result of what Oxford did in real life…and the what ifs that follow. Hodder supplies us with a second Edward Oxford, one who is a descendant of the Original (as the historical Edward Oxford is called in the book to distinguish him from his name sake). This new Edward Oxford is born in the 22nd century and at the beginning of the 23rd century has perfected a suit that will allow him to travel back in time and stop his ancestor from putting a black mark on the family name by attempting to assassinate the queen.

So we have a time traveler from the future arriving to do one little thing – stop his ancestor from taking the pistol from his coat and firing it. As we all know, it only takes something extremely small to start the changes snowballing.

And unfortunately, the man from the future is instrumental in getting the queen killed now. At one point in the story, the Edward from the future calls Burton a Victorian to which Burton replies, "what's a Victorian?" If anything, this Burton is living in the Albertian era.

But back to our cast.

Algernon Swinburne. A poet both historically and in the Hodder's book. He is a friend of Burton's and ends up being the explorer's partner/assistant on the case King Albert and Palmerston, the Prime Minister, have set Burton to. It is doubtful that Swinburne ever considered disguising himself as a chimney sweep lad as he does in this tale though.

Oscar Wilde. Burton's link to a Baker Street Irregular sort of network is through the newspaper boy he calls "Quips". It isn't until quite a bit into the story that we discover Quips' real name is Oscar Wilde. Historically Wilde was never selling newspapers on the streets of London as a boy.

Spring Heeled Jack. Apparently there was a mysterious "thing" that was given this name who appeared in the late 1830s, and again in the 1860s. Hodder simply made the Edward Oxford from the future his Spring Heeled Jack, fashioning Edward's time travel suit and what it did to match the descriptions of Jack. Then he gave this Edward Oxford a reason to be attacking young girls as the original Jack did.

Charles Darwin. Not everyone cared for Darwin's theories about evolution, but he wasn't ostracized historically as he is in Hodder's tale, which has him going into hiding and having another intellectual's brain surgically grafted to his. Darwin is one of our villains, you see. So is ***Florence Nightingale*** who to save the Marquis of Waterford's life, implants his brain in the body of an orangutan.

Henry Beresford, Marquis of Waterford. Our major villain in Hodder's tale. He meets an injured Edward Oxford, the time traveler, and while nursing him back to health learns about all the marvels of the future. As he knows inventor ***Isambard Kingdom Brunel,*** who is another of our historical characters, he mentions what Oxford has babbled and this sets in motion further alternations to this book's historical period. He wants Spring Heeled Jack's time travel suit so that they can learn how to make others like it. In the meantime, he jollies Edward Oxford along, sending him after each young girl in a search for the girl who married the Original and is thus his ancestor as well.

Hodder also uses the name of the constable who as at the scene of the attempted assassination in 1840 and promotes him to Detective Inspector at the Yard by 1861, giving Burton someone to work with in the law enforcement community. Otherwise, the constable had just that one bout with fame and faded from historical record.

COMMUNICATION

Hodder gives us three different ways for the Albertians to send messages.

1) There is a system that sounds very like an old pneumatic tube system (sort of like those at the drive up windows at the banks today). In this story we only learn of a few places it is connected to: the King's desk, the Prime Minister's office, two agents who work behind the scenes cleaning up things like bodies left behind – cleverly named by Hodder after the most famous Resurrectionists of the early 19th century – and Burton. For a message to reach the King, the tube is sent to "1", to the Prime Minister to "2". Burton is "4" on the list and urged to rarely ever send anything to Albert unless it is specifically requested.

2) Some biological tinkering has been done and a breed of dogs created that, in answer to three piercing toots of a whistle, will arrive at the door. They must be fed, and have voracious

appetites, then the message is handed to them, they take it in their teeth, the destination is given verbally to them, and off they go.

3) Parakeets. Another of the biological innovations here, these birds can be verbally given a message, rather in the format a telegram would be written out, and they will fly off to deliver it. They will even wait for and take a message back to the original sender. Unfortunately these birds have a defect as well (the dogs' appetites are their defect). The parakeets swear foully and insert insults into the messages.

TRANSPORTATION

There are seven different types of transportation used in *The Strange Affair of Spring Heeled Jack*, eight if you count the biologically enhanced giant horses bred to pull heavily loaded wagons; nine if you count regular conveyances that use regular horses. Ten if you count walking!

So what are those that are out-and-out Steampunk conveyances?

1) Hackney carriages pulled by steam-powered mechanical horses

2) Kites large enough for one person to ride in pulled by large swans

3) Large rotoships with more than one deck and accommodations for a crew as well as passengers

4) Rotochairs (my favorite actually) which are armchairs on runners with steam engines powering the roto blades that lift the single person conveyances above the fog, treetops, and houses. These are used quite a lot by Scotland Yard

5) The atmospheric railway system which runs on air pressure or pneumatic pressure rather than steam

6) Velocipedes, early motorcycles, and another of the Yard's requisitionable transports

7) And of course the suit the time traveler arrived wearing

THINGS TAKEN FOR GRANTED

Again, we're talking small things here. In this case there are crablike creatures who scuttle about the streets "eating" the refuse – including that...er, deposited by the animals pulling conveyances.

The Prime Minister has had a few alterations made to his appearance to appear younger, in other words he's had a bit of plastic surgery done.

THINGS THAT STAY THE SAME

The fog in "the Smoke" (i.e. London) is still dense, foul smelling and foully colored.

The Thames is still...well, gross is as pleasant a word as I can come up with and still be accurate.

The clothing everyone wears as well as the style of beards and mustaches remains. We have only a few women in the story so there isn't much about how they are turned out.

The correct Prime Minister is in office. Burton is still known within society for the things he did in real life prior to 1861. He is still engaged to the woman he historically wed, though here he breaks their engagement to her. The correct man fired a weapon at Victoria and Albert in 1840. Even our villain broke his neck in a riding accident at the right time, though in real historic time he died. And finally, as noted earlier, Spring Heeled Jack is portrayed as he appeared in all the reports of his historical appearance, even though he's a bit like the Mothman, more rumor and evidence free reports.

**CUTTING BACK ON THE WORLD BUILT:
THE NOVELLA AND THE SHORT STORY**

When you write a novella, you can still build a very believable world. It needs to be a slightly less "filled" world though.

For one thing, the cast is usually smaller. In *Victoria* (Spoiler! I feel like *Doctor Who*'s River Song), the hysterical novella from Paul di Filippo's pen, the hero is a biologist. Through his work, he enhances the growth of a newt to the size of a small woman. One that looks uncommonly like the queen, which is why he names the newt Victoria in her honor.

For the most part there are just four characters, if you want to count the newt as one of them, that is: our scientist hero, the prime minister, the queen, and the newt. The newt has no speaking parts, simply makes contented or fretful sounds.

What sells the story best is that our hero, who is the only character we follow, is very believable in his part. The consummate, out-of-touch-with-the-real-world nerd who is rather unassuming, he puts his foot down and demands his newt back at the story's close. The Steampunkishness of the story is that anyone could – or would want to – grow a newt to such a size in the Victorian era. As there was an underground of Victorian hanky panky (and Victoria's diary in the early years is quite enthusiastic about the marital bed) is accessed and used for every man who sees the newt wants to...er, have congress with it.

Otherwise, everything stays as it was historically. Well, almost. You can find the novella in *The Steampunk Trilogy* by Paul di Filippo, 1995.

For a short story, you'll be cutting back even further.

In "The Steam Dancer (1896)" by Caitlin R. Kiernan, which is included in the anthology *Steampunk II: Steampunk Reloaded* edited by Ann and Jeff Vandermeer (2010), the set up is very simple. This is more a "slice of life" tale as opposed to one where drastic events take place. The main character has lost limbs thanks to disease and vermin. A mechanic made metal parts to make her whole again and married her. They live in one room in a boarding house in a frontier town and to add to the coffer, she goes to a Chinese woman's place of business and, though untrained, dances in her own graceful combination of flesh and machine to the music. The story stays with this one character, though the husband and the Chinese woman are seen briefly. Other than the main character's rebuilt condition, there really isn't much in the world of the story that is distinctly Steampunk.

But it doesn't have to be. Too much would clutter the story.

The trick, then, is to tweak the history in a manner that a reader can feel is a logical progression. Yes, even the giant newt makes sense in *Victoria*. It's all in the presentation, the weaving of elements within the story, and the type of personalities given to the main characters. You can dream up all sorts of Steampunk elements to include, but if the characters headlining your cast can't sell it as "normal" within the story, the goal of having a saleable tale will fall short.

As you're writing a novel, take a look at the elements you've come up with so far. Do you have some that impact the "community" of the story, that is, they are not elements that only the characters on stage are use to or react to, but ones that are are everyday things anyone in your Steampunk world would call "normal" – like those transportation and message delivery systems I noted in *The Strange Affair of Spring Heeled Jack*, for instance.

Here are your classifications again:

TRANSPORTATION

WRITING STEAMPUNK

COMMUNICATION

ALTERATION OF HISTORICAL EVENTS

THINGS THAT DON'T CHANGE

THE SMALL THINGS
TAKEN FOR GRANTED

These will add layers to your background, to your setting. Don't just "invent" them or alter them. Go the next step and describe what they look like, how they are propelled or mutated, any defects that still need to be worked out, what they sound like, what they can and can't do.

The progression must be logical, believably possible.

Using these things can also add elements to the scenes as they play out. And can you have too many ideas on what could happen in the large playing field that is the middle of your book? No such thing as too many ideas.

Using them all is not always advisable though. Too much of a good thing is…well, a bad thing.

THE MONSTER

Remember I said – somewhere along the way – that the one thing every Steampunk tale I have ever read had was a monster? It doesn't have to be a scary one, just something that is abnormal, like the giant newt grown via scientific tinkering. It looks like Queen Victoria and when Vicky runs away, fills in for her on the throne until she can be convinced to return to her royal duties. Not that the men who get really turned on by the newt Victoria are anxious for the exchange. Extremely funny story.

I will admit that most of the monsters that appear in Steampunk tales are scary and usually were created by megalomaniacs or insane mechanics, scientist-inventors or biologists or via wizardry.

Think about what you already have put together for your storyline, about the characters you have waiting in the wings to take the stage.

Which of them is most likely to have created this artificially "different" being?

Why would they create it?

How would they create it?

The hero in "Victoria" is a scientist, a biologist, who was trying to breed a better newt and got a real whopper.

In other stories the creation has been a mechanical man or one that is part machine and part human – sometimes to give the "creator" a minion or worker and other times to make themselves more powerful either physically, mentally, or to achieve fantastic longevity.

Genetic tinkering results in "ships" that are animals in *Leviathan*, with crews maintaining them.

There is a short story set in Australia where the new wife finds her husband has a mechanical maid that runs via programming on punch cards. She finds that one of the programs is to satisfy what she sees as her husband's unnatural urges. The wife, left alone at the station, indulges her interest in mechanics and installs a few changes then leaves the station. When she learns that her husband is dead, she feels guilty because she had insured that the robotic maid's "administrations" would result in his death. Changes she had meant to disengage before leaving.

The main character in "The Steam Dancer" was the "monster" because she had been "repaired" and was now a combination of biological and mechanical parts.

The "monster" doesn't always have to equate to MONSTER. It simply has to be created using the things that were beloved of the Industrial Age or part of the Victorian (like Darwin's ideas).

And, yes, this being can still be created via magic as well. And it can be a paranormal being, like a vampire or a were-creature if it is a major character or "works" for or with a main character. Ditto in regards to members of the fae or spirit worlds. Or from other dimensions or alternate universes. The "monster" can be chosen from a wide pool of possibilities in other words.

Let me give you some examples, some categories, that might help you construct one of these.

MECHANICAL: Servants, workers, minions, aliens

1) Non-sentient robot, no biological grafts or parts. Mad scientists can turn these suckers out by the hundreds, maybe thousands depending on the scope of your story. These can be large, hulking monster vehicles that are wound up, powered by steam boilers or electrical current or they can be related to C3PO and R2D2, resemble dogs, cats, rats, mice, large bugs, small bugs, or tiny bugs. Unless they come from the future or a location off-planet, they shouldn't be nano-sized because with a Victorian or 19th century Earth or Earth-like setting you're limited to what a scientist can see. Part of the charm of Steampunk is that it is possible to see working parts, gears, pulleys, punch cards, etc.

Examples of this sort of robot or programmed mechanical (such as a computer) is the infamous HAL, the computers that have turned the human race into batteries, robots who have followed their programming to cannibalize available materials to repair a ship and have used human parts to do so (a *Doctor Who* episode), and any spider or roach-like creation that can emit poisonous steam or stab poison into the person they were sent to attack and overcome. These robots can also serve as waiters, office staff, assembly line workers, or sexual playthings (which references the example I gave earlier with the short story set in Australia). Even cylones for any of you *Battlestar Gallactica* viewers – the original show, not the remake. Even Data of *Star Trek Next Generation* is of this genesis.

2) Sentient robot, no biological grafts or parts. While robots like C2PO and even R2 appear to be rather sentient, they aren't. They might be personable and have personalities and even emotions but they can be turned off. A sentient robot can't be. They are alive. They could be killed and disassembled though. Examples are Johnny from *Short Circuit*, and the robot accused of murdering its creator in *I, Robot*. These beings no longer function as programmed, but make their own decisions.

3) Combination of mechanical and biological grafts or parts, mechanical dominant, non-sentient. Here you can think cyborgs, if you like. An evil scientist has usually helped themselves to living tissue they wish to use to enhance the mechanical properties of their creation. As these creations are far more mechanical than biological, since they aren't sentient, they act via program. However, that doesn't mean they can't be very humanoid in appearance. Perhaps we should call them androids.

4) Combination of mechanical and biological grafts or parts, biological dominant, non-sentient. This category is the android upgrade. A physical, biological body that works as a human (or other creature's body, for it doesn't have to be humanoid) but has a programmed brain. It is not sentient, therefore can not make decisions counter to its programming. The androids in any number of sci-fi flixs meet the criteria here, even when characters can't at first tell them from non-mechanical beings. In Steampunk, one probably CAN tell they aren't true living creatures simply because technology is still in its infancy, even

technology borrowed from the future – say, ours! They could be humans whose brain has been preempted by a technological feed, something implanted in their brain, that has stripped them of the ability to think for themselves, taken away their free will, stolen their humanity. Of course, there might be a very good reason for this. At least as far as the scientist who performed the alteration is concerned.

5) Combination of mechanical and biological grafts or parts, mechanical dominant, sentient. If you need a supervisor for the minions, a sentient creation would be a handy upgrade. No longer running on a program, this being could be grateful to their creator or out to get even with them for making a freak. Could also serve as librarians, office workers, chefs, soldiers, what have you. While an inventor might THINK they are the one in control, because this being is sentient, the tables could be turned.

6) Combination of mechanical and biological grafts or parts, biological dominant, sentient. Much the same as above but less of a mechanical appearance.

MECHANICAL: Lords, masters, leaders, aliens

1) Non-sentient robot, computer, machine, no biological elements. Programs run amuck here and because the creation can compute faster, is stronger, is whatever, it rides roughshod over its creator and any who try to stop it. Anything that doesn't match the programming is eliminated. Or stored. There is no evil intent, no intent at all other than to follow the program. While taking over and rearranging the way things are done, this creation can be inherently evil or benign.

2) Sentient robot, computer, machine, no biological elements. Same as above except that this creation has grown beyond the programming, has becoming a thing capable of original thought, decision making, etc. Could have emotions, might not.

3) Combination of mechanical and biological grafts or parts, mechanical dominant, sentient. This could be a case of medical science in action – the inventor, scientist, who requires limb replacement or aid to normal biological functions to stay alive and thus has mechanical parts implanted or attached or is placed

inside of a mechanical body to maintain life. The Daleks of *Doctor Who* are a bit like this, for there is a small, helpless, biological body inside a large mechanical one. And remember the little alien trying to protect the galaxy in *Men in Black*? While it's outer form looked biological, it was created of another material and wasn't living at all.

4) Combination of mechanical and biological grafts or parts, biological dominant, sentient. A lot like above but with a biological appearance. Could be confined to a mechanical chair or have tubes attached to sustain life, but otherwise, more an enhanced biological body. A bit more than a hip replacement, and using far larger parts if engaged in keeping the lungs moving or the heart pumping. Again, the reminder is that this is Steampunk and it has to look like a Victorian attachment. Think of the spider legs Dr. Loveless attaches to his legless torso in the movie version of *Wild, Wild West*, or the wheezing machine that keeps Queen Victoria's lungs functioning in George Mann's Newberry and Hobbs Steampunk mystery series.

BIOLOGICAL: Servants, workers, minions, aliens

1) Altered by mixed genes in breeding by nature, sentient. While nature can be fickle, usually these sort of alterations take place as part of evolution, a species adapting to their habitat, to the climate. An overly large gorilla, like King Kong, might be the result. Dinosaurs that didn't quite die out but are in a "lost world" such as that spun by Arthur Conan Doyle with Professor Challenger's adventures. These sort of things.

2) Altered by mixed genes in breeding by man, sentient. This is coming up with a cockapoo in a way, interbreeding two animals. Rather than mating a cocker spaniel and a poodle to create a new breed, this is mixing two different species to create a new one (perhaps in an attempt to recreate a griffin) or giving evolution a helping hand but with an agenda in the free hand. The Darwinist creatures in *Leviathan* fall under this category.

3) Altered by DNA grafting, sentient. Bringing back an extinct species, such as the dinosaur or mammoth and filling in any "holes" in the available DNA with what is available from similar creatures. Think *Jurassic Park*. And yes, DNA can come into it

for Friedrich Miescher actually did discover DNA in 1868. It doesn't mean Victorian scientists could actually do anything with it, at least not in real life, but in Steampunk...well, Darwin tinkered with it in the backstory of Scott Westerfeld's *Leviathan* series.

4) Cloned, sentient. Can't be done in Victorian times? Yeah, well, but this is Steampunk, so maybe it can if you dream up a good way to actually make it sorta believable. Clones don't always turn out to be exact duplicates of what was cloned any more than identical twins are totally identical, even though they were once a single cell.

5) Altered through accident by nature, sentient. Nature does this all the time: two headed goats, Siamese twins, extra limbs, missing limbs, that sort of thing.

6) Altered after accident by man, sentient. Whatever is done to sustain life, such as amputation. Your Steampunk scientist could get very creative with replacement parts.

7) Altered by accident by man, sentient. Oops! Drank the formula! Result: Dr. Jeckle turns into Mr. Hyde; the Invisible Man...er, disappears and can't reappear; bit by a radioactive spider a geek turns into a webspinning superhero. Get the idea?

8) Created by man, sentient. One word for you: Frankenstein. And I'm not talking about Victor, but his creation.

9) Natural beings, sane but not quite all right mentally (as in intellectually or mentally handicapped) and/or physically (handicapped or deformed). The Igors of the world?

10) Natural beings, insane due to a mental unbalance or the result of an event in their life.

BIOLOGICAL: Lords, masters, leaders, aliens

1) Altered by mixed genes in breeding by nature, sentient. Much the same as #1 under Biological servants but this time around they take control.

2) Altered by mixed genes in breeding by man, sentient. Ditto.

3) Altered by DNA grafting, sentient, a scientist or magician's creation inadvertently more powerful than they are

4) Cloned, sentient, the more forceful and/or intelligent personality emerges in the duplicate

5) Altered through accident by nature, sentient, much the same as #5 for servants, except that the force of will, power, intellect as been increased

6) Altered after accident by man, sentient, in attempting to cure or repair a person or creature a super "thing" is created through use of a formula or something else

7) Altered by accident by man, sentient, the formula tested on oneself, the dose of radiation, the step through the time vortex, the experiment gone wrong (like *The Fly*).

8) Created by man, sentient, Frankenstein's monster may look perfect, attractive, and possess charisma now that Victor has experience tinkering with parts but if he got Jack the Ripper's mind, or George Custer's or even Abe Lincoln's, the scientist is no longer in charge.

9) Natural beings, sane. Of course this doesn't mean they don't want to change the world or take over running the world or do away with certain things in the world. The cold bloodedly determined scientist, inventor, politician, businessman – could be any of these or another type equally focused. Could be beneficent or evil or somewhere in between.

10) Natural beings, insane. Jack the Ripper and other serial killers, but also any megalomaniac who has stepped way passed sane, though they could appear sane most of the time.

MAGICAL: Servants, workers, minions

1) Created accidentally by man, sentient, the spell missaid results in a new creature or spirit

2) Created purposefully by man, sentient, the spell altered purposefully and done correctly results in a new creature or spirit

3) Created accidentally by non-human beings, sentient, a demon, angel, djinn, or a member of the fae new on the job missays the spell and creates a new creature or spirit

4) Created purposefully by non-human beings, sentient, a demon, angel, djinn, or a member of the fae does the spell right and creates a new creature or spirit

5) Created purposefully by man, non-sentient, this would be a golem, created of mud or perhaps something else with a magic word written on a piece of paper and inserted in its mouth to animate it. Could also be a mummy or a zombie

6) Created purposefully by non-human being, non-sentient, a demon, angel, djinn, or a member of the fae creates and animates the golem, the mummy, or the zombie

7) Created purposefully by a paranormal creature, sentient. There's no other kind here for a vampire or were-creature can turn the human or animal they bite into a creature like themselves, and that bite probably has more to do with some original magic passed down in the "venom" or what you wish to call it, than it does with a biological process

8) Natural beings, sane, who can be put under a spell, mesmerized, to do one's bidding

9) Natural beings, insane, who can be put under a spell, mesmerized, to do one's bidding

MAGICAL: Lords, masters, leaders

1) Altered by nature, sentient. Born with dark magic, or white magic, powers they are unaware of when young, but still makes them a leader. The idea of a little magical power is dangerous but a lot of it can be deadly or do immense good

2) Altered by man, sentient. A mentor or the person themself finds a spell or magical artifact that increases their abilities

3) Altered through accident by nature, sentient. Falling into a magical vortex or absorbing power from a crossroad of ley lines or something along those paths increases the magican/wizard/witch's abilities

4) Altered after accident by man, sentient, a non-practitioner tries to do a spell to heal an injured or dying magican/wizard/witch

5) Altered by accident by man, sentient, a non-practitioner steals into the sorcerer's quarters, attempts a spell, and the sorcerer get the blast or ends up absorbing something in trying to prevent a disaster.

6) Created by man, sentient, the sorcerer/wizard/witch is sent by the king or their employer or via a trick to a place where the power inherent in the task will change him irreparably into another sort of person or feeds more power to him for use than he was capable of exercising before

7) Natural beings, sane. Merlin really ticked off? Queen Mab or Tatiana or Oberon or Puck

8) Natural beings, insane. Morgan Le Fay when not pictured as a member of the fae (she has so many incarnations). A banshee?

It's almost boring when broken down this way, isn't it? But it does show how many ways one can go when creating the "monster", be it good or bad, in your Steampunk story.

CHAPTER SIX
HUMAN AND MECHANICAL CHARACTERS

Whether they are main characters or minor characters, a Steampunk story usually has some humans and some of their mechanical brothers, or a human-mechancial conjunction thanks to a mad or no-so-mad scientist, in pivotal positions. I haven't run across a story where the main character was a machine – yet – but that doesn't mean the concept need be avoided.

Keeping your humans to categories that the early science fiction writers (Verne and Wells in particular) used puts you in safe territory. As these are frequent the type of gentleman and lady who actually lived in the Victorian era, research could be simply choosing a historical personage to model a character after. While mentioned briefly back in Chapter Two, let's look at a couple of these with an eye to actually hiring them as cast members in the story.

RESEARCHING EXPLORERS

The 19th century, of course, saw people going everywhere, looking for everything, and sometimes getting lost or dying or becoming famous in the process.

Very early in the century Merriweather Lewis and William Clark set out with a group to find what lay on the way to the American Pacific Coast.

Others headed into jungles on various continents or followed rivers upstream to discover their source. You might follow some of them (Stanley and Livingstone, Richard Burton, Frederic Caillaud, Charles Darwin, and others). There are some handy dandy primary sources to help you know what they might be up against.

Sir Frances Galton in particular went traveling, came back and wrote numerous tomes about the experience. You can still get his books, some POD, some Kindle, some reprints. Look for these:

The Narrative of an Explorer in Tropical South Africa with colored maps, plates, and woodcuts. 1853. Available in a POD of the original or via Kindle.

The Art of Rough Travel
Vacation Tourists and Notes of Travel 1860

I also found *Hints to Travellers* from the Royal Geographical Society (paperback reprint) which was used by late 19th and early 20th explorers like Shackleton, Scott, Burton, Fawcett, "and other legends who carried it into the field as a practical state of the art manual of gentlemanly exploration. Indiana Jones no doubt has his own copy, too," the website I found the information on gushed.

For accounts, or at least excerpts from accounts, written by the explorers themselves see *Dead Reckoning: Great Adventure Writing from the Golden Age of Exploration, 1800-1900.*

There is a list of 59 names of 19th century explorers on Wikipedia should you care to investigate a few.

Another web search resulted in *19th Century Exploration of Australia.* A slight warning: I could only get this to come up by feeding the name of the article into the search engine. You'll know you have the right link when **http://people.wku.ed/charles.smith/Australia/** is indicated as the site.

Also found an article from *The Guardian* (Tuesday December 8, 2009 edition) online which mentioned the local guides explorers used, many times women. Well, Lewis and Clark did have Sacajawea.

Men weren't the only ones exploring though. With the odds against finding a husband (women out numbered men by 4% in the population of England, Wikipedia told me), the more adventurous ladies who could afford to follow their passion for knowledge headed off as well.

Try *Victorian Lady Travellers* by Dorothy Middleton
Living With Cannibals
How High Can We Climb by Jeannine Atkins
Women Into The Unknown
www.distinguisedwomen.com

If you want a contemporary late 19th/early 20th century novel to get the feel for the adventure, try reading Conan Doyle's Professor Challenger Lost World adventures, H. Rider Haggard's Allan Quartermain tales such as *King Solomon's Mines*, or Edgar Rice Burrough's Tarzan stories.

RESEARCHING AUTOMATONS

Fortunately for us, the 19th century was considered The Golden Age of Automatons. In reality these were clockwork toys for adults to gaze upon with wonder rather than for children to enjoy, though no doubt they did as long as they kept their hands off them. The 17th century supplied the first human robot though...I think we can merely consider this a humanoid form, not a robot as we might think of it. HOWEVER, there is that possibility that we can jump our version back in time.

Try

www.allonrobots.com/automatons.html
and
www.automates-avenue.fr/web/historique/
or
www.handworx.com/au/gearwork/history/19.html
for other information.

And if anyone has seen the *Doctor Who* episodes with Madam Pompadour or the Space Ship *UK*, both have what might be called the typical historic look of an automaton.

IDEA PROMPTS AND SOME OTHER BEGINNING SOURCES

The Victorian Age can date to a few years before Victoria took the throne.

The First Industrial Age began in earnest in the 1760s, and continued to around 1850. It was mechanical in essence. Thus the Regency and the years prior to Victoria's reign can be settings for Steampunk as well.

The Second Industrial Age is more science related but very, very chocked full of inventions. Edison's Menlo Park complex is turning things out lickety split, but they aren't alone. This era begins around 1850 and moves toward the Diesel Era with motor driven vehicles beginning to make their appearance in the 1890s and early 20th century. Tales set in the 1900 through 1919 era (and a bit beyond) are more often referred to as Dieselpunk, of course.

The Edwardian Era begins in 1901 when Edward succeeds his mother Victoria. Although he dies in 1910, historians stretch this era to cover all of World War I, thus ending with the Treaty of Versailles signed in 1919. By this date the entire world appears to have changed nearly overnight.

While we talk about the Victorian and Edwardian a lot in Steampunk, the novels can also be set in the New World with North American characters. In the US the period most like Victoria's is the Gilded Age, basically the 1870s and 1880s, when wealth boomed…for some. These tales can also head out onto the frontier for Weird West tales (as can the Australian frontier). There is no reason they can't take place in post Civil War New York City, Boston, Chicago, St. Louis (which actually was the 4th largest US city in the early 20th century and hosted both the World's Fair and the Olympic Games in 1904), Philadelphia, Pittsburg, Cincinnati, Cleveland or New Orleans. Louisville, Memphis, and Nachez might also fit the bill. Any large city with a population large enough to have manufacturing, rich people, and neighborhoods of the poor works, and NYC, Boston, and Chicago all fit that bill. West of the Mississippi we really only have Denver and San Francisco as large cities. San Francisco benefits from that lovely fog, of course.

While Britain might have been sailing high (and around the world with all those bits of Empire scattered about) Europe was a bit slower to adopt the Industrial Revolution. The best era to equate to the Victorian and be called Europe's golden age is the Belle Époque. It comprises 1870 to 1918, or begins with the Franco-Prussian War (just a year long) and ends with the close of World War I.

And in respect to Steampunk, you can pick and choose, mix and match, and move things about to your heart's content. Cherie Priest has stretched the American Civil War out from four years to twenty, moved the gold finds of the Klondike from the late 1890s to where she wanted it, and populated the skies with airships. Scott Westerfeld let Darwin discover DNA, the British to leap into genetic manipulation to create living ships and the German/Austrians to concentrate on mechanical transport with spiderlike legs, then he started World War I.

You might access some of the following:

Dicken's London
The London Underworld in the Victorian Period
The Victorians
Looking Back at Britain: 1860s Peace and Prosperity
Looking Back at Britain: 1870s Holidays and Hard Times
King's Handbook of New York City 1892
*This Fabulous Century 1870-1900 (*Time-Life book*)*
Boston's Back Bay in the Victorian Era
Portsmouth, New Hampshire in the Victorian Era
The Englishman in China During the Victorian Era
Lights and Shadows in New York Life (available at **gutenberg.org/files/19642/19642-h/19642-h.htm**)
The Barbary Coast (for San Francisco)

To keep up on new books out, keep an eye on HistoryBookClub.com and periodically search your category via the online book retailers. Bibliographies are always helpful in leading you to sources.

Newspapers of the period, such as *The London Times* or the *New York Times*, are usually available on microfiche at a university library if not at your main library. Online you can find old newspapers as well at places like Newspaper Archives, but unless you are going to be using it a lot, the membership fee might be prohibitive.

Magazines also are a good source: *Godey's Ladies' Magazine, Demorests' Magazine, Frank Leslie's Magazine*, and others are helpful for stories set in the U.S. I used Frank Leslie's account of traveling cross country on the train from coast to coast in the 1870s when writing a historical romance, and it would certainly (and probably will) work well as a source for a Steampunk tale that involves train travel.

Find old maps, such as Britain's Victorian Ordinance Maps to give the names of brooks, creeks, etc. On a map in a book on Montana mining in the 19th century I discovered that the Ruby River was called the Stink Water River at one time. You can't make up a better piece of detail, can you?

And of course we have the Internet to hit. Try all kinds of variations on Victorian: England, era, homes, fashion, architecture; Victorians at home. Also try 19th century, and a mix with countries, cities, etc. Don't forget all those wars that might benefit from a Steampunk creation or two.

My first port of call is Wikipedia anymore because it supplies names, and sometimes sources, for me to search out. If you can get a reference librarian on your side willing to cruise primary sources or show you how to find them better, the search can expand in marvelous ways. I discovered a year's worth of *Demorest's* magazines bound on a shelf at the local university library, and via a bibliography got interlibrary loan to find and bring in four volumes about Chicago written in the late 19th century that supplied the names of sections in the red light district, the names of saloons, gambling parlors, of madams and the city officials who owned a number of these places. You can make these up but I like using as many real names of things as I can when writing a historical of any sort be it straight-factual based fiction or 52-Pick Up Steampunk.

Research is like stepping in a time machine without needing a wardrobe change or doing without central heating or air conditioning and knowing you won't die from drinking the water.

CHAPTER SEVEN
NON-HUMAN, NON-MECHANICAL CHARACTERS AND MAGICAL ELEMENTS

Steampunk is a mashup of elements from a number of genres, but I think that's what makes it such a fascinating style of story to write.

If you are writing a Steampunk romance, then the romance section will need to follow guidelines in the romance market, such as at least 50% of the story dealing with the relationship between the two characters.

If it's a whodunit style of mystery, then you need to play fair and have the clues before the reader's eyes, if a bit disguised and surrounded by things that lead them – and the sleuth – astray.

When it comes to paranormal characters and magic, these are both elements that have surfaced in nearly every fiction genre in the past, though at times they were barely seen, manufactured rather than real, and at other times the major focus of the story.

That changes with Steampunk. The paranormal and magical are equal partners in at least half or more of the Steampunk stories published today. Gail Carriger's main characters are (Spoilers!) nearly all paranormal for werewolves are govern pencil pushers, vampires are members of society, and our heroine's paranormal existence as one of the soulless allows her to touch either were or vamp and strip their paranormal nature away as long as her fingers linger on them. In Mark Hodder's *Spring Heeled Jack* story (new Spoilers! warning), the mad scientists have been experimenting, turning wolves into what equates to weremen, though they are still called werewolves, and one of the villains was "blended" with his white panther, giving him the cat's quick reflexes.

But there are other types of creatures that can meet your cast requirements. There's also more than enough sources to feed your tale's needs. It's what YOU DO with them that defines the style of Steampunk you write.

MYTHS

This is one humongous category. There have been myths told around the fire, turned into religions, and used to scare children into behaving...or as morality tales for their parents, considering there are two ways to look at these things...for at least seven thousand years – which takes us back to the earliest known settlements in Mesopotamia in the Chalcolithic Period of 5300 BCE. Of course, we probably aren't going to find anything to use from that period, we'll have to move up to Sumer in the 4th millennium BC to harvest a nice god or his pet monster.

If you don't care to evoke the old gods of the Fertile Crescent or another part of the world (China was up and running – and possibly even writing – in 4000 BCE), move forward in time and a bit west or north. This will place you in Egypt or Greece. As Rome borrowed and renamed a lot of the Greek gods and monsters they bred and fought, you have a choice of what to call them. Head further North and the Celts begin to supply some nice myths. And the Celts are everywhere – nudging the Britons (who have their own library of otherworldly folk) out of the way.

Move to the Americas for a different take on many of the same tales; to the various regions of Africa, to India, Australia, the Himalayas, the jungles of Malaysia. Wherever there are people, there are stories of gods, monsters, and their adventures. Pluck some free if you like, then reshape them to suit your needs. (See *The Anubis Gate* for a sample from Egypt; and based on the 3rd of Gail Carriger's books, it looks like Book the Fourth will dip into this as well.)

LEGENDS

I'm taking the stand that Legends are a bit different than Myths. Myths are full of stories but they are more often than not the mythology of a religion. I'm going to say that Legends are about the children of the gods, the ones half human, who still have to go up against monsters, who are also oddly enough the children of the gods.

Ever read the oldest book in existence? *Gilamesh* – it's short, it repeats a lot (hey, but so does the Old Testament) but it's a classic. Very harvestable for unlikely...er, cast members. And Gilamesh deals with the Flood long before Noah starts building that ark, it predates the earliest Biblical tales, the ones in Genesis. What if Gilamesh traveled forward in time...a long way forward in time...and still thought he was ruler of all that he could see? Might cause a few problems, eh what?

The people in the Bible deal with Legends. And not all legends are heroic, either. Goliath is a legendary type character but he was on the wrong side and falls by the hand of our more astounding legendary hero, David. He could have had family though, family that went in for those begettings wholeheartedly. They might rule a hidden valley somewhere where Victorian explorers dare to tread.

Heroes in the Bible have mysterious talents as much as those in the Greek tales. Look at what Samson can do when his hair goes unsheared. Daniel doesn't do badly in the lion's den, either, does he? And Joseph has a cool hand when spelling out the meaning of dreams. Maybe Yahweh hasn't stopped doling out those kind of gifts.

Some of the legends end up based on actual events – like the Trojan War, though Helen might not have existed. And *The Iliad* made *The Odyssey* with all those adventures possible. Fiction? Perhaps, but spun from tales long told of such monsters. Odysseus might not have killed them all, you know. Could be it isn't just the Hydra that comes back with more heads than were cut off.

Let's take a giant leap in time – forward, not backward – and consider another legend: *Beowulf*. Grendel is a monster in need of crushing, isn't he? It? Urban fantasy folks comb through these tales and pluck things free so why not us? (Jim Butcher has a grendel in one of his Dresden Files short stories, not Steampunk but Urban Fantasy.) After all, Steampunk is quite like Urban Fantasy, just set in a non-contemporary setting. A lot of times it uses the same cities – London is very popular with the otherworldly. Monsters work so well with places that are foggy, able to pop out of the shadows and do what needs to be done according to the job requirements you've given them.

There are a lot of legends, and there were many more dreamed up as people moved further and further west (like Paul Bunyan, John Henry, Pecos Bill), but the all time favorite legendary character has got to be King Arthur. He's got Merlin. He's got knights to battle a whole bestiary of creatures that never existed, and has he ever got staying power! And he's supposed to return.

FAIRYTALES

While we think of Jakob and Wilhelm Grimm when it comes to Fairytales, all they did was collect them from peasants and spell them out in a format that wouldn't change as the verbal versions might do. Oddly enough, there are tales of Cinderella like girls told in China, among the American Indians, and in many other cultures. We're going to concentrate on the Grimm tales though. The brothers were well surnamed for these tales. If you read their originals, you will find very little to recognize when comparing them to Disney versions…and, heck, Disney can scare a few months growth off a kid (which kids seem to love…we did, right?)

Fairytales give us dwarves, witches, fairies of godmother persuasion and evil ones as well, wolves that are cross-dressing grandmothers, dragons, pixies, elves, trolls, and this list is just off the top of my head.

But fairytales are a different type of legend, too, the type that can scare one: vampires, werewolves and other were-creatures, mermaids, sirens, shape shifters that aren't weres, demons, djinn, devils, angels.

Ah, I'll bet you thought the demons, devils, angels and djinn belong to the religious mythology, didn't you. Well, they aren't gods, are they? And that's my criteria for mythology. They do appear in the Bible and the Koran (which has the djinn) though. They appear in things outside of these two books, too, though. What if any of them were part machine (which they are in some of the more horror style of Steampunk, the dystopian type).

SIDE NOTE: I always have to look up the word dystopian to make sure I know what it means, Webster's says dystopia is an imaginary place which is depressingly wretched and whose people lead a fearful existence. Bet you've come across some storylines featuring this type of scenario (or thought one up) and never knew they were dystopian.

But back to our Fairytale category. Any and all of these creatures/beings/things show up in Urban Fantasy, and that means they can show up in Steampunk, too.

THINGS THAT WERE REAL (OR ALIVE) ONCE AND DON'T BELONG IN ANY OF THE ABOVE CATEGORIES

Well, you know what these are: ghosts! Be they spirits, wraiths, spooks, invoked memories, or stalled memories that keep repeating themselves, if they were real once, they fit the criteria here.

If you put your mind to it you can go beyond haunted places or séances, though séances were extremely popular in the 19th century. You can go with popular thought and bind them to a place or just a part of a place or you can rewrite their nature and make it what you will. Ghosts can be weak, they can benign, they can be poltergeists that are playful or vicious, they can be destructive, they can be strong and possess a person, or more than one person.

Things that were once real applies to Zombies, too. Mummies.

THINGS HELPED ALONG WITH SCIENCE

The Second Industrial Revolution was really the one of science rather than machines, remember. We have great strides being made in laboratories, in observatories, at dig sites – particularly those in Egypt

(Tut was uncovered in 1924, I believe). Darwin's idea about evolution had taken the fancy of many (while sneered at and banned by others). In *Leviathan* a dollop of DNA was added to the mix for the British to begin breeding their own creations.

We have Dr. Frankenstein's monster as a good example, and *Frankenstein* was written during the Regency, long before science really took off.

We have Robert Louis Stevenson's tale of *Dr. Jeckle and Mr. Hyde* and H.G. Wells' *The Invisible Man*, both of which are science related Victorian tales.

Science also gives us the first artificial intelligence. Metal men and women can be either robots that are wound up or steam powered but do tasks via a deck of punched cards (like looms did to create patterned cloth or computers did in the 1960s and early 1970s) or they can be cyborgs, part flesh and part machine. Usually not very pretty specimens, but that doesn't mean you can't tidy them up. Need a visual? Again, think Daleks or Cybermen in *Doctor Who* or the cyborgs of *Star Trek The Next Generation*, then give them visible clockworks and some nice engraving for a Victorian look. Or create your own.

Think cloning. True they didn't have cloning in the Victorian era, but that doesn't mean we can't drop it in, put a Verne or Wells' spin on it.

Think genetic blending. My great grandfather spent the first twenty-five or so years of his life in the 19th century and he had a tree in his backyard when I was very little that was a mashup: he'd grafted an apple tree and a pear tree together. It had one giant trunk but grew both fruits. I see these in plant catalogues now, but it was apparently new fangled when he did it. If you can do it with plants, who's to say some mad scientist wouldn't attempt it with animals…or people.

Lest we forget, we have electricity. Oh, it had been around for a long time, more as a toy than a tool, but that changed in the late Victorian. It wasn't just Thomas Edison's labs that were working on the light bulb. Nicola Tesla had his own power company, a rival to Edison's, and was turning out things. If you haven't seen it, watch *The Prestige* with Michael Caine, Hugh Jackman, Christian Bale, and David Bowie as Tesla. Quite a nice Steampunk take on what electricity MIGHT be able to do. And how does this fit into the created creatures? Watch *The Prestige*. I don't want to ruin it for you.

THINGS THAT DON'T FIT ANYWHERE ELSE

Well, what sort of things don't fit anywhere else? Really only one thing: IMMORTALS. Not gods, not monsters, not any version of the fae or paranormal being, simply things that just don't die.

Your hint is *The Highlander*, but there have been other mysterious people who show up occasionally.

There are Eight Chinese Immortals, beings that figure in Taos literature.

There are the Four Horsemen of the Apocalypse.

Anyone who has managed to create a philosopher's stone, like Nicholas Flammel, is an immortal (unless they can't get a fresh hit of stone as I understand it).

According to an old Anne Rice novel, Ramses II is immortal.

We'll add any mysterious personage who has surfaced and then disappeared in this category, because there is no telling where they came from or who they were.

While this isn't a Steampunk tale, the man being interviewed in *Below The Salt*, a very old (well, mid-20th century) book, was a boy at the signing of the Magna Carta and is now a US Senator. He wasn't reincarnated, he simply aged very slowly over the centuries.

Whether they are born that way or drink something to become immortal, either way works for a Steampunk story.

THE RESEARCH

Now, from a research standpoint, what you need to do is find out what the original myths, legends, fairytales, and data is regarding whichever of these things you think would fit well in your Steampunk tale.

Then you decide what to keep and what to change. Gail Carriger's heroine, as I mentioned, can simply touch a vampire and its fangs disappear, or touch a werewolf and have it become merely a human again, albeit a naked one.

Oddly enough, angels can have just as vicious and evil inclinations as demons or devils do, without being fallen angels. It's only the God of the New Testament who has mellowed. He wasn't quite so layback in the Old Testament and not a single god in any other pantheon lacks a selfish agenda. Must go with the godling code or something.

But the key here is, if you are using something that already has a data bank about it, read it! Decide what to keep and what to change (if anything) or what to recreate for your Steampunk story.

It can be done. We're professional dreamer-uppers, after all. We tell lies for a living (or hope to if you're still striving for that "published" tiara or scepter). So let's tell some whoppers.

MAGIC

In a Steampunk tale, the magic can go two ways: occult magick or stage magic. Stage magic, of course is slight of hand, the illusionists, the escape artists, the entertainers. And even if you don't intend to have any "real/occult" magic (spells, chants, manifestations, callings), working in some stage magic effects might be just the ticket.

In fact, one heck of a lot of these sort of tickets were sold to Victorians around the world, but more specifically in the English speaking sections and Europe during this period. The art of prestidigitation is said to have originated with the Persians (among others) and their Magic-men were called Megh, derived from "Magus" a Greek word that got stretched, mutated, garbled into "Magic." In the 19th century some stage magicians donned flamboyant names, such as The Fakir of Ada, The Great (fill in the blank), Professor (so-and-so) or went by a single, brand, name at times, like Houdini.

Bartholomew Bosco was doing magic tricks in Siberia after being captured and imprisoned for being part of Napoleon's march on Russia. Once free he spent another 18 years on the road with simple apparatus (pasteboard boxes and tin cups), amazing all comers.

Professor Libholz took magic in another direction, with mechanical apparatus of all kinds to aid in the first performances of the Indian basket, the Hindu Box Trick, the Speaking Head...well, you get the drift. The secrets of his tricks were shared with his colleagues and a new wonder, the amateur magician, via the wood turner (Oscar Lischke) who made many of the Professor's tools of the trade and a few extras to sell on the side.

Hermann, one of the most noted modern stage conjurers, was the son of a conjurer. When he went into the biz professionally around 1848 his dexterity and the effects, managed without any apparatus, won him fame in the courts of Europe. He made and lost a fortune a number of times, but died a millionaire in 1887.

Professor St. Roman performed in theatres built specifically for performances of magic.

Agoston turned a ship into his own magic drawing room and toured up and down the Rhine stopping to give performances in the cities along the river in the 1860s. He was noted for ghost shows. His wife donned Oriental costume and found success of her own as a magician.

Bellachini took up magic in 1846 and frequently arrived for performances in traveling clothes, and would apologize to the audience as he stripped off overcoat and gloves, saying, "Unprepared as I am..." which of course he wasn't at all. He lacked dexterity so slight of hand was beyond him but he did use modern apparatuses worked by electricity and mechanism. He also did a side business in magical apparatus sold to amateurs "at cost prices only." Or so he said.

Dr. Hofzinser of Vienna was the most celebrated card performer. He actually WAS a doctor and according to Vishwas Purohit, who wrote the article I'm referencing here, "his manipulation of cards has never been excelled."

Ben Ali Bey might have been born to the family Auzinger in Bavaria but he was the inventor of Black Art, which I take it to be part of his Oriental Magic – a bit hit in Berlin.

Purohit sites H.J. Burlingame as his source for much of this. However, his list leaves out Harry Kellar, Harry Houdini's mentor, who was instrumental in the founding in 1877 of the Martinka Magic Company, the family he went to to have all his apparatus created. They are still in business today and still creating tricks for contemporary magicians, such as David Copperfield.

He doesn't mention the Fakir of Ava, aka Isaiah Harris Hughes, who created numerous tricks, a list appears at Magicpedia **TheGeniimagazine.com/wiki/index.php/Fakir_or_Ava**.

One would think that Harry Houdini was the most famous magician in American, but he wasn't. But then, Houdini is far more early 20th century than 19th. No, the title goes to Alexander Hermann who was so successful that he was able to afford a mansion on Long Island, to own his own railroad car, and have a personal yacht.

Magic without the "k" is separate from stage tricks, though it appears to be more the choice of the author writing the word. However, should you want more occult magick than stage conjuring, the Internet can supply occult magick, occult magic spells, occult magic books, the history of occult magic, and occult magic tricks. Most of the time the Internet keywords don't use the "k" version of magic.

Practitioners of magick to read up on are Aleister Crowley (1875 – 1947, very into his work in the 1920s) and Alessandro Cagliostro (1743-1795) who was also an Italian Adventurer. Yes, I know they are rather out of our time zone, though Crowley brushes it. That doesn't mean you can't get a handle on what an occult magician might be up to when it comes to building your characters.

CHAPTER EIGHT: RESEARCH AIDS
WARDROBES AND COINAGE

Whether you decide to keep this as it was or change something about any of it for your story, knowing what you're dealing with comes in handy. What I'm going to do is give you a few nudges in the right direction.

You're probably thinking corsets, goggles, that sort of thing, but those are just the image of Steamunk. There has to also be reality behind the closet doors.

Knowing what coins to have in pocket or purse makes purchases easier – I particularly like that size and consistency of paper money exchanging hands in the movie *Sherlock Holmes*.

So let's see what is out there to inspire us, what to use, what to contort to fit our specially built Steampunk world.

WARDROBES

We're talking women's wardrobes more than men's here simply because a woman's wardrobe was far more complicated and changed with the times more drastically than a man's did. While the skin tight pantaloons and jackets of the Regency dandies gave way to more relaxed trousers and boxy jackets, the ladies' ensembles went from classic Grecian looks to the glories of Worth, the matronly silhouettes of the 1890s to the slim, straight line cut gowns that appeared in the early 1920s.

I'll give you some details but more particularly, I'll give you sources to head to for ladies wear. Ready to go shopping?

19TH CENTURY

Because the 19th century isn't as far back as the other centuries have been, there is a lot more that has survived and turned up in museums. Even delicate muslin Empire/Regency gowns that are now two hundred years old can be viewed courtesy of some very hard working website folks.

We also benefit from one of the technological advances that was sadly lacking in prior centuries – the photograph. Oh, they won't begin showing up until around the 1840s as tintypes and then progressing on from there to moving pictures, thanks to Mr. Edison's team of hard workers, but they will be available.

Let's get to these awesome – and don't mean that lightly – websites. **www.cwrl.utexas.edu/~ulrich/19cdress/00s-20s.htm.** This will take you to the Empire/Regency fashions. Actually I stopped counting the different pieces when I hit 50 and I was only halfway through the first section at that point. There is also a very large section for the 1870s-1880s. Sadly, when I accessed it the website was a work in progress and they didn't have items from the 1890s up yet. That doesn't mean they don't have anything dealing with the closing years of the century for the Timeline doesn't begin until 1840 but it does go to 1899.

At this site just in the Regency wardrobe I found evening gowns, day dresses, court gowns, pelisses, redingotes, walking dresses, a riding suit, spencers, a coat, an Indian shawl, a visiting dress and wedding dresses.

The 1830s supplied a dress with a Pelerine, an 1835 manteau; a rare workdress appeared in the section dealing with the 1840-1850; and a half-mourning gown from the early 1860s surfaced. There was also a carriage dress from 1889. A dress with both a cloak and a hat from 1850-1869 (and there are frequently hats shows on the mannequins dressed for the out-of-doors). Charlotte Bronte's going away dress from 1854 is here. There is a dressing gown from 1878. A to-die-for Worth gown (well, actually nearly all of his gowns are that) that was one of the court dresses of Empress Elizabeth of Austria in 1877.

This website also has THE BEST GLOSSARY of apparel because the descriptions include museum pictures of what is being explained.

The next real time dissolver is the British Fashion Museum, which is located in the Assembly Rooms in Bath, England.

www.fashionmuseum.co.uk.

They have both Regency and Victorian gowns.

The Victoria and Albert Museum offers a wonderful 19th century fashion reading list at

www.vam.ac.uk/collections/fashion/ resources/booklists/19th_century/index.html.

Also "shop"

www.luxemag.org/fashion-history/19th-century-fashion.html.

The McCord Museum **www.mccord-museum.qu.ca** has Form and Fashion 1810-1898, the museum's gown collection with fabric and era/year on 18 slides. For fun click into their games section and mix and match the dress pieces on the mannequin. Under Collections look for "Those Parasol Days" for photographs of women with parasols and a couple parasols without women.

For a diagram of the length of a girl's skirt by age (since it kept falling as she got older) head to **www.angelfire.com/ar3/townevictorian/victorianfashion.html**. There is also a "flash" picture showing the underpinnings of the 1850s then the gown over them. They also have a timeline but compared to some of the others it is vague and incomplete. It does tell when puff sleeves were in fashion and horsehair was used to stiffen petticoats and when hoops and bustles came and went into style – but even that isn't as detailed as I'd like it. I know bustles were in then they were out around 1880 but came back into fashion much larger after that, and that's from what I learned in reading a year's worth of *Demorest's Magazine* from 1879.

Another real time grabber was the Fashion Plate Collection (drawings from fashion magazines) which can be found at **http://content.lib.washington.edu/costumehistweb/index.html**. What was fascinating about this was that it gave the name of the magazine and the issue and date on nearly all the fashion plates. And there are a lot! 37 items under Empire (1806-1813), 72 Georgian (1806-1836), 19 Regency (1811-1820), 72 Romantic (1825-1850), 85 Victorian (1837-1859), 77 Late Victorian (1860-1900), and 188 Edwardian!

19TH CENTURY SOURCES

There's an interesting article that serves as a nice window into the 1830s-1840s at **http://xroads.virginia.edu/~HYPER/DETOC/every/fashion.htm**.

Need to know about hoop skirts, bustles, etc.? There's a brief article called "A Brief History of 19th Century Women's Fashion" by Kim Kenney at **www.americanhistory.suite101.com**. Is your heroine a lady who wants to be on the move but not have the bother or expense of upkeep on a horse? "Women and Bicycles: Fashion for the Active Woman, 1894 Style" by Jone Johnson Lewis can be found at About.com.

And **www.oldandsold.com/articles09/clothes-29.shtml** will give you the low down on what PASSEMENTERIE is among other tidbits of information.

When you have a chance to read rather than gaze at the lovely choices (and their descriptions) at the museum related sites, give a look at some of these books:

The Opulent Era: Worth, Doucet and Pingat by Elizabeth Ann Coleman, The Brooklyn Museum. Not only does it have pictures, sketches, and details, it tells about the three fashion houses, two of them I was unaware of until stumbling across this. Hated to return it to the library.

The Wishlet Series: Fashions 1806-1810 by Susan Sirkis. These are patterns for making gowns scaled to fit 5 ½ inch tall dolls but they do so from the skin outward and offer hair styling ideas as well. Never underestimate what you can get from such books...well, it's more pamphlet size. Chances are I found it at a museum shop.

These are all from Dover Publishing, bless them.

Ackermann's Costume Plates: Women's Fashions in England, 1818-1828. Edited and with an Introduction by Stella Blum.

Fashions and Costumes from Godey's Lady's Book edited and with an Introduction by Stella Blum.

Victorian Fashions and Costumes from Harper's Bazar 1867-1898, edited and with an Introduction by Stella Blum (she's a busy girl).

La Mode Illustrée: Fashion Plates in Full Color edited by Florence Leniston. These are from the 1886 issues.

Metropolitan Fashion of the 1880s: From the 1885 Butterick Catalog by the Butterick Publishing Company.

American Dress Pattern Catalogs, 1873-1909. Edited by Nancy Villa Bryk.

Fashions of the Regency Period Papter Dolls by Tom Tierney. It gives details about the original clothing recreated here.

Worth Fashion Review Paper Dolls by Tom Tierney. These paper dolls even get underwear! Again, details are given about the original clothing recreated for the paper girls. The fashions begin with 1845 and run though 1900.

Great Fashion Designs of the Belle Epoque....1890-1919 by Worth, Paquin, Lanvin and Others by Tom Tierney. Need I bother to say, details are given?

Victorian Fashion in America: 264 Vingate Photographs. Edited by Kristina Harris.

There are probably many more photographic collections available, if not through Dover, which makes things nice and affordable (probably why I have so many of them on my personal research shelves), then through other publishers. Going through your local library system to look up the book of photographs just given should supply the right Dewey Decimal (or Library of Congress) locale to find similar books, too.

Don't forget that biographies of 19th century performers will have photographs in as well. Sarah Bernhardt had some fascinating outfits, one a pant suit she lounged about in.

There are around 12 pages devoted to women's clothing in *The Writer's Guide to Everyday Life in the Wild West from 1848-1900* by

Candy Moulton. Oddly enough, among the resources given are many of the books I listed from Dover.

The Writer's Guide to Everyday Life in the 1800s by Marc McCutcheon offers a glossary that mixes men's and women's items together (around 22 pages long) but it does offer an interesting "Chronology of Hairstyles" for both men and women.

The Writer's Guide to Everyday Life in Regency and Victorian England: from 1811-1901 by Kristine Hughes. Only 4½ pages worth on women's clothing (and this book seems to think the only shops are ones where you purchase foodstuffs, too), but there is a rather extensive bibliography, a little over three pages worth. And, yes, it's got a number of those Dover books on it, too. They are just too darn handy!

What Jane Austen Ate and Charles Dickens Knew by Daniel Pool gives us the information has basically two pages on women's clothing but three on drinking alcohol just before it. Hmm.

Is this enough to get you started? I'd hoped that Pool would tell us WHERE to shop, but he didn't – just went on about livestock fairs that appear in Dickens, and that's no help at all when looking for clothing! But I do have some addresses to share.

ADDRESSES OF SOME OF THE EXCLUSIVE SHOPS

You can visit the House of Pingat in Paris from 1860 on into the 20th century at 30 rue Louis-le-Grand (which runs parallel to the rue de la Paix). There you will find "magnificent fancy articles, ready-made clothing for women, plain and unique silk fabrics for town and day dresses, ball gowns, court trains, hand-and machine-made laces." (*The Opulent Era*)

Prior to that there is a Mlle Pingat listed as a corset maker in 1855 at 371 rue Saint-Honore, but no one knows whether she was related to Emile Pingat of the House of Pingat or not. Still, if you need a corset made around 1855, she could be the one to see. (*The Opulent Era*)

M. Walles specializing in importing English fabrics to his shop at 148 rue Montmartre in 1873-74. He had an earlier shop selling textiles at 84-90 rue Richelieu from 1854 to 1963. There is a Mme Walles, couturier, doing business at 8 rue de Choiseul in 1878. In 1882 an A. Walles at the same address advertises that they make dresses and wraps. (*The Opulent Era*)

In 1816 the place to visit for lingerie in Paris is Doucet Lingerie on the Rue de la Paix. (Wikipedia). This is one of the world's most fashionable shopping streets, according to Wikipedia, "Located in the 2nd arrondissement [sorry, I've no idea what that means, never having been to or looked up things related to Paris before]...running north from Place Vendome and ending at the Opera Garnier." Cartier opened a jewelry store on the Rue de la Paix in 1898, and the House of Worth was always there, at 7 rue de la Paix. Charles Frederick Worth opened his doors at this address in 1857, and his boys kept the shop up after he passed on in '95. The House of Worth was still making gowns, and being run by a Worth, into the 1920s. (*The Opulent Era*)

By the way, it's rumored that Charles worked at Lewis and Allenby, London's most exclusive silk mercers until around 1845-46. Worth kept up his acquaintance with Lewis and Allenby and into the mid 1890s it was possible to purchase a Worth gown at Lewis and Allenby. (*The Opulent Era*)

In the mid 1800s Gagelin-Opigez of Paris snagged the gold medal for dressmaking at the 1851 Crystal Palace exhibition in London. They were also distributors of the "highest quality fancy goods, Indian embroideries, tasteful articles, silks and shawls". (*The Opulent Era*)

See why I loved this book?

Of course if you want to shop anywhere OTHER than Paris in the later part of the 19th century, you'll have to tell the hackney driver what you're looking for, then he can drop you off.

EARLY 20TH CENTURY/EDWARDIAN

So where do we go from here? Well, if you're thinking those skirts rose quickly, think again. The first fashion buzz was the Gibson Girl look.

The folks at Dover come to our aid again. We have...

The Gibson Girl and Her America: The Best Drawings of Charles Dana Gibson.

Victorian and Edwardian Fashion: A Photographic Survey by Alison Gernsheim. 235 photos from 1840 to 1914.

Victorian and Edwardian Fashions from "La Mode Illustrée" by JoAnne Olian. 1000+ illustrations from 1860 to 1914.

Fashion in Underwear from Babylon to Bikini Briefs by Elizabeth Ewing. Well, bras did come into being during our current time period.

Try *Fashion Illustration: 1820-1950* by Walter T. Foster.

Erte's Fashion Designs by Erte has gowns from 1918 to 1932.

Fashion Drawings and Illustrations from "Harper's Bazar" is another Erte piece.

Want to try the paper dolls again? *Great Fashion Designs of the Twenties Paper Dolls* by Tom Tierney. And we know from the previous ones that there are written details given.

Erte Fashion Paper Dolls of the Twenties by Erte...has 43 costumes.

Art Deco Fashions Paper Dolls by Tom Tierney, which probably applies more to the 1930s but should be fascinating...the era of the bias cut evening gowns.

American Dress Pattern Catalogs: 1873-1909 edited by Nancy Villa Byrk has over 3500 illustrations depicting "everything from bicycle suits to evening wear."

59 Authentic Turn-of-the-Century Fashion Patterns by Kristina Harris claims to have "575 illustrations detailing 59 different garments mainly for women."

Then there are the catalogs like *Everyday Fashions 1909-1920, as Pictured in Sears Catalogs*, edited by JoAnne Olian.

Now for the Net...

For the best idea of how the fashion silhouette changed year by year go to

www.fashionera.com/C20th_costume_history/1900_silhouettes_1.htm.

www.oldmagazinearticles.com has a 1917 fashion show film that might have shown as an ad at the theatre, shows shoes, stockings, hats, fur pieces...is a hoot really. The Impossible Glamour of Paris was not available any longer though it was still listed. However there is a film called French Fashions 1900-1967 where three models are on stage, they pose in the gown, strip to the lingerie and pose again and then go on to the next era and do the same. There was also a set of slides of corset and lingerie ads from the 1900-s 1950s from magazines and newspapers.

Costumers Manifest (**www.costumes.org**) didn't really have as much as I'd hoped but they do suggest that period movies are a good source for a visual. For the 1910-1915 try *My Fair Lady* and *Titanic. The Music Man* would fill in the period earlier than that.

I'm sure there are other websites out there, they simply didn't surface easily. It depends on what you've still missing. Unfortunately, those sites I found for the Regency and Victorian gowns don't include the Edwardian, though you'd think the museums had plenty of those as well.

Don't forget you can always use photographs of your ancestors, too. And baring that, a search on eBay sometimes turns some up (I have a friend who collects old photos she finds on eBay – she has a thing for ones of young men to use as models for her heroes).

FILTHY LUCRE

As one needs local coin to purchase supplies whilst traveling, bringing the right coins along is an excellent plan. For those unfamiliar with the symbols for British money here is a guide: £ stands for pound; "s" stands for shilling; and "d" fills in for pence or penny (though I've no idea why considering neither word has a "d" in it).

COINS IN THE RAJ

Should you get so far a field that you find yourself shopping – or gambling! – in India, in the Raj, anywhere from 1835 to 1947, here's what you and your native servant will need along:
Mohur, worth 15 rupees = £1
10 rupees = 13s 4d
5 rupees = 6s 8d
1 rupee, worth 16 annas = 1s 4d
½ rupee, worth 8 annas = 8d
¼ rupee, worth 4 annas = 4d
2 annas = 2d
1 anna, worth 4 pice or 12 pies = 1d
½ anna, worth 2 pice or 6 pies = ½d
¼ anna, worth 1 pice or 3 pies = ¼d
½ pice, worth 1½ pie = ½ of ¼d, or 1/8th of a pence
1/12 anna, worth 1 pie = 1/3rd of ¼d or 1/12th of a pence

GERMAN COINS

The Mark was introduced in 1871-1873. It may or may not have had the same worth as the English Mark of an earlier period, which was 13s 4d. It replaced the Thaler which had been in use since the 15th century.
1 Reichsthaler, worth 23 Groschen = 3 shillings
1 Speziesthaler, worth 32 Groschen = ? (Sorry, my source wasn't specific. Obviously more than 3s)
5 Reichsthalers equal one Friedrich d'or or Louis d'or = 15 shillings

DUTCH COINS

The guilder was the currency in the Netherlands from the 17th century until the 21st when the euro replaced it. (It was the same as a florin in English though that was already archaic in our period.) Worth? 100 centen, or cents, in 1817.
Between 1810 and 1814 the French franc was used since Napoleon had gathered the Netherlands to his bosom.
In 1817 the copper 1 cent piece and the silver 3 guilder were introduced. The following year came the copper ½ cent, silver 5, 10 and 25 cents, the ½ and 1 guilder, and the gold 10 guilder. In 1826 gold 5

guilder coins entered the mainstream.

In 1840 the 3 guilder was replaced by the 2½ guilder. 1874 saw the 10 cent piece disappear for 50 years – it came back in the 1890s. Gold 10 guilders weren't struck from 1853 to 1875. A bronze 2½ cent coin dropped into pockets in 1877.

BRITISH COINS

The gold half guinea, valued at 10s 6d, had been introduced in 1669 but was discontinued in 1813.

In 1822 the silver fourpence, threepence, twopence and penny all became standard Maundy ceremonial coins.

The first large copper penny was minted in 1797 but became the norm in 1825.

(A Side Note: the regal halfpence produced in 1770-1775, 1799, and 1806-1807 were frequently counterfeited.)

In 1833 it became a regular issue and gained a new name: the half penny. It was in use until 1967.

Farthings were produced only during certain periods in the 18th century and saw another release in 1806-1807, but they were a regular issue of the mint from 1821 until 1956.

US COINS

The US was only getting coinage up and running early on, still getting by on all the foreign coins that had been used during the colonial years. Folding money doesn't come in until later in the period, and it is frequently printed by banks rather than a federal press. The coinage is as we are used to it now for the most part:
Penny
Nickel
Dime
Quarter
Half dollar
Silver dollar
$20 gold piece

Naturally it won't be a good idea to attempt to purchase anything with any Confederate bills in the North or after early spring 1865.

CHAPTER NINE: RESEARCH AIDS
WEAPONS

If there is one thing that explorers, detectives, soldiers, diplomats, gamblers, and those living on the various frontiers will be interested in owning and carrying in a Steampunk tale, it is a handgun and, if in the "wilds", a rifle, so we're going shopping for some likely additions to the story's arsenal.

We have to backtrack a bit because weapons that were around in the 18th century were still being used into the 19th. But once inventors really get their teeth into things, the weapons – particularly revolvers and rifles really take off. Unfortunately, we need to backtrack to the flintlock at the moment.

A BIT OF BACKGROUND INFO

The flintlock combo of cock, frizzen and pan came in both musket length and convenient pistol models. Barrels on pistols were a foot long, so it was handy that long skirted coats began to be popular with men – the better to pocket their weapon, for there are no holsters other than those on saddles at this point. In fact, the civilian version of the cavalry pistol went by the moniker "horse pistol" simply because you had to have a horse to carry your pistol. Quite a large accessory! Don't forget that these pistols needed a ramrod as well. The horse pistol's smaller relative was the "travelling pistol", a weapon easily stashed in a coach in the event a highwayman with a brace of horse pistols tried to stop your wagon. The Scottish pistol discarded the idea of using wooden stockbutts and went for iron all the way; it also tossed out the trigger guard. No matter what style or model was used, the flintlock musket was THE musket for any European army from 1660 to 1840.

While a musketoon sounds like it should be used by musketeers or animated Disney characters, it is really nothing more than a shorter barreled musket – think shotgun or carbine with a flared muzzle in an earlier period. It was popular with seafarers be they of military or pirate persuasion, and could be either wheellock or flintlock when it came to the mechanics of firing one. Enfield was making musketoons as late as 1861 though.

The Brown Bess is synonomous with the Redcoats, the British version of a musketeer. The Brown Bess weighed around 10½ pounds, had a barrel 42 inches long, and an all-over length of 58½ inches. It was effective within 50 to 100 yards (though 175 yards was mentioned as a possibility) and could fire up to four rounds a minute, though three might have been a better average. That's a lot of rounds flying. It had no sights but came with a bayonet. Ramrods were wooden at first then iron, though many wooden ones continued to be issued. Designed in 1722 it saw service in many wars and with many nations. The British carried the Brown Bess until 1838, but it saw recycled service in the Maori wars, the Zulu, the Mexican War, and at least one showed up at the Battle of Shiloh in 1862. "Brown Bess" was a slang term for the rifle, already long in use by 1785. However, it was the India pattern model issued during the Napoleonic Wars that proved the most accurate, coming in with accuracy rates of 75% to 95% within 175 yards. It was lighter (just a little over 9½ pounds) and shorter (barrel 39 inches and over all length 55¼ inches).

The blunderbuss has a flared muzzle and a shorter barrel. An early shotgun, if you will, when fired the blast evoked the fancy of a fire-breathing dragon, thus it was frequently called a "dragon" from whence the military designation of "dragoon" evolved. Word is it was as often loaded with rocks, scrap iron and anything else that could hurt the enemy, although this ended up maiming the bore of the barrel. It was created to blast out a number of small lead balls, so no matter what was loaded in, the effect was that of a scattered spray of pellets or shrapnel (though the word shrapnel hadn't come into usage yet). It had a range of around 80 yards. The blunderbuss was used from 1788 to 1816 by the British mail service. Some had 14 inch long barrels but a model could go up to 17 inches and have a two inch wide muzzle. In addition, the blunderbuss had a spring loaded bayonet. The Pilgrims brought a few over; the American colonists during the Revolutionary War used them – on redcoats; and the Lewis and Clark expedition carried a number of blunderbuss style muskets but by the 1850s it was obsolete. Blunderbusses came in both musket and pistol styles.

The famous Joseph Manton produced an air-powered, breech-loading pistol in 1820, though it was underpowered compared to the blackpowder weapons. Perhaps he was trying to cut down on the smoke from all those rounds fired in his shooting gallery by Regency bucks. While his innovation didn't take, the Forsyth lock introduced the first "hammer", the modern replacement for the flintlock's cock.

THE NINETEENTH CENTURY:
THE CENTURY OF INNOVATION

Around 1815, Manton and Joseph Egg, another English gun maker, were working on the same idea an American and a number of European smiths were trying to perfect as well: the percussion cap. However, it wasn't until the 1830s that the update to the hand gun (and this category includes pistols and muskets) was ready for major production.

What the percussion cap did was make a weapon fire dependably no matter what the weather, something no weapon before had been able to do reliably. What exactly is it or what does it do? Here's what Wikipedia says: "The percussion cap is a small cylinder of copper or brass with one closed end. Inside the closed end is a small amount of a shock-sensitive explosive material such as fulminate of mercury. The percussion cap is placed over a hollow metal 'nipple' at the rear end of the gun barrel. Pulling the trigger releases a hammer which strikes the percussion cap and ignites the explosive primer. The flame travels through the hollow nipple to ignite the main powder charge. Percussion caps were, and still are, made in small sizes for pistols and larger sizes for rifles and muskets." Aren't you glad you asked? Still lost? It's a bullet. But not one like we're used to seeing...yet.

Unfortunately, popular as they were, the percussion caps were small and easy to fumble if the reload was in the midst of a battle, even more so if astride a horse as well. A number of ideas were developed but the one that worked was the metallic cartridge of the 1850s, and it made the percussion cap obsolete.

There are still plenty of lovely weapons your hero could use a percussion cap in though. Particularly the derringer. The first true pocket gun.

THE DERRINGER

Henry Deringer himself was a gunsmith busy with government contracts for rifles and shotguns, but around 1825 he added pistols to his inventory. The first ones were the same sort everyone else was producing, but Deringer realized there was an untapped market just waiting for a different weapon – one easily concealed. It didn't need to have range, it needed to protect the person carrying it when they were being held up, or their life was threatened by someone else with a weapon. His small caliber, one-shot mini-pistols became the hit of the barroom crowd. Can we even picture a riverboat or frontier gambler without one? I don't think so.

Deringer never bothered to patent the gun which lead to a host of similar pistols being turned out, but the workmanship that went into a derringer (the misspelling of his name that now refers to the weapon) put the true Deringer derringer above the rest. It was a Deringer, by the way, that John Wilkes Booth used to assassinate Abraham Lincoln at the theatre.

A SAILING MAN'S WEAPON

The percussion cap also lent itself to a remodeled pistol marketed as a boot gun or bootleg gun featuring the hammer beneath the barrel allowing the weapon to slide into and out-of a boot without snagging the hammer in fabric. The oddest of the new weapons was a pistol/cutlass made for naval use in 1837. The undercarriage of the 4-inch long barrel was a wide 9-inch blade that protruded beyond the muzzle of the pistol rather like a bayonet. The wicked looking thing required a special holster but that didn't daunt the US Navy from arming an expedition to the South Pacific with them in 1838. By the time they returned in 1840, the company responsible for the pistol/cutlass was bankrupt.

THE COLT

Samuel Colt hired a gunsmith to work up a few of his designs and once he was happy with the result, he headed for England to take out a patent, then returned to the States for a US version as well. It was 1836 and he was 21 years old. Production on the first Colt, the "Texas" model or "Paterson" model, named after the town in New Jersey where he opened his factory, began the same year. The 5-shot weapon found favor with the Texas Rangers. By 1839 Colt was making changes, and sound ones. He patented the built-on loading lever "which could be used to load and ram the bullet into the cylinder chambers." Before much could be done with the modification, the company backing him went bankrupt and the factory closed, stock and tools sold off for a mere $6,000. Fortunately for Colt, there was a war brewing and the government needed weapons. General Zachary Taylor liked the sort of pistols Colt made and sent one of his officers, Sam Walker, to work with Colt on the sort of thing they needed. The result was an order for 1000 pistols in 1847. Since Colt no longer had a factory, he contracted with Eli Whitney, who had a large weapons factory in Massachusettes, to make the weapons. Gun production had moved from the hands of a single craftsman into the mass production field, using standardized parts. The Whitneyville Walker model was big – 15½ inches long with a 9-inch barrel. The hammer had to be thumb-cocked for each shot which became known as the "single-action" lock. When a second order for 1000 pistols arrived in November, Colt had his own factory up and running again. The first weapon off the assembly line was the 1848 Dragoon, the "Old Model Army", similar to the Whitneyville Walker. This was followed by the "Baby Dragoon", a shorter 5-shot weapon that came in a variety of barrel lengths.

All these models appeared in response to the Mexican War, but it was the discovery of gold in California in '48 that sent the young men of many nations to the foothills of the Sierra Nevada in '49 that really let the model take off. The 49ers wanted protection – they bought Colts making the Colt revolver "the" gun to own in the American West. These were still percussion cap pistols, and the most famous to roll off the production lines was the 1851 "Old Model Navy", a graceful weapon with a 7½-inch barrel and a six-shot cylinder. After the 1851 Navy model was displayed at the Great Exhibition in London, an order for 9500 of the weapons was placed. When a Lancers division headed to South Africa, they carried the 1851 Navy Colt made at the factory in England in 1853.

A note when it comes to description in your manuscript: "As was common with all Colt designs of that period, the circumference of the cylinder was engraved with a martial scene; previous models had depicted battles with Indians and a stage-coach ambush, but the 1851 pistol cylinder showed a naval battle between the Texas navy and the Mexican navy which had taken place in 1845, and it is this, and not any official adoption, which led to the pistol being called the 'Navy' model."

Colt's success obviously led to other gunmakers following his lead. Brit Robert Adams was in competition with Colt and his answer to the Navy model was a "solid-frame" rather than an "open frame" design like the 1851. This meant Adams made the barrel, frame and butt all one piece with an opening cut for the cylinder. An axis-pin could be removed to take the cylinder off for cleaning. The lock mechanism differed, too, being "self-cocking" so that pulling the trigger alone fired the weapon – no thumb to the hammer to draw it back was needed. The system wasn't new, simply reworked and made more efficient by Adams. The British militaries were looking for accuracy and long range though, elements Colt's 1851 Navy had in abundance. Until officers who'd purchased an Adams proved that the self-cocking features and heavier caliber were better in the field, that is, and the British government sent their new orders to Adams. In 1855 Adams built a pistol that incorporated both the self-cocking and the single-shot features and created what is called the "double-action" lock, which is the standard today. (Actually, when it came time to arm the hero in my 1877 western set historical, I put an Adams in his hand.)

The U.S. Civil War saw soldiers equipped with the Colt New Model Army 1860, a 6 shot pistol with an 8-inch barrel. After the war, it found its way into the hands of folks on the frontier: farmer, cowhand, and bandit alike. Smith and Wesson were in the business of manufacturing cartridges and gravitated to making pistols and rifles for their ammunition. They went into the pistol building business as The Volcanic Company, but were bankrupt by 1857. A fella name a Winchester, a haberdasher and one of their stockholders, bought them out. He dumped the Volcanic repeating pistol of 1854, hired a top-notch mechanic, one Tyler Henry, and put him to reworking the repeating idea into a rifle. The level-action rifle was born. But we'll come back to rifles in a bit.

THE RIMFIRE

In Europe in the 1850s it was the pin-fire cartridge that was in favor. And the same inventor had something else up his sleeve as well – the rim-fire. He wasn't interested in creating and patenting both the pin-fire and rim-fire cartridges though. So others took up the idea, like French gunsmith Louis Flobert, who produced a series of single-shot pistols and small caliber rifles suitable for use at indoor shooting galleries. Flobert managed to improve both the power and velocity of the rim-fire cartridge and that had Smith and Wesson looking over existing patents in regards to their own product. They found an ex-Colt employee with a patent for "extending the chambers through the rear of the cylinder for the purpose of loading them at the breech from behind." Colt had turned the idea down. Smith and Wesson bought it. The Number One model was a five-shot with a frame known as a "tip-top", which allowed for easier loading, unloading of spent shells, and cleaning. By 1864 Smith and Wesson needed to contract with other firms to manufacture it – they were two years behind in filling orders. In 1871 Smith and Wesson's .44 Open Top Rimfire model won accolades from pistoleers. Wyatt Earp, Jesse James and the ill-fated George Armstrong Custer carried them. (Buffalo Bill Cody carried a Colt.) The Russians liked the Smith and Wesson, too, and, though they requested a few modifications (a spur on the grip, a finger rest on the trigger guard, and a 6½ inch barrel), placed an order for 215,704 pistols. The factory turned out 175 pistols a day for five years.

THE PEACEMAKER

With Smith and Wesson busy with European orders, Colt stepped into the batter's box again on the home front and produced the Model 1873, perhaps better known as "the Peacemaker." One reason for its popularity was that it was always usable. "If the trigger spring broke, you could thumb back the hammer and let it slip; or you could slap the hammer back with the free hand, the practice known as 'fanning'. If the ejector broke you could pull out the cylinder pin and poke the empty case out. If the mainspring broke, you could bang the hammer with a rock to make it fire. As a weapon for use in the rougher and more remote corners of the world, it was without equal, and, added to all that, the proportions were such that it pointed instinctively and was the perfect weapon for "snap" shooting at fleeting targets." The Peacemaker stayed in production until 1941, too. In 1873 it was adopted by the US Army, all in .45 caliber with 7½ inch barrels.

Because it's hard to top a Peacemaker, we're going to turn to the long guns, the muskets and rifles that built the British Empire and tamed the American West.

THE REMINGTON RIFLE

We already know that the Brown Bess was a real stayer in the flintlock line, but let's talk American muskets for a bit. The name Remington resonates firearms, doesn't it? It is certainly one of the oldest names in weapon manufacture, as it all began in the early years of the 19th century. Eliphalet Remington was sent off to learn how to make a better barrel so his father, a blacksmith, could add a sideline to his forge, and apparently it was something he saw that put the younger Remington to designing and building a flintlock himself. The weapon was demonstrated to locals when Remington entered a shooting match – and came home with enough orders for muskets like his that he no longer worked for his father. The year was 1816. By 1828 the business had to move to bigger quarters and moved to the company's current location in Ilion, New York. Oddly enough, they got out of the firearms business and into producing a really newfangled gadget in 1873 – typewriters. It wasn't until the 20th century that they returned to the firearms business. And thus, unless it's really early on, your hero can't carry a Remington.

THE HENRY RIFLE

By 1850 he could carry a Henry rifle though. This was the improved version of the old Volcanic Repeating rifle that Smith and Wesson had attempted. They were really in great demand at the start of the American Civil War with the factory turning out 290 lever-action rimfire muskets a month in 1864 (the peak of production). And why not want a Henry? They could fire 28 rounds per minute so soldiers saved up and bought their own, seeing it money well spent when it came to survival. The Confederates called it "that damned Yankee rifle that they load on Sunday and shoot all week!" Actually, it held 16 rounds, and took a specific type of ammunition, not easily available to a Johnny Reb if he was lucky enough to pick one up from a not-so-lucky Union skirmisher. The Henry was used by some Confederates, most notably President Jefferson Davis's personal bodyguards. It evolved into the Model 1866 lever-action Winchester.

The lever action on the Henry ejected a spent cartridge on the downstroke and cocked the hammer. The next round was shoved into the magazine via a spring and once the locking lever was back in position, everything was sealed up and ready to fire again. As it had no safety, it was always in the firing position. It was in production from the 1850s through 1866.

THE SHARPS RIFLE

Now the Sharps rifle surfaced around the same time as the Henry, but the Sharps had Abraham Lincoln's eye come 1861 and so he placed his order. And the order was big: 2.5 million muskets, 11,000 rifles, and 90,000 carbines, the shortened versions of regular muskets which used the same size ammunition. Carbines were created for cavalry because the shorter length had two benefits: 1) it was easier to handle on horseback, and 2) once holstered it didn't get in the way when swords were drawn as longer muskets would. Actually, it was the same length as a sabre.

Although carbines as a rule were known for poor long-range accuracy and a shorter effective range, these didn't seem to be components of the Sharps rifle. THESE carbines had an effective range of 500 yards and a maximum range of twice that. The sights were the open ladder type, the rate of fire was 8 to 10 shots per minute, one round fed at a time. It weighed 9½ pounds, and was 47 inches long, butt to muzzle. It was used by Union sharpshooters during the Civil War, then went west to fight Plains tribes and decimate buffalo herds. Wyatt Earp, Pat Garrett, and Bill Cody favored the 16 pound, cartridge firing Sharps Sporting Rifles, some equipped with mounted scopes. First designed in 1848, the Sharps weapons saw service from 1850 to 1881. If you ever watched *Quigley Down Under*, the weapon Matthew Quigley (Tom Selleck) brings to Australia is a Sharps.

CONFEDERATE RIFLES

But what were the Confederates carrying? They were up against both Sharps and Henry rifles and only acquired them if found on a field of the dead. Well, they were armed with Springfields (nearly six-foot long) and muzzle-loading Enfield muskets.

The Springfield Model 1861 was a 9 pound rifled musket 56 inches long. It had an effective range of 100 to 400 yards and a maximum range of 900 to 1000 yards. It was muzzle-loaded, so it's no surprise to hear of battlefields where muskets with up to eight or ten rounds were still found rammed in the barrel, the man furiously loading it seemingly unaware that none of his rounds had fired. The Springfield could be had for $20 a piece from the Armory where they were made, and came with a flip-up leaf sight set to 300 to 500 yards. These were fairly scare in the opening years of the war and when they did become more numerous not all soldiers were aware that the bullet left the barrel with a "rainbow" or arch trajectory that had them firing over the enemy's heads. This resulted in the order to "aim low."

The Confederates also favored the Pattern 1853 Enfield, a British rifle with the ladder-sight system. This was a rifle-musket, which meant it was the same length as the musket it replaced. The barrel was 39 inches long, with another 16 inches in stock. It weighed 9½ pounds unloaded, had a percussion lock, could fire three or more rounds a minute with a maximum range of 2,000. But it, like the Springfield, was muzzle-loaded. Enfield also produced a Pattern 1861 musketoon with a 30 inch barrel which was imported for both artillery and cavalry units. We'll come back to the Enfield in a bit when we fall back to weapons that the Empire carried in the 19th century.

After the war was over, the Springfield Model 1871 Rolling Block breech-loading rifle was nearly put to use by the U.S. Navy and the U.S. Marines. The government placed an order for 10,000. But when the weapons arrived it was discovered that the rear sights were incorrectly positioned close to the chamber and thus considered unsafe. But the French didn't seem to mind and bought them for use in the Franco-Prussian War. The recovered funds were turned into fulfilling an order for an additional 12,000 rifles from the Navy Ordinance Department, but they weren't manufactured again after 1872.

THE SPENCER REPEATING RIFLE

The Spencer repeating rifle saw action with both sides during the American Civil War then went west to fight the tribes. It could fire 20 rounds per minute, the hammer was cocked manually with a level action, it fired Spencer rimfire cartridges, from a barrel either 22 or 20 inches long (overall length of the rifle was 30 inches). There were only two problems troops armed with Spencer repeating rifles encountered: 1) the smoke and haze from such rapid fire made it difficult to see the enemy, and 2) the supply trains had never had to deal with a weapon that ran though ammunition so quickly, and rarely managed to keep the Spencers' sufficiently "fed." The Spencer Company went out of business in 1869 and Winchester took over, but ammunition for the Spencer rifle was still available in the US until around 1920.

COLT RIFLES

Let's see what Colt has been up to, besides making Peacemakers. The weapon adopted by the US military in 1855 was the Colt Revolving Rifle Model 1855, an early repeating rifle. The design was almost pistol like with a rotating cylinder stocked with five or six rounds. These saw action with the 21st Ohio Volunteer Infantry Union forces at Chickamauga during the Civil War, laying down a fatal volume of fire convincing the Confederates that they faced not a single regiment but an entire division. Despite this the weapon had a fault, a gap between the firing cylinder and barrel that occasionally resulted in "chain fire", which though relatively common in early percussion weapons, tended to injure the man firing it. The military decided to stop using the Model 1855 and sold off the majority of the 4,712 they'd purchased for a modest 42 cents a piece. (A hero who has the knowledge to fix the weakness of the Model 1855 could get himself quite a bargain!)

From 1884 to 1904, they turned out the Colt Lightning Carbine, a slide-action or pump-action rifle. It came in three different frame sizes, so there was practically a Lightning style to suit everyone. It was a weapon fancied by sportsmen and the San Francisco Police Department. Colt did much better when it came to pistols.

THE WINCHESTER 1873

The Winchester Model 1873 has a moniker: The Gun that Won the West. It was in production from 1873 to 1919 with 720,000 built during those years. A little over 49 inches long with 30 inches of that barrel, the rifle was a lever-action carbine weighing in at, what I'm beginning to feel was the norm for muskets in this period, 9½ pounds. There were plenty of earlier models, too, beginning in 1866. What the 1873 had going for it was that it used the same type ammunition as a pistol, offering convenience to the customer. The U.S. military wasn't the only major customer either. In 1883 the Canadian Northwest Mounted Police purchased 750 Winchester Model 1873s. Teddy Roosevelt was one of the civilian's praising Winchester's products. He had an engraved, pistol-gripped half-magazine

1876 that he used on hunting expeditions in the West.

Before we venture into British territory, let me mention the coach gun here. The term dates from 1858. Wells, Fargo & Company had begun stagecoach service from Tipton, Missouri to San Francisco and back, a 2,800 mile route one way. As they traveled through a barren frontier and Indian country, a lone coach needed protection. No particular manufacturer or model qualifies as a coach gun. The term merely applies to any shotgun used by the guards and drivers on a stagecoach traveling a wilderness route. This not only applies to the US west of the Mississippi River, it applies to the Australian frontier as well.

THE BAKER RIFLE

Okay, let's see what those boys in the red coats are using. We've already talked about earlier weapons and the Brown Bess, so we're going to jump into the 19th century and the Napoleonic Wars.

Oddly enough, the Brown Bess is still holding her own, but it is the Baker rifle that the 95th Rifles and the 5th Battalion, 60th Regiment of Foot are shouldering. Production began in 1800 with the first order for 800 rifles. Over the years it underwent modifications and changes in length finally averaging out at just shy of 46 inches long, a little over 30 inches of that being barrel. A flintlock it was muzzle loaded with a lead ball and could fire two or more rounds a minute. It could not be reloaded as fast as a musket due to the balls being wrapped in patches of greased leather or greased linen. An experienced rifleman, particularly a sharp shooter who could practically fell at will, could reload in twenty to thirty seconds. (This is probably why the majority of the army was still issued the trusty Brown Bess musket which could get off four rounds a minute.) If you are a fan of Bernard Cornwall's Richard Sharpe, you probably already know what weapon he's carrying – a Baker.

The Baker was actually made by a number of different companies and was considered fairly accurate at medium distances, but not at long range. To increase the odds, 60 to 80 muskets were fired in a volley. (Actually, the French claimed the British could fire frequently and in great volume without actually hitting any of the French. Naturally, this is not what the British said.) In fact, "the accuracy of the rifle in capable hands is most famously demonstrated by the action of Rifleman Thomas Plunkett of the 1st Battalion, 95th Rifles, who shot French General Colbert at an unknown but long range (as much as 800 yards according to some sources) during the retreat to La Coruña during the Peninsular War. He then shot one of the General's aides, proving that the success of the first shot was not due to luck."

THE ENFIELD 1853

From the Brown Bess and the Baker, the British moved to the Enfield. The Pattern 1853 Enfield saw action in India during the Mutiny, in the Crimean War (think Charge of the Light Brigade), and the New Zealand Land Wars. We already know it put in an appearance in the American Civil War. With a maximum range of 2,000 yards, it is no wonder men's faces lit up at the sight of one. While user dependent, the 55 inch long muzzle-loading, percussion lock could get off three or more rounds a minute. The British trained by shooting at a man-sized target, six foot by two foot. When set 650 to 900 yards out, it was given a three foot bulls eye and any man managing to get seven points on the target within 20 rounds was ranked as a marksman.

The Enfield 1853 saw its first action in the Crimean (1854-1856), then went to India where it caused trouble. The sepoys of the British East India Company's armies got the new rifle in 1857 and believed the rumors that the paper wrapped powder and projective cartridges (not metal ones yet) were greased with pig fat or beef tallow, a giant no-no for either Muslin or Hindu soldiers, which pretty much was the religious affiliation of the sepoy contingent. And since part of the drill to load a rifle was to bite the bullet, so to speak, they choose to bite the hand that fed them – well, at least the hand that supplied wages. The Enfield was also carried by the New Zealand Armed Constabulary between 1845 and 1872, and found its way into the hands of both the Maori and civilians when the updated version came along. Enfields were still being used into the 20th century by British troops.

And that is where we are going to leave things. Believe me, this has been just a glimpse.

Why did I give it? Basically to show the innovations made to one very dangerous piece of machinery – and these were all accomplished historically. Think what the genuses in your Steampunk story could do with whatever you put in their hands! If you care to follow the gleam in your character's eye to track down more information in regards to historic weapons of his or her choice. Here are some of the places to go:

SOURCES

Muskets: Musket, Brown Bess...Spring Field Model 1842...Model 1816 Musket by Books LLC

Pistols: History, Technology and Models from 1550 to 1913 by Adriano Sala

WRITING STEAMPUNK

The Blunderbuss 1500-1900 by James D. Forman
English Guns and Rifles…15th Century – 19th Century by J.N. George
The Brown Bess: Identification Guide and Illustrated Study of Britain's Most Famous Musket by Erick Goldstein and Stuart Mowbray
The 'Brown Bess' Musket by Peter Pinard and John Mosker
The Complete Black Powder Handbook by Sam Fadala
Black Powder and the Old West: Frontier Cartridge Guns and Cap-n-Ball by Shoot Magazine
Flintlock Fowlers: The First Guns Made in America 1700-1820 no author noted
Firearms in American History by Charles Winthrop Sawyer
Pistols: An Illustrated History of their Impact by Jeff Kinard and Spencer Tucker
Texas Gun Trade: A Guide to the Guns Made or Sold in the Lone Star State 1780 to 1899 by Chris Hirsch
Weapons of Mississippi by Kevin Dougherty
Colt Single Action: From Patersons to Peacemakers by Dennis Adler
Colt Rifles and Muskets from 1847 to 1870 by Herbert G. Houze
Single Action Six Guns by John Taffin
Percussion Pistols and Revolvers: History, Performance and Practical Use by Mike Cumpston (19th century weapons)
Percussion Revolvers: A Guide to Their History by Mike Cumpston
The Springfield Armory: Shoulder Weapons 1795-1968 by Robert W. D. Ball
Guns of the Old West: An Illustrated History by Dean K. Boorman
Guns of the Wild West: A Photographic Tour of the Guns that Shaped Our Country's History by David Kennedy
Guns of the American West by Dennis Adler
Arming and Equipping the U.S. Cavalry 1865-1902 by Dusan P. Farrinton
Rifles of the US Army 1861-1906 by John D. McAulay
The Sharps Rifle: Its History, Development and Operation by Winston O. Smith (pub date 1943)
Lincoln's Choice by J. O. Buckeridge (pub date 1956). The table of contents mentions going from the Kentucky Flintlock to the Seven-Shooter (the Sharps Rifle) and follows the Sharps though the entire Civil War.
Winchester: The Gun That Won The West by Harold F. Williamson (pub date 1952)
Percussion Pistols and Revolvers: History, Performance and Practical Use by Mike Crumpston and Johnny Bates

Handguns of the World: Military Revolvers and Self-Loaders from 1870 to 1945 by Edward C. Ezell (the cover says "Historical reference on handguns from Great Britain, the U.S., France, Italy, Spain and much, much more" – just imagine!)

For French weapons of the 19th century all I can give you is a place that sells reproductions, but they do give a tiny bit of history about the original of the model shown: **www.armae.com/Zenglish**.

If you got confused in trying to figure out what sort of weapon your hero would carry, or change, during the American Civil War, Wikipedia's "List of weapons in the American Civil War" might help.

DUELING WITH PISTOL OR SWORD

Dueling with Sword and Pistol: 400 Years of One-on-One Combat by Paul Kirchner

Pistols at Dawn: A History of Duelling by John Norris

Gentlemen's Blood: A History of Duelling by Barbara Holland

Gentlemen's Blood: A Thousand Years of Sword and Pistol by Barbara Holland (could be the same book but I found these two slightly different titles listed)

Code of Honor: A Civil War Era Rulebook for Duels and Duelling by John Lyde Wilson. This is a Createspace reprint of an 1838 title. I have no idea where they got the Civil War reference from as Wilson's book was out over twenty years before it and he died thirteen years before the opening volley.

And that brings us to the end of weapons, at least for the 19th century. Well, with the exception of various knives but I'll leave those and the 20th century gunnery alone. The pistols and rifles I just gathered are heavy enough without adding tommy guns.

CHAPTER TEN: RESEARCH AIDS
SLANG

Your Steampunk characters live in a world that is only partly altered from the historical record, so the more you know about the words used by common folks, particularly if you are going for a setting that involves the London rookeries of St. Giles and other slums, the more alive your own personal Steampunk world can appear.

Because we have both British and American landscapes commonly acting as the stage in Steampunk, I'm going to concentrate on the words, and places to find them, that might be used most often. These are by no means the only sources you can use. Starting places only.

BRITISH CANT OF THE REGENCY

For those who have dipped into a Regency set tale by Georgette Heyer a number of the words in this first section will remind them of those dripping from a Corinthian's chiseled lips or that of his tiger or a Bow Street Runner. For those who haven't been exposed to Regency era thieves cant, it's a treat.

Fortunately for us, there are a number of places to go to find the right words to put in a character's mouth.

1) A number of writers of Regency set novels have blogs and/or websites where they list some words. These will be your smallest offerings though – I looked, that's how I know.

2) Websites, like **www.rugglesrag.com** for a 19th century slang dictionary (will cover more than just the Regency era) and **www.thenonesuch.com/lexicon.html#A-B** will give you a leg up

3) The Best Bet – Captain Grose's 1811 Dictionary of the Vulgar Tongue. The original version was called A Dictionary of Buckish Slang, University Whit, and Pickpocket Eloquence. Really tells us what we're likely to find, hmm?

WRITING STEAMPUNK

Here are some examples from Grose's book:

ADAM'S ALE water
ADDLE PLOT a spoil-sport, a mar-all
AEGROTAT at Cambridge a certificate written by an apothecary that you are Indisposed
AIR AND EXERCISE being whipped at the cart's tail or the cart's arse
ALE POST a may-pole
ALL HALLOW to be beat until no chance of winning
AMUSERS rogues who carried and threw dust or snuff in the eyes of the person they intended to rob
BADGE-COVES parish pensioners
BAKER-KNEE'D one whose knees knock together in walking as if kneading dough
BALSAM money
BENE FEARERS counterfeiters of bills
BENESHIPLY worshipfully
BEN a fool
BESS or BETTY a small instrument used to force open doors
BETWATTLED surprised, confounded, out of one's senses, betrayed
BEVER an afternoon's luncheon, also a fine beaver hat (make sure you look closely before chewing!)
CLOVES thieves, robbers, etc.
DEVIL'S BOOKS cards
FACER a glass filled so full as to leave no room for the lip, also a violent blow on the face
FACE-MAKING begetting children
FOGLE a silk handkerchief
TO FAN to beat anyone
FASTNER a warrant
GENTLEMAN COMMONER an empty bottle (university joke)
GENTLEMAN'S MASTER a highway robber
HERTFORDSHIRE KINDNESS drinking twice to the same person
KATE a picklock
JUMBLEGUT LANE a rough road or lane
NECKWEED hemp
PONTIUS PILATE a pawnbroker
POSTILION OF THE GOSPEL a parson who hurries over the service
SHE LION a shilling
SHE NAPPER a woman thief-catcher, also a bawd or pimp

A SWELL'S SCREENS a gentleman's bank notes
TILBUKY sixpence
TIFFING eating or drinking out of meal time, disputing or falling out, also lying with a wench
TIP-TOP the best
TITTUP a gentle hand gallop or canter
TIZZY sixpence
TO TWIT to reproach a person or remind him of favours conferred
TWITTER in a fright

Not surprisingly, a number of the phrases from the 18th century surface here as well, but 1811 isn't that far into the new era to make much difference. Which brings us again to *The Dictionary of Nautical, University, Gypsy and Other Vulgar Tongues: A Guide to Language on the 18th and 19th Century Streets of London*.

Another source of cant in daily usage is *Richmond: Scenes in the Life of Bow Street Runner, Drawn Up from His Private Memoranda*, which is actually fiction but it was written in the 19th century, so it can stand in for a primary source nicely. Bow Street Runners, by the way, predate Scotland Yard, being salaried thief takers (an upgrade from bounty hunters style thief takers) from the mid 1700s to 1829.

Jane Austin's characters would be loath to utter such vulgar words, but reading Austin with a pen in hand will supply words commonly used in the era. For the same sort of period detail took to Mary Shelley's *Frankenstein*, Bryon, Mrs. Ann Radcliff, and even Sir Walter Scott, though he's writing historicals, his phrasing may still be early 19th century. His novels were published from 1814 through 1829.

The Regency is really a very small part of the 19th century, so let's leap into...

THE VICTORIAN ERA

We have plenty of literary giants to pick through if need be: all three Bronte sisters, Conan Doyle, Conrad, Bulwer-Lytton, Wilkie Collins, Dickens, Disraeli, George Eliot, Hardy, Kipling, Stevenson, Stoker, Thackery, Trollope, Wilde, Lewis Carroll, H.G. Wells, Tennyson and the Brownings as well as plays by Wilde, Shaw, and Gilbert and Sullivan. Don't overlook *Tom Brown's School Days* by Thomas Hughes as school boy slang is probably there, though tamed.

Here are some others:
Soldiers of the Queen: Victorian Colonial Conflict in the Worlds of Those Who Fought edited by Stephen Manning.

WRITING STEAMPUNK

Passing English of the Victorian Era: A Dictionary of Heterodox English, Slang, and Phrase by James Redding Ware (circa 1909)

www.victorianlongon.org has *Flash Dictionary of Slang of Street Patterers, Words and Expressions.*

www.londonslang.com/db/a/ is not necessarily Regency or Victorian, but simply London-ese. In fact, that was the most difficult element – things that told me they were taking me to a Regency or Victorian slang site, dumped me in a "London" one, or a Cockney Rhyming slang site with names that were most definitely 20th century ones...shall we say Cockney Rhyming slang is still alive and morphing with the times?

www.victorianweb.org/history/slang2.html has an article about "back slang" which is basically saying words backwards. It appears to have its start in the 1830s and is still used a bit today. In back slang "man" would become "nam". Bob's yer uncle? John Hotten's *The Dictionary of Modern Slang, Cant, and Vulgar Words* (1859) has back slang in it.

Here are just a few of the delightful bits...and they are moving away from the Georgian/Regency cant of the good captain's 1811 book.

BLAG to steal (still used today)
BONNET a covert assistant to a Sharp
BROADSMAN a card Sharp
BUG HUNTING robbing or cheating drunks
BUTTONER a Sharper's assistant who entices dupes
CHAUNTING LAY street singing, hopefully for money
CLY FAKING to pick a pocket of its handkerchief
CRACKSMAN a burglar, safecracker, a high end "profession" set apart from other thieves
CRUSHER a policeman
DEB bed (back slang)
DIPPER pickpocket
DEVICE tuppence
DOWNY cunning, false

And for further words of the period: *Hobson-Jobson: Colloquial Anglo-Indian Words and Phrases* will tell you what someone stationed in the Raj or just home from the Raj might be inclined to drop into the conversation. The word "nabob" is just one that was added to the English language as a result of colonization in India.

Otherwise, here are a couple titles that I'm not quite sure what era they belong to:

Bingo Boys and Poodle-Fakers: A Curious Compendium of Historical Slang Collected for the Best Authorities.

Balderdash and Piffle by Alex Ganes and Victoria Coren.

I'm also going to suggest a modern novel that will feed thieves cant in generous wallops: *The Great Train Robbery* by Michael Crichton (or watch the movie of the same name with Sean Connery and Donald Sutherland where you'll hear Sutherland drop the words crusher, cracksman, and many others).

19th CENTURY AMERICAN

There is a delightful bit in Mark Twain's *Roughing It* where a miner is trying to arrange for the funeral of a friend with a minister and neither of them can understand what the other is saying. The minister is upright, proper and educated; nearly every word out of the miner's mouth is slang related to sports. It's hilarious.

Does this mean we're about to talk about sports slang? No. We're talking 19th century America.

While the country covers a lot more territory than the whole of the isle of Britain does, and industry was going great guns (and we aren't just talking Colts, Winchesters and Remingtons), there is very little showing up on the Internet in regards to what the lower classes spoke in the cities. This could be because 1) these were the immigrant populations and they were speaking their native language at home and broken English otherwise, or using the thieves cant of London, 2) because while books set in cities in Victoria's England are popular, books set in New York, San Francisco, St. Louis, Chicago, New Orleans, and Denver (the major cities of the last half of the century…only New York need apply prior to that) just aren't in great demand and thus no one has bothered to compile things yet, or 3) when anyone thinks about 19th century America they follow Horace Greeley's misquoted advice to head West – which means cowboys, miners, mountain men, gamblers, and outlaws.

There's always a separate category for Civil War speak, probably because of all the reenactment groups.

But let's go to the miner's first.

MINING CAMP SPEAK

We're a bit crippled here. When it comes to what was being said in the mining camps. Trouble is no separate website or dictionary of era specific words came up in any of my searches. In fact, a search for 49ers gave me far more modern sports related sites.

All is not lost though for there are some things words can be culled from should you need any mining related words, either for the 1849 rush to California for gold or the late 1850s and early 1870s silver rushes to Nevada, or similar rushes to Colorado, Idaho, Montana, Arizona...well, you get the drift.

For 19th century vocabulary words culled from an 1830s book, try Eric Ferguson's website at **http://celticfringe.net/history/vocab.htm**.

A few of them are:

BY THE BY means the same thing today though we usually say "by the way"
GRANDSIRE grandfather
GRANDMA'AM grandmother
AS WARM A PATRIOT to be patriotic
FOR AUGHT I KNOW for all I know
WARRANT guarantee
ELBOW RELATION a distant relation
OVERREACHED gulled, conned, tricked
SAWNEY slang for Scots
BUCKSKINS fur traders or Westerners in general
RAISED HIS IDEAS made him angry, aggressive
PUSILLANIMITY cowardice
PALAVER useless talking

Let's move on.

Nearly anything by H.H. Bancroft can be used to find period words. He was the 19th century historian who chronicled western expansion in volume after volume. Although his work is available online, it's separate PDF pages so ferreting out the actual book from your local library or university library will give you a better idea of which volume and which pages you might want to copy. Look at the terms used for most of the miners, particularly in the later periods, learned a bit about geological formation to help them pinpoint likely veins of gold, silver, or copper.

You can find True Tales of the 49ers at
**http://nevada-outback-gems.com/
gold_rush_tales/california_gold_rush1.htm**

Mark Twain's *Roughing It* will give you a lot of dialogue to fill in your word specialty needs since most of the book deals with his life in Nevada, in Virginia City, and writing for the *Territorial Enterprise*. And let's face it, Twain always had a layback style that seems to epitomize the common man in 19th century America. I'd take note of the "big" words that are worked into things by characters who aren't educated beyond the local level…and that warn't much. My maternal grandmother was born in 1886 and by her era's standard, was a sufficiently educated girl when she graduated from the 8th grade. From then on she was expected to work outside the home either in the local factory or tending house and children for others before she married. Boys frequently fell into the same category, out making a living when a pre-teen. And yet you can read letters written by these people that have startlingly uncommon big words dropped in…and used correctly, too! So don't overlook any family treasures, hey?

But let's go back to the mid-19th century and Nevada for a moment.

Another of the reporters at the *Territorial Enterprise* in Virginia City, Dan DeQuille (neither Dan nor Twain used their real names at the newspaper), wrote his own book of tales at Twain's urging. Look for *The Big Bonanza*, which is what the second silver strike in the 1870s was called. Trawl for words.

In 1848 John Russell Bartlett put together a *Dictionary of Americanisms*. It's still available as a POD through Amazon for under $20 and it's also available at **http://openlibrary.org.**

CIVIL WAR SPEAK

Of course between the two silver strikes a little conflagration occurred. We call it the Civil War nowadays. Because there are a lot of Civil War enthusiasts and reenactment groups, there are a lot of places to find words. A lot of them repeat the same ones, but careful cruising over their lists will supply a new phrase or so at each of these sites. You'll find a lot of them start off with the word "absquatulate", meaning to take leave or disappear. (What did I say about those "big" words?) After a while you might want to absquatulate yourself. In the meantime visit:

**http://freepages.geneology.rootweb.ancestry.com/
~poindexterfamily/CivilWar.html**

http://cwslang.tripod.com/

The listings here are by the letter so it will take a while to look them over.

http://34nc.com/slang.html

This is the site of the 34th North Carolina Reenactment Group Company H. Might give you a few more Confederate words than any Union based site would, though they don't usually identify themselves as either one side or the other.

WRITING STEAMPUNK

www.angelfire.com/me/reenact/terms.html

www.mogenweb.org/mocivwar/cwslang.htm

www.civilwarhome.com/terms.htm

Book-wise I was attracted to *The Encyclopedia of Civil War Usage: An Illustrated Compendium of the Everyday Language of Soldiers and Civilians* by Webb B. Garrison and Cheryl Garrison .

The Life of Johnny Reb and/or *The Life Billy Yank*, both by Bell Irwin Wiley, might be of use.

For the language of generals we have *The Memoirs and Personal Letters of General U.S. Grant, The Memoirs of General P.* (Phillip) *H. Sheridan* (who moved on to battling the Plains Indian tribes after the Civil War), *The Memoirs of William Tecumseh Sherman, The Memoirs of Robert E. Lee*, and there are no doubt memoirs and letters of many, many others. These were just the Big Four, well, as far as I'm concerned, at least. There are also various collections of letters from common soldiers at the front, the ones they wrote home that were saved in attics and are now being found by historians who get all tingly just looking at them. These might be harder to find though they do surface at The History Book Club frequently. A librarian might be able to help you find some. They might be privately published and only found in local libraries or museums or come from a university press, although some make it to the major publishing houses – think it depends on who the author is or who the soldier was or what battles he was involved in.

Personally, I've used *Civil War Wordbook Including Sayings, Phrases and Expletives* by Darryl Lyman in the past. Here are some of the words found within its pages:

BUTTERNUT GUERRILLA Union scout wearing Confederate uniform to infiltrate the lines

CAMP CANARD false report widely believed among the men of a camp

DANDYFUNK a navy stew of hardtack soaked in water and baked with salt pork and molasses

DRAWN OVER THE LEFT to be drafted

DRAW OVER TO THE LEFT to steal

EVACUATION OF CORINTH diarrhea or dysentery among Confederates prior to Shiloh 1862

FAITH PAPER paper currency not backed by gold or silver

HELLFIRE cheap whiskey

WRITING STEAMPUNK

HOW COME YOU SO liquor (term in use since early 1800s)
LARK a foraging expedition
LAYOUT a skulker
MCCLELLAN PIE Union term for army-issue hardtack cracker
OLD HORSE corned beef
PEAS ON A TRENCHER breakfast call
PEDDLE LEAD to shoot repeatedly and quickly
TO RAG OUT to dress up
RIFLE KNOCK-KNEE hard liquor, Southern term
SECESH Northern term for a Confederate soldier
THE STREET already the nickname for Wall Street in 1863
VEAL an experienced soldier's term for a new recruit

So what's happening after the war? Well, the real action is in the cities, isn't it? And just as in London, the lower element is active in all the majors…New York, Chicago, San Francisco.

Allan Pinkerton wrote a number of books detailing how crooks worked. Oddly enough, a number of the same words used in the London Underworld are used in America. But you can check out Pinkerton's *The Burglar's Fate and the Detectives, The Expressman's Fate and the Detectives, The Somnambulist and the Detectives, The Murderer and the Fortune Teller* (no idea what happened to the detectives here), and *The Spiritualists and the Detectives*. All are available for download free through **www.gutenberg.org**.

There are also a number of books about various criminals in New York that will supply some nice terms and neighborhoods. *Lights and Shadows of New York City Life* is a lovely primary source, available at **http://openlibrary.org**. For San Francisco look for *The Barbary Coast* by Herbert Ashbury (1933) a nearly primary source about San Francisco's red light district, also at Open Library.

COWBOY SLANG

It's Western words, you know, cowboy slang, that gets nearly the same kind of representation that the Civil War does.

There's a lovely long list of cowboy or western words (by the letter so you have to keep clicking to move from one group to the next) at
www.legendsofamerica.com/we-slang.html.

Here's a selection from the pages I did click on:

ABISSELFA by itself

ABANDONS foundlings but also prostitutes
ACOCK knocked over, defeated, astounded
ACTUAL money
AIRTIGHTS canned goods
ALL MY EYE nonsense, untrue
ASK NO ADDS ask no favor
BANDED hungry
BARED shaved
BARREL FEVER hangover
BETTER MOST the best
BOSTON DOLLAR a penny
GO HEELED carry a six-shooter, packin' iron
RAG PROPER dress well
RAILROAD BIBLE deck of cards

Book-wise take a gander at:
Western Words: A Dictionary of the Old West by Ramon F. Adams
Western Lore and Language: A Dictionary for Enthusiasts of the American West by Thomas L. Clark
Happy Trails: A Dictionary of Western Expressions by Robert Hendrickson
Cowboy Slang by Edgar R. "Frosty" Potter
Cowboy Lingo by Ramon Adams, et al
A Dictionary of the Old West by Peter Watts

I also recommend reading any of Louis L'Amour's westerns to pick up tidbits.

OTHER SOURCES

For 19th century words and expressions, you can always go through the classics to pluck free what appears worthy of usage once more. Tomes from folks like Harriet Beecher Stowe, Washington Irving, Fennimore Cooper, Hawthorne, Emily Dickenson, Emerson, Whitman, Thoreau, Melville, Louisa May Alcott, Conrad, and Twain. Don't overlook any of the dime novelists either…their audience really was the common people and they phrased things for that audience – their readers. My personal favorite dime novelist is Colonel Prentiss Ingraham who supposedly had quite an adventurous life himself before he began cranking out stories (over 200, I believe) and doing promotion work for Buffalo Bill Cody's Wild West Show. There were a lot writers scratching out 30,000 to 75,000 words every couple of weeks (Louisa May Alcott was one of them, doing so under various names). Look for things published by Beadle and Adams or Smith and Smith or *Frank Leslie's Magazine* and other story papers. University libraries catering to Popular Culture or Western History departments tend to have these on microfiche if nothing else.

A couple general books to consider are *The Writer's Guide to Everyday Life in the 1800s* by Marc McCutcheon who devotes his first chapter to slang and lingo and *The Writer's Guide to Everyday Life in the Wild West from 1840-1900* by Candy Moulton, who holds off until chapter 15 to talk the talk.

I wanted to end this with some words from the end of the century but the closest I came was the 1890s edition of *The Dictionary of Slang, Jargon and Cant* by Barrere and Leland. You can find it 1) through your local library, the call numbers are 427.09 for Dewey Decimal and PE 3721.B32 for Library of Congress or 2) you can get it through **http://openlibrary.org**. Open Library lets you read it online or has a PDF copy that was taking forever to load. I ended up looking at it online. It has pages that turn but you need to enlarge them to be able to read them. However, once you get past the forward and preface, it's nice columns of words with definitions. It supposedly covers American, Australian, British, Anglo-Indian, Tinkers, etc.

At **www.alphadictionary.com/slang/** they offer words grouped by the letter and the slang jumps back and forth with most of it being 20th century. I cruised a few of the letters of the alphabet and came up with these offerings for the 1890s:

ALSO RAN unsuccessful in a competition
LIVE WIRE as in exciting, energetic
LOADED drunk
LUSH alcoholic
And from the 1870s: LOONEY meaning crazy
From the 1850s: ANKLE BITER child
From the 1810s: BANG-UP exciting, excellent
From the 1780s: LOOT as in proceeds of the theft

A FEW MORE HEAD'S UP

It isn't as if the slang of the late 1800s evaporated over night…say at 12:01 a.m. on January 1, 1900. No, much of it was still used in the early 20th century. However, what with motorized vehicles gaining in popularity and men taking to the skies from 1903 to 1910, a new age is most definitely in the dawning. And, oh, what words they are tossing about!

WRITING STEAMPUNK

To know what words were being used prior to the Jazz Age, there are a number of ways to begin your search.

1) Newspapers. Your local newspaper is probably available on microfiche. In larger cities and at universities you can find the New York Times as well. Reporters will use words in common usages, including slang ones. Same goes for British newspapers (perhaps not so much the *Times*, but there are plenty of others, though not as easy to find on the west side of "the pond", i.e., the Atlantic Ocean) and other major cities.

2) Novels. In particular, mystery novels, adventure novels, and short stories in various magazines. For Brit-speak read early P.G. Wodehouse for what the gay (as in carefree) young lads and lassies are sprouting. His first short story was published in an English periodical in 1903 and by 1909 he was in the U.S., actually working in NYC and living in Greenwich Village, although his tales are nearly all set in Britain. American Mary Roberts Rinehart's first romantic-suspense tales were released in 1908, 1909, 19—well, basically one or sometimes two a year throughout the period. G.K. Chesterton's mysteries were first published in 1911 and 1914. Of course we still have the literary giants: Faulkner, Conrad, Woolf, Lawrence, Joyce, Shaw, T.S. Eliot, Galsworthy, James, Doyle and Forester. Jack London was in the Klondike gold fields during the hoopla there but back in San Francisco in 1898 and writing. His work moves us into the new century (he died in 1917, by the way).

3) Song lyrics. Tin Pan Alley was turning out melodramatic ballads but also comedy novelty songs and we can sort out what young sparks were saying to their lady loves. I pulled the following from 1910's "Some of These Days", "Come Josephine In My Flying Machine", Irving Berlin's 1913 "Snookey Oookums" and a few others (courtesy of **www.perfessorbill.com**): BILL AND COO, CUT IT OUT!, KID, OH, HIGH HOOPLA!, GEE!, MY BABY, TOGGED UP IN HIS BEST SUNDAY CLOTHES, and CUDDLE.

And of course plays, particularly those after WW I, that included music – nearly all the popular songs showed up on Broadway, either in a Ziegflield *Follys'* production or one of George White's *Scandals*, or in a musical/play – you'll get a lot of Cole Porter songs from these and George

Gershwin wrote for White's *Scandals* extravaganzas.

The coming of the Great War bought out the most melancholy songs but once it was over, Jazz music, and catchwords, ruled the day. But that's Dieselpunk, so we'll back away from slang and move on to Entertainment. I can see Steampunk creations taking the stage by storm!

CHAPTER ELEVEN: RESEARCH AIDS
ENTERTAINMENT

If you thought there was a lot of different weapons, hold on to your derby. There's even more variety in the entertainment available, the using some of it will make your own personal fictional world even more alive to the reader.

Entertainment features an excellent place for some Steampunk innovation, too.

I will warn you, the first instances given here may not sit well with animal lovers. We're talking history here though and one can't write historical characters or settings believably without knowing what was acceptable and considered normal or even "fun" in the past. And thus we go to what our ancestors thought was a great time to be had by all: blood sports.

COCKFIGHTING

Cockfighting has been around since 2000 BCE in the Indus Valley Civilization, but in Tudor times, the Palace of Westminster made sure there was always a handy arena for the royals and the court to enjoy a good fight. The Cockpit-in-Court was a permanent cockpit AT the court. The "event" pitted two specially bred gamecocks against each other. Their comb and wattles were usually cut off to prevent freezing in colder climates, a standard recommended by the Old English Game Club and the American Gamefowl Society – yes, the "sport" came across the Atlantic with the settlers. And the fighters were bred specifically for the arena, receiving the best of care and conditioned for the fights that would begin when they neared two years of age. Wagers were placed and the cocks were set in the pit, no doubt hooded until the last minute among the elite fanciers. Some fights were to the death but even when they weren't the cocks were bloodied, maimed and would still have attempted to take on another contender since they possessed a "congenital aggression toward all males of the same species."

Fighting cocks were expensive to own so only wealthy men bred the competitors and got them in fighting shape. But once in the pit, all classes of society from low to high came to bet on the outcome.

Cockfighting was banned outright in England, Wales and other parts of the British Empire through the Cruelty to Animals Act of 1835...except in Scotland. It had been a common sport there since the 18th century but that ended when cockfighting was banned there in 1895 in Scotland as well.

BEAR AND BULL BAITING

If you think blood sports are enjoyed only by brutish male types, you don't know much about Good Queen Bess. She loved to watch big brutish animals battle for their lives, as did nearly everyone else. There was a Bull and Bear baiting ring in nearly every town by Elizabeth's reign. Bull baiting had been around since the 1200s, so it was seeped in tradition as an entertainment feature.

And just as with sporting events today, a lot of cash exchanged hands as everyone bet on their favorite.

In London the epitome of arenas for the sport was the Bear Garden located within the Paris Garden in Southwark. For Bull Baiting one went to the Bull Ring Theatre. Audience capacity was 1000 people all perched on tiered seating for the best view and protected from the animals by walls of flint.

Lest ye think the Bull and the Bear battled each other, such was not usually the case.

With Bull Baiting the bull was tethered by a 15 foot rope – or chained by one hind leg or by the neck – to a stake to keep his movements within a diameter of 30 feet. For a full hour specially trained and bred dogs – the origin of the breed known today as bulldogs – were set to nip at its heels and attack it – to "worry" it. Sometimes pepper was blown in the bull's nose to enrage it before the contest began. There were variations on the set up, too. A bull could be confined in a whole in the ground or be the recipient of "pinning the bull" where the Old English Bulldog was considered the winner if it managed to set its teeth soundly about the bull's snout. Bull baiting was far more common in England than bear baiting because bulls were plentiful compared to bears, which were also costly.

This wasn't just an Elizabeth pastime though. Such entertainments surfaced in mining camps and other desolate areas in the US in the 19th century and trained bears could still be seen being lead around to do their little dance for the "entertainment" at country fairs if not in the cities.

Have we left the blood sports? Sadly, no.

BADGER BAITING

In the 18th century and through the first half of the 19th century, a relatively "quiet and docile creature" joined the pit. The badger had a lot less bulk than a bull or a bear, weighing in at 35 pounds fully grown, but when cornered it was not only courageous, it had an "extraordinarily dangerous bite" and wasn't afraid to chomp down on its persecutors. It also had powerful claws since it dug in hard earth for its dinner. To gamblers and breeders looking for new adversaries worthy of their dogs, the badger was the new pick.

How the dogs felt about this – well, they liked to keep their masters happy. So when put in the artificial badger dens, which meant harrying through a tunnel after its opponent, the dog was on the clock – literally. The more often the dog managed to latch onto the badger and drag it out within a minute, the more often the task was repeated to see how many times it could be done by a particular dog. It became quite the sideshow and easily staged away from the bull and bear pits as an attraction in cellars and taverns. It was very big during the Regency as numerous paintings and drawings attest.

But it declined, replaced by an even more profitable pitting of dogs against rats during the Victorian era.

RATTING

It didn't matter to anyone that the Cruelty to Animals Act had been passed in 1835, forbidding such things. When it came to ratting, everyone looked the other way. Possibly because there were so many rats. Hard to say.

There was a referee and a timekeeper. A dog was placed in the pit and the rats were dumped from bags for the contest to begin. The setting was lit by gaslight, full of smoke from patrons' pipes and cigars, and the smell was…well, less than pleasant – a whole lot less. Turnspit Quakers Alley was one such place, The Graham Arms was another. The Paris Dog Show had mirrored walls in the pit, though whether this was to confuse the animals or allow patrons to catch all the action, I don't know. It could have gone either way. As a popular gambling sport, London alone possessed 70 rat pits at one time.

If you could call it that, there was a delicacy to the dog's ability. It had to deliver a killing bite, one per rat "customer" and move on. And as if that wasn't enough, herding the rats before it took them out one at a time was also required. Speed was the name of the game, too.

The dogs weren't large, they were mostly terriers and breeding them was a good business. In fact, the breeders' names were murmured with the same awe given trainers of thoroughbred horses today – they were famous despite the fact that they were engaged in an illegal business. Another entrepreneur of the ratting business was the rat catcher who was called upon to supply thousands of rats for the pits each week.

On April 22, 1832 a dog named Billy, a 26 pound Bull and Terrier with a pedigree of proud ratting ancestors, went down in ratting history by dispatching 100 rats within five minutes and 30 seconds – a record of one rat every 3.3 seconds. No other dog bested that until Jacko came along, a 13 pound black and tan Bull and Terrier who, according to the Sporting Chronicle Annual, took out 60 rates within 2 minutes and 42 seconds on July 29, 1862, or one rat every 2.7 seconds. On May 1st of the same year, Jacko slightly bested Billy's record of 100 within the first five minutes and 28 seconds. Within a ten-week period that ended that day, in a total of less than 100 minutes Jacko had rid the world of 1000 of the nasty vermin. The more normal rate at which a dog dispatched his prey was one rat every five seconds but fifteen rates a minutes was excellent. I'll bet a demonized mechanical Steampunk "ratter" could best that easily.

The last public ratting competition was in 1912 in Leicester when the owner of the pit was arrested, prosecuted, fined and assured the court he'd never promote another ratting event.

EXECUTIONS OF FELONS

Sadly, people also attended the hangings at Newgate gaol in London and in nearly every other location a scaffold was built or a handy tree grew. And they did this for entertainment, some betting on how long it would take the unfortunate human at the end of the noose to die. Venders sold food and toy scaffolds complete with a doll hanging by a noose to the crowds. But how would they execute a killer cyborg? Should your Steampunk world have laws written to cover this sort of situation?

FOX HUNTING

Using dogs to hunt is an ancient practice that was popular with the British Celts prior to the arrival of the Romans, who had their own hunt practices. In medieval times foxes were only one of the "beasts of the chase", with red hart and hind, martens, and roes also marked for extermination – or at least for the dinner table. While dogs were used, the first instance of a "hound" dates to 1534 in Norfolk, England, with farmers doing the chasing rather than the landowners.

In the 16th century the fox hunt began to take on the form of a ritual in Britain as aristocrats saddled up and followed their hounds in a cross country gallop after a red fox, usually, which was considered vermin if you were a country landlord. The oldest recorded fox hunt, the Bilsdale, using hounds took place in the late 17th century in Yorkshire. Hares were also hunted in this manner.

By the late 17th century, fox hunting was the main method of protecting poultry from the fox population, but it had morphed into a sport by the early 19th century with a season that began the first Monday in November and lasting to the following Spring. It wasn't just the chickens, ducks, and geese that were being protected though. As shotguns improved during the 18th and 19th centuries, game shooting became very popular. Gamekeepers hunted the fox and birds of prey to protect pheasants for their employer's shooting pleasure. The red fox and some birds of prey became nearly extinct in some areas.

Once riding to the hunt, or even walking behind the beaters, had been a sport reserved for royals and aristocrats, because the game on their land was considered private property – had been for centuries. Such laws resulted in the common man in England unable to feed his family in quite the same manner as his colonist relatives might in the New World. However, at long last there was a relaxing of the game laws in 1831. Those who might have poached the landowner's reserve before could now take rabbits, hares and game birds themselves.

Fox hunting as we picture it with riders in their "pinks" drifted to North American shores as well, though the Hunt seems to have settled in the southeast and Pennsylvania. The first pack of English foxhounds arrived in 1738 and their descendants are still leading the chase today.

All things involving animals and entertainment didn't result in the death or mauling of the creature in question though.

THE MENAGERIE and the ZOO

Charlemagne had three menageries; William the Conqueror had one that grew to be today's London Zoo, but until the 19th century only a select few ever got to admire it. If you lived in the right quarter outside the Tower of London you probably could heart the beasts though.

The Zoological Society of London was established in 1826 and sat on the boundary line between the City of Westminster and Camden at the north edge of Regent's Park. The Zoo opened in April 1828, was granted a royal charter in 1829 by King George IV and opened to the public to aid funding in 1847. A reptile house was added in 1849, an aquarium in 1853, an insect house in 1881 and the first children's zoo in 1938. Because they felt tropical animals could not survive London's colder weather, these animals were kept indoors until 1902.

In 1831 most of the animals (32) were transferred from the Tower menagerie to the newly opened London Zoo in Regent's Park. The rest were (and my sources differ on this) either shipped to the Dublin Zoo or sold to an American showman and shipped to the US, and the Tower Menagerie closed in 1835 by order of the Duke of Wellington.

Wouldn't it be interesting to find the animals were lifelike automatons when they left the Tower though?

CIRCUSES

The first circus-like traveling shows were those in the 14th and 15th century, and rather than be formalized as we know the performances to be, these were basically gypsy caravans. They did, however, have trained animals and many of the circus skills still performed, if a bit differently, by modern performers, acrobatics and horsemanship in particular.

The "father" of the modern circus is Philip Astley though. His first exhibition in England on January 9th, 1768 featured trick horse riding. Astley's program offered "astounding acts of physical skill, danger and comedy, all accented with music." Later he added pantomimes and difficult riding moves, which he performed himself. At first his shows were presented in small fields but the crowds soon made that venue unsatisfactory. The circus according to Astley resulted in a construction boom in the cities, all for the purpose of offering Astley's performers an arena. The London Hippodrome was one such place. There were wild animals (lions and elephants), a decorated ring, acrobatics, trick riding, and a variety theatre in the decorated ring.

The first circus entrepreneur in America, John Bill Ricketts, not only amazed audiences with a blend of equestrian feats and theatrical performances, he was befriended by President George Washington. Ricketts abilities on horseback made him a favorite, particularly with feats known as "Flying Mercury" and "Egyptian Pryamids". Unfortunately, by 1799 Ricketts' good fortune had turned to financial ruin.

The 19th century is when the circus came into its own. In 1825 Joshuah Purdy Brown forewent the arena and put up a large canvas tent – the first "big top." Clowns like Dan Rice were circus pioneers.

P.T. Barnum's name says "circus" to some, though he was primarily a museum owner. When fire claimed his museum in New York City in 1868, he retired for a few years, but reentered the entertainment world via the circus. His contribution is the sort of things that had been featured in his museum: the freakshow and sideshow elements. He was only ever a part owner of a circus, but it was with a number of traveling circuses from 1871 to 1880. One of those partners was William Cameron Coup.

In American Coup was the first to commission a circus train, transporting his shows from town to town – an event that still happens, with a parade of animals and performers from the rails to the fields where the tents go up. Coup also added more than a single ring to his arena under the canvas. The Barnum and Coup franchise merged with the Ringling Brothers at the close of the 19th century to become the Ringling Brothers and Barnum and Bailey Circus of the 20th century.

Circus innovation happened in America in the 19th century. When Thomas Cooke, an equestrian performer, left the US to head home to England, he took the idea of the circus tent with him. Adam Forepaugh was the first with a dual roundtop, separating the menagerie from the circus performance. His circus tent was a half-mile in circumference.

Ringling Brothers were at the top of the circus heap, earning as well as broadcasting via barker and flyers that they were the "World's Greatest Shows". Their innovations were to install family values – no profanity, no crooked gaming devises, no short-changing. Honesty and integrity were their bywords and with the help of railway transportation, they performed in over 150 cities from late April to early October every year.

THE WILD WEST SHOW

The first Wild West Show was held in 1882 in North Platte, Nebraska to celebrate the 4th of July. The town fathers asked local resident Colonel William Cody to put on a show for them. It wasn't quite the wild west show he became famous for, it was more the first rodeo ever held, and went by the rip snorting name "The Old Glory Blowout." But it was so successful, Cody went into showbiz. The next year "Buffalo Bill's Wild West" played to the populace in Columbus, Nebraska. Before the start of World War I it had played all the major US cities a couple times over, and toured Europe. Queen Victoria came for a performance when the troupe was in London. The Wild West Show featured trick riding, much like a circus, but the features that brought in the crowds were the shooting exhibitions by Frank Butler, Annie Oakley, Bill himself, and reenactments of Indian raids (using Plains tribesmen off the reservations, including a couple famous chiefs) and fake holdups of the Deadwood Stage. It was the most successful touring show of all time.

SPORTS

The following research aids don't reflect all the various sporting contests being played but are a selection of those more applicable to being twisted to Steampunk purposes.

BOXING

Popular in 4th century BCE Athens and in Rome from the 1st century BCE to the 5th century CE (around about the time Rome lost it all to the barbarians), but REALLY popular in the 18th century with the British common man...the one who couldn't be involved with the sort of things the aristocrats were enjoying.

At first it was bare knuckle competitions, four men in the area (a cleared space surrounded by spectators rather than a ring or pit), and the winner was the last man standing. Very few rules so fighting dirty and street fighting techniques were probably much in evidence.

In 1719 James Figg had made a real name for himself in the boxing matches, enough to be proclaimed English Champion. Jack Broughton had fought as well between 1734 and 1750, but he devised a set of rules to follow: a man had 30 seconds to get to his feet and his opponent couldn't set upon him while he was down. Not much but enough to catch the fancy of gentlemen who took up boxing as a sport. To give them a hand – or a way to punch – up, Broughton opened a boxing academy in Haymarket.

Daniel Mendoza was the champ towards the end of the century, but he lost it to John "Gentleman" Jackson in 1795. Before his fall, Mendoza had introduced a style that was subtle and had written a book, *The Art of Boxing*, in 1789. Jackson opened a boxing academy in Bond Street that was a big hit with fellows like Lord Byron and other aristocrats eager to learn the art of the pugilist. The Prince of Wales enjoyed a good fight as well, and when he was at long last king, Jackson and other fighters dressed as pages and guarded the entrance at Westminster Abbey during Prinny's coronation in 1821.

1830 brought more rules to the sport. The London Prize Ring Rules disallowed kicking, biting, and gouging. The infamous Queensberry (Queensbury) rules weren't even formulated by the marquis himself, but he approved of them in 1867. These regulations added gloves, limited the rounds to three minutes each, and allowed an opponent only ten seconds to get back on his feet. Also, wrestling moves were outlawed in boxing.

American boxers began arriving in England early in the 19th century. In 1805 Bill Richmond, a former slave, entered the London ring. John L. Sullivan came in 1882, bested all comers, and was the first boxer to ever be awarded the honor of being the World's Heavyweight Champion.

Nowhere in the rules does it say the fighter must be 100% human though. Hint, hint.

CRICKET

The game of Cricket dates to Henry VIII though a similar version is recorded as played in 1301. The first professional cricket players appear in 1660 with the Restoration which seems to indicate Charles II fancied the game. The 18th century saw adjustments being made to the game and in the 19th century underarm bowling (pitching a baseball player would call it) replaced round arm and over arm throws. In 1844 the US played Canada in a Cricket match. The Golden Age of Cricket was the two decades before WW I. For the most part this is a game associated with Britains and played at home or in one of their colonies.

What sort of match would it be with one team made up entirely of specifically cricket programmed bio-mechanical players?

BASEBALL

A purely American game first played in the 19th century. There were already professional teams touring the country playing in the 1870s. Ditto the cricket idea.

RUGBY

And what baseball is to America, Rugby is to England. It is named after the school where it originated – Rugby – and was played by the boys at the school from 1750 to 1859 without a change in rules. Innovation appeared in the game in the 19th century with the first written rules being penned in 1870.

Could those rules have included a restriction against genetically engineered players? Something that goes WAY beyond steroid use?

AMERICAN FOOTBALL

Like Rugby, American football was first played at school – universities and colleges though rather than grammar schools. It's a 19th century game that began in the early part of the century, experienced changes in the later part, went professional in the late 19th century and saw regulations written in the early 20th century.

How about a game against werewolves or vampires though?

BASKETBALL

Basketball is a very young game, its birthday 1891 in, you guessed it, America. It underwent a number of changes in the early years but now has a rabid following, whether the players are college teams or professional ones.

Surely those extremely tall players are the result of interspecies breeding? Perhaps with aliens or elves?

SOCCER

Soccer began in England in the 19th century though it is played world wide now. The first rules were written in 1863 and it only began to be termed "soccer" in 1880. See suggestions for Rugby and American Football for ideas on corrupting the game to a Steampunk arena.

HORSE RACING

While people have been racing each other on horseback for thousands of years, modern horse racing is rare before the 17th century. There are instances of an annual race in Chester before 1500, but the sport really takes off during the Restoration because Charles II likes horse racing. This is also when the first thoroughbred breeding for race horses begins. The Byerley Turk, the Darley Arabian and the Godolphin Arabian stallions are introduced to England from 1690 to 1730, and most thoroughbred today have one of these fellows in their pedigree. The first racing calendar was published in 1727 and the General Stud Book was published in 1791.

There are actually three different types of horse racing: flat racing (like the Kentucky Derby), steeplechase (similar to a run after foxes as jumps over fences and other obstructions are the course), and sulky racing (a small two wheels cart behind the horse, though aristocratic bucks would have races their sporty carriages in unofficial races down turnpikes or streets).

I'm sure all three would benefit from a Steampunk touch.

BILLARDS/SNOOKER/POOL

The origin of billiards is murky. In an early form of the game in the 1340s, it resembles croquet. The cue, or mace, was developed in the late 1600s but it looked more like a hockey stick used to shove the balls – table shuffle board in some ways. It evolved from a lawn game, moving indoors and up onto a table. Mary Queen of Scots complained in a letter written in 1576 that her billiard table has been removed. As the game was popular in France and she'd spent most of her life in France, she no doubt brought it with her. The cue as we know it came into being in the 19th century as did the type of table used. Billiards was popular among those who could afford the table from the 1770s until the 1920s when it had evolved into Snooker.

Pool is the late 19th century American version of the game, though billiard tables are being mentioned in ads for various saloons in the Old West in the 1870s. No doubt they were just as popular and had been in demand in the eastern cities long before this.

Can't you see a recently sentient robot taking up the game and besting all comers? Maybe even "snookering" them when it comes to betting on the outcome of the game? A robot, even if it's alive, still needs to purchase oil for its joints.

TOYS

So what's a fond Steampunk inventor going to give his children at Christmas or for their birthday? How about an upgrade on one of these toys? It's quite possible to make some of them quite diabolically scary.

JACKS or jackstones, jackrocks, fivestones, onsies, knucklebones or snobs

Considered by most of us as a child's game, Jacks has been around for a long time. Children collected whatever was found where they lived (thus the diverse names), tossed them in the air, and played the game much as it is played today. Earlier jacks sets were five cubes made of stone, clay, wood, ivory, bone, and today metal or plastic. Jacks' origins are cloaked in history but chances are that whether it was ancient Rome, Greece, Egypt or a setting in Europe or the New World, when two tikes had their heads together over a game on the ground, it was likely to have been jacks. What early children used as a ball would have been a non-bouncing stone or wooden ball, but once rubber balls were available (and that was dependent upon the discovery of rubber trees by explorers) the game got an upgrade.

CUP AND BALL
or BILBO CATCHER

Drawings seem to indicate that these toys date to at least the 17th century if not before. A wooden cup is attached to a spindle to which is tied a ball on a string. The object is to fling the ball in the air and catch it in the cup. The Bilbo catcher is similar but lacks the cup, having instead a saucer to catch the ball. Adults played with these as well as children. It's the forerunner of the paddle and ball, or at least a close cousin to it.

WHIRLIGIGS or BUZZERS

Mentioned in literature in 1686 and found in Native American cliff ruins, the whirligig was made of hammered led musket balls or worn coins though a flat piece of bone no doubt worked, too. It features two holes punched in the center with string run through each and attached at a distance to sticks that act as handles. From the name it's apparent what it does – whirls along the strings, probably due to spinning it by the handles. Have to admit, I've never tried one.

A Buzzer has a shaped edge that makes a buzzing noise when the whirling is at top speed, otherwise, it's merely a modification (and upgrade?) on a whirligig.

CAT'S CRADLE

String games like Cat's Cradle are another of the world's oldest games to play, and variations of it have shown up in civilizations around the world, including those in Borneo and sub-Saharan African tribes. It has also gone by a number of names, Jack in the Pulpit and Cratch's Cradle among them. In 1858 it is referred to as Cratch's Cradle in a *Punch* cartoon and the name was included in an 1898 dictionary as the correct designation. There are a number of different figures to be woven with a circle of string, zig zagging from thumb to various fingers, which means it could keep those engaged in playing it from being bored for hours at a time if necessary.

TOPS

You'd think there were only one kind, right? Nope, there were five types, and they'd been around for centuries. In 16th century England they had the peg tops (with a turnip shape that was wound by string), whip tops (which has the string attached to a hand held stock), hand spun tops and two other kinds that my source kept to itself.

JACOBS LADDER

Considered by no less authority than *Scientific American* magazine to be a "simple toy – very illusive in action" in 1889, the Jacobs Ladder was said to have mysterious movement and having an inexplicable motion. It is made of six solid wood segments attached with ribbon. Again, I have no personal experience to say any more on this toy.

DICE

A favorite used in gambling games as far back as ancient Egypt where they were used in Senet, the ancestor of Backgammon, considered the oldest game in recorded history.

Dice came in wood, ivory, pewter, and bone. While used in tavern and gambling house games like Hazard, and disapproved of by proper sorts in the 18th and 19th century (read that as religious or crusading groups who were anti gambling or anti games of any sort), dice were still the most common game piece to be found in homes as many board games called for their use.

MARBLES

Like Jacks, marbles have been around for a long time – at least 2000 years – for the game didn't require the glass marbles prized by children in the 19th century and early 20th century. All it took were pebbles or round bits of clay. My Dad had a large collection of marbles that he'd played with as a boy in the 1920s and 1930s, but his own children managed to lose all those rainbows, cats-eyes, target marbles and glass shooters.

ROLLING HOOP

Another ancient game, thought to have originated with the ancient Greeks, it was very popular in the 19th century as hooks could be rolled along as a solitary game or be raced against other players. Hoops were 28" in diameter, 1 ½" wide and 1/4th" thick and whipped into action and guided by a stick.

THE GAME OF GRACES

Take something that looks very like 10" diameter embroidery hoops, attach ribbons to them and hand a group of girls each a 22" long wand then put them in action tossing and catching the hoops to each other and you have the Game of Graces. Boys joined in for a lark but it was basically a game for young ladies in the early 1800s.

FOX AND GEESE, SOLITAIRE, and NINE MEN'S MORRIS

Fox and Geese is a peg game that has been around since the 14th century and uses a 33 hole board. In it, one peg (probably made slightly different by the way the top is carved or how it is painted) serves as the fox and it has to stop the other pegs, the geese, from surrounding it. I say we electrify it!

Solitaire is basically the same game using a 37 hole board, and is thought to have been invented by someone confined in the Bastille. In it all but one peg needs to be removed from the board, and it needs to land in a designated hole. This makes it more like those folk games we find on tables in places like Cracker Barrel, though not exactly like them. I'd like to think something drastic is building throughout the game and gaining that final hole rewards the winning player with something they'd much rather not have.

CROQUET

A late comer to our list for it arrived on the lawns of middle class families in the mid 19th century, having travelled from France to Ireland to Britain to America around 1850. It was very popular with women, but rules were iffy. John Jacques was selling croquet equipment and rule books by 1864 though. In America it was Milton Bradley who grabbed the croquet bull by the horns in the 1860s. Having stringent rules led the game to fall out of favor with the ladies by 1874 but the men were still all for it. There were clubs and tournaments devoted to croquet, in particular the All England Lawn Tennis and Croquet Club. In America the Newport Croquet Club was inaugurated in 1865 in Rhode Island and by 1882 there were 25 clubs that made up the National American Croquet Association. As has happened with many things (spelling among them), there was a division on elements of the game between the way it was played in Britain and in the US. England fancied the 6-wicket layout while American kept to the traditional 9-wicket one. Croquet was actually played at the 1904 Olympics in St. Louis, but it was the last time it was included on the program.

Am I tempted to corrupt it? Not this time – an inventor does deserve some downtime!

GAMES COMPANIES

It might be handy to note that **Milton Bradley Company** began manufacturing games back in 1860, which makes them the oldest game company in the US. In the 1870s they had dozens of games and puzzles, word games, games of knowledge, traditional games and a game that allowed a player to buy and sell property with play money, but it was called "The Way To Make Money." They also sold croquet sets with mallets, balls, wickets, stakes and rules on how to play the game since there was a controversy in the 1860s about the correct way to play. The rules were written by Bradley.

Bradley heard a lecture in 1869 about the kindergarten movement headed by Elizabeth Peabody who felt creative activities should be developed at an early age. It lead to his company producing educational materials but when the recession of the 1870s hit, he lost two investors who felt the "art supplies, multiplications sticks, movable clock dials, toy money" and other educational games were a waste of good money. He also produced parlour games for adults, which were popular in the late 19th and early 20th centuries, and had a best selling jigsaw puzzle line that was popular with young boys for the theme pictured – wrecked vehicles. By 1920 there were five factories turning out games in Springfield, Massachusetts, with sales figures hitting $3.5 million – and that was in an age when a million was really worth something!

Parker Brothers was originally George S. Parker Company, for young George published his first game in 1883 when he was just 16. When his brother joined the company in 1888 the name was changed; a third brother got an office in 1898. But it was George who designed games and wrote all the rules. Parker Brothers had games that reflected the times, turing out *Klondike* when the Alaskan gold rush was on and *War in Cuba* when the Spanish-American war was in the news. In 1906 they produced the most successful card game – ROOK – but the game they had trouble keeping up with demand for first shipped in 1934, a time when many companies were going bankrupt. Its name was *Monopoly*.

What if the game company was run by an evil genius who'd been programming/brainwashing people for years via gamboards?

OTHER EVENTS

The **Olympic Games** had been a yearly event for over 1000 years before the flame was allowed to go out in 393 CE, but the games were renewed in the late 19th century. They joined the list of events that became familiar activities in the 20th century, urging global harmony as the locale moved every so many years. These were the world's fairs (first inadvertently begun by the British at the Crystal Palace exhibitions), the Pan-American games, and various other sporting and technology events.

There were also the pleasure gardens: Vauxhall from 1661 to 1859; Ranelagh from 1742 to 1803; Cremorne from 1845 to 1877. Dinners, dancing, flirtation, all topped off by a fireworks display of an evening. While we have a variety of colors exploding in the sky at special holidays today, by the 1830s the displays were not only colorful, they were frequently blazing away on forms at ground level or, for reflection and sound amplification, on floats in ponds or on the river. A display that featured a couple dragons squaring off for battle was always popular, and the fire masters (we call them pyrotechnicians today) were happy to oblige.

Balloon ascensions were big from the late 1700s. One of the first of which took place at Versailles, watched by King Louis and Queen Marie Antoinette. These continued into...well, today at some places!

Nearly all the new technology was introduced with hoopla and rides for the daring on steam powered trains is just one such example. The Great Exhibition of 1851, aka the Crystal Palace exhibition was very well attended, as were events like the World's Fair, the first of which is that sponsored by the Society of Arts in London in 1756 according to the list at

http://en.wikipedia.org/wiki/List_of_world%27s_fairs.

Other than the Great Exhibition, the best known ones are probably the 1889 one in Paris for which the Eiffel Tower was built, the 1893 World's Columbian Exposition in Chicago which had sideshow amusements, one of which was Little Sheba doing the belly dance (was she real though, or were there ballbearings in her hips?), and the 1904 Louisiana Purchase Exposition in St. Louis for which "Meet Me in St. Louis, Louie" was written.

THEATRES

We'll be breaking this up into British and American, so hold on tight. I'll try to be brief. After all, once you've got the names, you can always look up more data.

The BRITISH Actors (just a sampling of them)

- George Frederick Cooke. First appearance on stage at age twenty in 1776; in Dublin in 1794 where he grew as an actor. Back in London in 1801 was a rival to Kemble though he acted alongside John Kemble as with Mrs. Siddons from 1803.
- Sarah Kemble Siddons
- John Kemble
- Sir Henry Irving
- Ellen Terry
- Mary Anderson made her London debut at the Lyceum in 1885.
- Edmund Keene

- Arthur Lloyd performed at the Victoria Theatre in 1881 and 1892, and at the Middlesex Music Hall, Drury Lane in 1892.
- Marie Lloyd

There were plenty more, I simply wasn't seeing many names when collecting information on the theatres themselves.

British THEATRES and MUSIC HALLS

The Strand was considered the place for theatres late in the Victorian era.

Her Majesty's Theatre in Haymarket was the center of ballet in London in 1843.

The Theatre Royal, aka Drury Lane, still has patrons flocking to shows in the 1890s, though it had fallen out of favor for awhile prior to 1879.

Wyndham's Theatre opens 1899.

The Tivoli Music Hall 65-701/2 The Strand opened in 1890 with a capacity of 1,510.

The Adelphi Theatre was across from the Trivoli.

The London Pavilion, 1, Piccadilly Circus, Westminster opened 1885, the first building erected at the Piccadilly Circus end of Shaftesbury Avenue. Currently the site of Ripley's Believe It Or Not.

The London Pavilion Music Hall, 41/2 Tichbourne Street (now part of Windmill Street) was an entertainment room attached to the Black Horse Inn which opened in 1859. Bowling alleys were added later.

The Trafalgar Square Theatre (now Duke of York's) opened 1892.

The Lyceum Theatre was rebuilt when Wellington Street was constructed, reopening in 1834. The Wellington Street Lyceum was improved in 1882 and in 1884 the circle fronts were altered and redecorated.

The Old Vic opened as the Royal Coburg Theatre in 1818 opposite Bridge Road, Lambeth. Renamed the Victoria Theatre in 1833.

The Garrick Theatre opened in 1889 on Charing Cross Road. Backs up to The Duke of York's Theatre.

The Prince of Wales Theatre at the corner of Coventry Street and Oxendon Street in Leicseter Square. It opened in 1884 as the Prince's Theatre with a capacity of 1,062, and included a hotel and restaurant. Was renamed the Prince of Wales Theatre in 1886.

The Palace Theatre built as the Royal English Opera House on Shaftesbury Avenue in 1891. It was a failure and was converted in 1892 to The Palace Theatre of Varieties.

The Lyric built on Shaftesbury Avenue in 1888. Its stage door is on Great Windmill Street. It's façade is that of the house that preceded it at the location, built in 1766.

The Gaiety Theatre

The Windmill Theatre

The Shaftesbury, facing Cambridge Circus, opened in 1891.

The Surrey Theatre

The Savoy Theatre opened 1881, and had its main entrance on the Embankment. In 1903 a hotel was attached. It was the first to light the auditorium with electricity rather than gas, though it did have gas lighting installed as a backup should the electric power go out.

1848 Eagle Public House in Mile End Road, renamed Lusby's Music Hall. Destroyed by fire 1884 and rebuilt as the Paragon Theatre of Varieties in 1885. Became the Mile End Empire in 1912 and converted from music hall to cinema.

1870 Foresters' Music Hall in Cambridge Heath Road in Whitechapel, closed in 1917. In 1885 Dan Leno was paid £5 a week to perform his clog dance, sing two comic songs, and "very soon became immensely popular pioneering the style of stand up comedy which is still with us today."

The Sebright at Hackney

The Eagle in the City Road

1888 The Alhambra Opera House and Music Hall, 85 King's Road, Brighton. Closed in 1912, converted to a cinema, the Palladium Cinema with a capacity of 1,200.

17th century Mogul Tavern in Drury Lane. Glee club meetings and sing songs in adjoining hall from 1828. Altered in 1847 and renamed the Mogul Saloon, which had a capacity of 500. Music hall performances followed and in 1851 it became the Middlesex Music Hall. Main entrance at the angle of Drury Lane and Shelton Street. Remodeling and additions occurred in 1868, 1872, and 1875, and 1892. Auditorium is 88 ft by 80 ft, capable of seating 3000 in two tiers. Ground floor is divided into orchestra stalls, stalls, and pit-stalls, all with upholstered seats, the balcony/gallery also features upholstered seats and roomy comfort of dress circles in better houses. In 1911, demolished and a new building, 155 ft by 115 ft, named The Winter Garden Theatre of Varieties was built. It remained a music hall until 1919 when new owners acquired it. Remodeling done with the original tavern section renamed the Nell Gwynn Tavern. Theatre reopened May of 1919 with the musical "Kissing Time" by Guy Bolton and P.G. Wodehouse.

The Oxford Music Hall, 6 Oxford Street, opened 1861. Burned and was rebuilt in 1869 with a "sanded floor ...more in the style of most music hall audiences than one luxuriously carpeted." A new Oxford was going up in 1892 and opened in 1893, with entrances on both Tottenham Court Road and Oxford Street.

THE AMERICANS

There probably were theatres in America prior to the 19th century, but far more was happening during the 1900s, so there were a lot more places to go and things to see.

In fact most of was happening in the second half of the century. Why? Well, technology, of course! Gaslight and limelight and electricity made all things better when one was on the stage.

In 1869 the remodeled Chestnut Street Theatre in Philadelphia reopened. Newspapers raved about the "comfortable seats, convenient boxes, lovely decorations...excellent visibility, good ventilation" and décor.

Audiences in the first half of the century had a reputation for being loud, uncouth and unruly. The improvements, it was hoped, would bring in a better class of customer.

Acting styles were...well, hokey, melodramatic, with lots of posturing, overblown gestures, physical comedy and outlandish costumes, particularly early in the century. A "more naturalistic acting style came into vogue" at mid-century, although "travesty", aka burlesque (a type of variety show, not strippers), was also popular.

"In the antebellum period, beginning actors' salaries ranged from $3 to $6 per week" but "stars" doing the circuit could demand and get $150 to $500 for a 7 to 10 day engagement, plus a few more benefits. There were also an amazing number of child stars treading the boards.

The ACTORS (a sampling)

- Fanny Brown
- Joseph Jefferson III
- Edmund Booth
- John Wilkes Booth
- John E. Owens
- Charlotte Cushman
- Sarah Bernhardt
- Fanny Davenport
- Jenny Lind "The Swedish Nightengale"
- Lilly Langtree "The Jersey Lily"

The THEATERS

The Bayview Opera House opened in 1888 at 1601 Newcomb in San Francisco.

The Jenny Lind Theatre opened at 750 Kearny Street at Merchant in 1850.

The Market Street Theatre opened in 1889 in the 900 block of Market in San Francisco

The Elitch Theatre opens in Denver in 1891.

20TH CENTURY

Shaftesbury Avenue was London's street of theatres during the Edwardian era.

The BRITISH ACTORS

William Gillette starred in "Sherlock Holmes" in 1901

Charlie Chaplin (he was British but he'll show up in the American list, too)

Again, there are far more than two, obviously, but they escaped me.

The BRITISH THEATRES

1911 New Princes' Theatre opened on Shaftesbury Avenue near the new Oxford Street end. Suffered in the great gas explosions in the district and rebuilt in 1911. In 1919, 18-weeks of Gilbert and Sullivan opera filled the autumn schedule.

The Wellington Street Lyceum received yet another upgrade in 1904 and some minor touch ups in 1919. In 1937 it was converted to a cinema.

The London Hippodrome, Hippodrome Corner, Cranbourn Street, Westminster, opened 1900.

The Apollo in London opened in 1901.

The Globe (now the Guilguid) opened in 1906

The Queen's opened in 1907

The new Shaftesbury opened in 1911.

THE AMERICANS

The type of actors we have showing up now are quite different. While some appear on the stage, the majority of them are stars in the silent movies.

The ACTORS

- Mary Pickford
- Douglas Fairbanks
- Erico Caruso, opera
- Charlie Chaplin
- Buster Keaton
- Rudolph Valentino
- Clara Bow, the "It" Girl
- George M. Cohan
- Anna Held
- Fanny Brice
- W. C. Fields
- Eddie Cantor
- Josephine Baker
- Bert Williams
- Will Rogers
- Ed Wynn
- Sophie Tucker
- Billie Burke
- Mae West

(see a further list of Ziegfeld Follies and George White's Scandals stars at the Wikipedia entries)
- The Marx Brothers

The THEATERS

The Alcazar Theater opened at 650 Geary Street in 1917 in San Francisco.

The Geary Theater opened at 415 Geary Street in 1910, yep, in SF.

The New Mission Theatre opened at 2550 Mission Street in 1916, again in SF.

The Victoria Theater opened at 2961 16th Street in 1908 in San Francisco.

The Ogden Theatre opens in Denver in 1919.

The Iroquois Theatre opens in 1903 in Chicago on the Loop with "absolutely fireproof" mentioned specifically in the promotions, yet it burns down within five weeks.

The Ziegfeld Theatre on Broadway in New York built at 6th and 54nd in 1927, but the shows had been performed since 1907. The last show was in 1931.

SOURCES

It was easy to find historic places for San Francisco, at least ones still standing, via **www.noehill.com/sf/landmarks/default.aspx** where they had a list of historic sites. Not so easy for New York where at **www.musicals101.com/bywayhouses.htm** the list of "New York Theatres: Past and Present" noted only the names of theaters to click on and…well, there were far more than I felt up to clicking on. After all, it did say "and Present." I didn't want to keep clicking on theatres that came into existence after 1919.

There are a number of links in reference to historic Boston theatres at **http://arcadia.org/boston-theatre/**, including an essay "Boston Theatre, 1753-2003".

Fires apparently kept the theatres of Chicago frequently out of business, or so was the impression as no names of any were given for the 19th century at **www.encyclopedia.chicagohistory.org** in the Theatre Buildings listing. They didn't make it easy to figure out which of the 20th century houses that were named dated prior to my 1919 cut off date either.

Books are good. You might look out for:
The Great Theatres of London
Golden Gate Theatre
The Directory of Historical American Theatres
Historic Photographs of Broadway: New York Theatre 1850-1970

There are two books about the Iroquois Theatre fire in 1903: *Chicago Death Trap* and *Tinder Box*.

The Theatre Historical Society of America has a number of publications, so check the book listings on their website.

For a nice primary source, try:
The Theatre; Its Early Days in Chicago, a Paper Read Before the Chicago Historical Society on February 19, 1884.

What might also be of interest is the Encyclopedia of Chicago websites listings of maps, the oldest dating to 1812. None, unfortunately, was a map of theatre locations.

Had to draw the line somewhere, so I didn't go into early vaudeville or the variety acts that hit every theatre in every town from one side of the US to the other. No doubt there were similar acts playing the music halls in England, which I also didn't go into other than list a few.

And why give you so many choice theatre info bits? Don't your characters need someplace to go to relax—or to have their gadgets perform?

WRITING STEAMPUNK

While I only hit a few categories in regards to research for period related elements for your Steampunk tale, the intent was to illustrate that there is plenty of historical fact to leave as is or corrupt to your own alternative history devices.

But research and then writing the manuscript is not where it all ends – no, you still hav eto take this story to the market.

CHAPTER TWELVE
THE MARKETS

Once you've done your research, tweaked your history, mixed and matched elements and characters and come up with a plot, it's time to figure out where to send your completed manuscript.

That's what this section is all about – and a logical point at which to end *Writing Steampunk*. There are some (hopefully) helpful appendixes following this chapter. They are there to round out some of the time period and also supply a list of all the Steampunk titles I could find that are currently, or about to be, available.

I'd be terribly remiss not to mention where you could find editors interested in reading Steampunk manuscripts, wouldn't I?

Never fear. Such was never going to be the case. Because Steampunk is a subdivision of fantasy, I have listed fantasy publishers here even through they may not have had a Steampunk title released…yet. Check the online catalogues for each to keep abreast of what they are releasing. Also keep an eye peeled for editors' announcements in blogs and tweets as they will frequently leak the word "Steampunk" when looking for new submissions.

I will caution you that some publishers will not look at even a query letter much less a manuscript submission without it having an agent attached to it. Others will take a query letter but not a proposal without a request to see it. And then there are the third type, the ones who will not only look at an unagented submission package, but prefer to see the entire manuscript. As there are always changes in submission policies, I urge you to check the publisher in question's website for an update on what they are looking for and how they want to see it.

DEL REY/BALLANTINE BOOKS
A division of Random House. Agent required.
www.delreybooks.com
Manuscript guidelines online
Advance against royalties

SPECTRA/BANTAM DELL PUBLISHING GROUP

WRITING STEAMPUNK

A division of Random House. Agent required
www.bantamdell.com
Publishes ms 1 year after acceptance
Advance against royalties

DAW BOOKS, INC./PENGUIN PUTNAM
www.dawbooks.com
Agented and unagented submissions accepted
Manuscript guidelines online
Advance against royalties

TOR/FORGE/ORB
Tom Doherty Associates
Agented and unagented accepted
www.tor.com
Manuscript guidelines online via FAQ

ACE/ROC
Penguin Group Publishing
Agented and unagented accepted
www.penguingroup.com
Manuscript guidelines online via FAQ
Looking for 80,000 to 125,000 words
Query e-mail **sff@us.penguingroup.com**
Check the guidelines first though

DRAGON MOON PRESS
Check to see if they are accepting manuscript without a recommendation
from one of their authors, which is the current policy
Unagented submissions accepted
www.dragonmoonpress.com for submission guidelines
Accepts simultaneous submissions
Electronic submission only
Royalty, no advance mentioned. Publishes 2 years after acceptance

EDGE SCIENCE FICTION AND FANTASY PUBLISHING/TESSERACT BOOKS
Accepts unagented, unsolicited manuscript proposals
www.edgewebsite.com
Manuscript guidelines online; 75,000 to 100,000 words
No simultaneous submissions or electronic submissions; no YA/MG

WRITING STEAMPUNK

Advance against royalties; publishes 18-20 months after acceptance

HADLEY RILLE BOOKS
Agented and unagented queries accepted by email
www.hadleyrillebooks.com
Guidelines on website
Advance against royalties; publication generally 6 months after acceptance

JUNO BOOKS/POCKET BOOKS
Accepts unsolicited manuscript, considers simultaneous submissions
Check to see if submissions are open or closed first
www.juno-books.com
Queries by email only
Advance against royalties
Guidelines on website

KENSINGTON PUBLISHING CORP.
Not a fantasy publisher but recently bought a Weird West romance series
Conflicted listing as it says agent required but also that unagented manuscripts are accepted
www.kensingtonbooks.com
Check website for submission policies
Accepts simultaneous submissions
Advance against royalties; publishes 12 to 24 months after acceptance

CARINA PRESS
Division of Harlequin – E-books
www.CarinaPress.com
Actually lists Steampunk as something they are looking for
See website for guidelines
Agented or unagented submission okay
Submissions Electronic Only

AVON IMPULSE
New e-book division for Avon romance at HarperCollins
Also the only way Avon accepts submissions without an agent now
www.avonimpulse.com
Submission guidelines on line
Electronic submissions only
But Steampunk is noted as a genre of interest, must be romance though

WRITING STEAMPUNK

LACHESIS PUBLISHING
Accepts unsolicited manuscripts, considers simultaneous submissions
www.lachesispublishing.com
Query with proposal package via e-mail only
Guidelines on website
Royalties; publishes 18 months after acceptance

LIQUID SILVER BOOKS
Accepts queries by e-mail – Must be Romance
www.liquidsilverbooks.com
Guidelines on website include font and point size
Royalties; published in e-book format 4 months after acceptance

LOOSE ID
Erotic romance publisher of e-books
www.loose-id.com
Query by e-mail; guidelines on website
Royalties; publishes 1 year after acceptance

MEDALLION PRESS, INC.
Minimum word count 80K for Adult Fiction, 55K for YA
No erotica or inspirational
www.medallionpress.com
Manuscript guidelines online
Advance against royalties; publishes 1-2 years after acceptance

MOUNTAINLAND PUBLISHING, INC.
Online submissions only
www.mountainlandpublishing.com
Considers simultaneous submissions
Royalties; manuscript published 3 months after acceptance

SAMHAIN PUBLISHING, LTD
Accepts unsolicited manuscripts
www.samhainpublishing.com
Guidelines on website
Royalties; publishes 6 to 18 months after acceptance

ST. MARTIN'S PRESS
Agent only
www.st.martins.com

WRITING STEAMPUNK

Manuscript guidelines online
Advance against royalties

ENTANGLED PUBLISHING
Accepts unagented submissions
www.entangledpublishing.com
Novels 70,000 to 120,000 words
Novellas 20,000 to 40,000 words
Manuscript guidelines online
Electronic submission only

YA or MIDDLE GRADE PUBLISHERS

CLARION BOOKS/
HOUGHTON MIFFLIN BOOKS
Does accept unagented submissions.
www.houghtonmifflinbooks.com
Manuscript guidelines available on website
Advance against royalties;
publishes 2 years after acceptance
No multiple submissions

DIAL BOOKS FOR YOUNG READERS/
PENGUIN GROUP
Accepts unsolicited manuscripts
www.penguin.com
Do not include SASE,
they will call if interested, recycle if not
Advance against royalties

HENRY HOLT & CO. BOOKS
FOR YOUNG READERS
Does not accepted unsolicited submissions;
queries only
www.henryholtchildrensbooks.com/submissions
for complete guidelines

LITTLE, BROWN AND CO. BOOKS
FOR YOUNG READERS
Agent required
www.twbookmark.com/children
Advance against royalties;

publishes 2 years after acceptance
Guidelines online

If you have never been published before or are just entering the fantasy market (having been published in romance or mystery or non-fiction before), the best thing to do is complete the manuscript first, then contact either an agent or editor about the story.

AND THAT'S ALL THERE IS TO IT

...which, of course, makes it sound like a slam dunk, a drop in the bucket, when it's really a lot of hard work, fevered creation, and fast pounding fingers, spilling the story unraveling in your flights of fancy onto the printed page – or computer screen.

You can do it. I have faith in you. In fact, I'd enjoy hearing of your success, that moment when an editor says, "we'd like to offer you a contract on (fill in the title of your book)". It's a truly magical moment.

WRITING STEAMPUNK

APPENDIX I
THE 19th CENTURY: WHAT'S HAPPENING

1800s: Napoleon becomes First Consul, his armies best the Turks and march on Cairo, the defeat the Austrians and head towards Vienna, after which he conquers Italy. The British snag Malta. The US Government moves from Philadelphia to the new city of Washington D.C. – population 2464 free inhabitants and 623 slaves. Tom Jefferson beats out John Adams's reelection bid. A plot to assassinate Napoleon is found out in Paris. Maria Edgeworth's *Castle Rackrent* is published, a gothic novel. Sir Walter Scott is also turning out novels. Goya, Turner and Canova are it in the art world. Beethoven, Paganini and Rossini are the musically inclined. Haydn dies. **Trevithick constructs his light-pressure steam engine while Volta produces electricity from a cell – the first battery; Fulton produces the first submarine, the "Nautilus", and propels a surface boat by steam power and then navigates on the Hudson River in his paddle steamer "Clermont". A German invents the water voltameter telegraph** (and I have no idea what it could possibly be). *The source of the Ganges River is discovered, Mungo Park heads up the Niger River to explore a second time.* **Dalton introduces atomic theory in chemistry; the term "biology" is coined.** On the Space frontier, **Herschel discovers infrared solar rays and dinary stars.** Great Britain and Ireland unite (not that everyone is pleased). The English enter Cairo; the French leave Egypt. Napoleon becomes President of Italy. Paris has 550,000 folks living there, London has 864,000, while New York has only 60,000. The Bank of France is founded. The first Debrett's *Peerage* is published. The Second Mahratta War ends with Wellesley (later Wellington) the victor; the East India Company bests the Holkar of Indore's army. Not satisfied with lesser titles, Napoleon goes for Emperor. Spain declares war on England. Alexander Hamilton is killed in a duel by Aaron Burr. Wellesley is top dog in India; Jefferson gets a second term as President in the States. Napoleon becomes King of Italy. England and Russia are joined by Austria against France by Treaty of St. Petersburg. Napoleon tromps the combined Russo-Austrian forces at Austerlitz. Austria caves to French control. England and the US frowning at each other over trade with the West Indies. The British find Continental ports closed to them thanks to Napoleon's dictates. The Holy Roman Empire comes to an official end. The first dahlias arrive in England. Napoleon abandons the French revolutionary calendar. **A scale is built to indicate wind strength by Sir Francis Beaufort**, the British cotton industries has 90,000 factory workers and 184,000 handloom weavers. Building on Dartmoor Prison is begun. The First Gentlemen vs the Players in cricket. The first Ascot Gold cup is awarded. England prohibits slave trade. **Street lighting by gas first appears in London**. The fashion for pigtails in men's hair (those pulled back ponytails at the nape) disappears (1808). *Extensive excavations at Pompeii begin.* Henry Crabb Robinson becomes the first war correspondent reporting on the Peninuslar War for "The Times of London". The Newmarket Races are established with the help of two thousand guineas (which if you watch your coinage denominations, you'll know are worth more than a pound sterling).

1810s: Napoleon at his height (in popularity and accomplishments, not inches). He also becomes a papa with the birth of his son. In England, George III is declared insane and the Regency begins with another son taking over for his papa. Wellington is chalking up victories in the Peninsular War. The British are in Java. William Henry Harrison trumps Tecumseh's gathered tribes at Tippecanoe, Indiana. Napoleon enters Russia but four months later is in retreat from Moscow. The US declares war on England. Prussia declares war on France. Wellington is on a roll and after a few more victories in Spain is pushing into France. Murat switches sides, leaving Napoleon, and the Allies enter Paris. Napoleon abdicates and is banished to Elba. The Congress of Vienna opens. The British burn Washington D.C. In India the English go back to war against the Gurkhas (Nepal). The US bests the Brits at New Orleans; Napoleon slips away from Elba and lands in France. The Allies hastily form up again; the Congress of Vienna ends. Napoleon gets squashed at Waterloo and is banished to St. Helena. Brazil declares itself independent, then Argentina does, too. More territory in India comes under British control. The border between the US and Canada is agreed upon as the 49th parallel. The East India Company establishes a settlement in Singapore. "Peterloo" Massacre of rioting (or at least vocally protesting) workers in Manchester, England occurs. Florida is purchased by the US. Scott's historical novels must make way for a certain Miss Austen's contemporary ones. Lord Byron's Childe Harold's Pilgrimage is released as is the Brothers Grimm's fairy tales. Shelley, Wordsworth, Coleridge, Keats are in print and a startling novel by Shelley's bride is released: "Frankenstein." The Drury Lane Theatre (not the first, but a replacement) goes up. Actor Edmund Kean has his debut performance at Drury Lane. The Elgin Marbles arrive in England. Nash begins design of Regent Street, London. **The "Comet", a steamship, is operating on the Clyde River in**

Scotland. Girard invents a machine for spinning flax. *The Great Temple of Abu Simbel is discovered;* Stephenson builds the first practical steam locomotive; Humphry Davy does his bit by inventing the miner's safety lamp. The "Savannah" becomes the first steamship to cross the "pond" (also known as the Atlantic) doing it in 26 days. Other scientists are working on the diffraction of light and the relation between specific gravity and atomic weight. The kaleidoscope and the stethoscope are both invented. The London "Times" is printed on a steam-operated press and St. Margaret's Westminster is the first district illuminated by gas. The first steam warship is the USS *Fulton.* There is an eruption of Sumbawa Volcano in Indonesia that kills more than 50,000. The last gold guinea coins are issued in England. The London Philharmonic Society is founded. The waltz conquers the European ballrooms. Beethoven, Rossini and Schubert are tops on the charts; Beethoven goes deaf in 1819. *Blackwood's Magazine* is founded in Edinburg. There is large-scale emigration from England to Canada and the US due to the economic crisis at home. There are riots in Derbyshire, England, against low wages. Waterloo Bridge is opened in London as is (shoppers take note!) the Burlington Arcade in Piccadilly. And there is a maximum working day set for juveniles in England: 12-hours.

1820s: Mad King George dies and Prinny becomes George IV; Napoleon dies, too. Oddly enough, so does Queen Caroline, the year after Parliament voted her an annuity of £50,000. Venezuela wins its freedom thanks to Simon Bolivar. Peru says "we're free, too!" Mexico becomes a republic. The Monroe Doctrine closes the American continent to further settlement as colonies by other nations. The final Act of the Congress of Vienna, which had returned to work, is passed. The Cato Street murder conspiracy is discovered, thus saving the British Cabinet from extermination. The leaders get exterminated instead. British Foreign Secretary Lord Castlereagh takes his own life two years later. The First Burmese War begins; the British take Rangoon. A frontier treaty is signed by Russian and US. The Egyptians conquer Crete. The French aristocrats get compensated for losses during the Revolution. Bolivia separates from Peru. The Burmese War ends; Russia declares war on Persia. The Treaty of London has the Allies deciding to force peace on the sultan, who says "no way!" Russia beats Persia and takes Erivan (Armenia) then declares war on Turkey. Wellington becomes Prime Minister. Uruguay frees itself from Brazil. Andrew Jackson becomes president in the US. The New Act in Parliament establishes an effective police force in London (The Metropolitan Police which becomes known as Scotland Yard due to the address). The Russo-Turk war ends. British emigration continues with folks heading to Cape Colony (Africa). In Britain, the death penalty for over 100 crimes is abolished. The Royal Thames Yacht Club is founded. Rugby Football originates at Rugby School. In Rochester, New York, a Baseball Club is organized. The Athenaeum Club is founded in London. British workers are now allowed to unionize. *The RSPCA is founded in London where there are now horse-drawn buses.* Tea roses are introduced in Europe from China. **The Stockton-Darlington railroad opens, the first line to carry passengers.** Portland Cement is developed. The Erie Canal is finished. **Charles Babbage is involved with early attempts to construct a calculating machine.** Daguerre and Bouton invent the diorama. **Charles Macintosh invents waterproof fabric!** *Lake Chad is discovered in Central Africa.* Oxygen-hydrogen limelight is invented. **The first railroad tunnel opens on the Liverpool-Manchester line.** Baedeker begins publishing his travel guides. The London "Evening Standard" is first published. **Sulfur friction matches are introduced.** London weekly periodical "The Spectator" is founded. **The screw propeller for ships is invented. Ohm's Law is formulated, defining electrical current potential and resistance. A sand filter for purification of London's water supply is constructed (and they really needed it!).** The study of elliptic functions begins. *An account of John Franklin's explorations in the Arctic are published.* The founder of phrenology dies. **The first photographs on a metal plate are produced. The Baltimore and Ohio railroad is built in the US. The Delaware and Hudson's gravity railroad opens – it was constructed with locomotive operation in mind. The breech-loading needle gun is invented. So is the earliest version of an electromagnetic motor. The screw-propeller can not get a steamship up to 6-knots an hour! Stephenson's "Rocket" engine wins £500 at the Rainhill trials.** The Suttee, the Indian customer of adding a living wife to a dead mister's pyre, is abolished in British India. The Royal Zoological Society takes over the menagerie at the Tower of London. *Champollion deciphers the Egyptian hieroglyphics using the Rosetta Stone.* Washington Irving, James Fenimore Cooper, and Edgar Allan Poe have tales available for sale in the US while Byron, Goethe, Victor Hugo, Alexandre Dumas ("Les Trois Mousquetaires"), Honoré de Balzac, Benjamin Disraeli, Edward Bulwer-Lytton, Keats, Shelley, Tennyson, and Scott have things out at the bookstores – then Keats dies and Byron dies in the Turko-Greek War. The "Diaries of Samuel Pepys" are published (he's been dead since 1703, of course).*The Venus de Milo is discovered.* Turner, Blake, and Constable are at their canvases, while Liszt and Chopin both make their debuts in Vienna, Bellini, Rossini, Mendelssohn, Schubert, and Beethoven have hits before Beethoven and Schubert both die. **And of great importance to us, the**

WRITING STEAMPUNK

first US patent on a typewriter is granted!

1830s: Stiff collars are the thing for men; women's skirts are shorter but the extra fabric is probably going into their enormous sleeves, which have nothing on the size of their hats which are overflowing with flowers and ribbons. **There are 26 steam cars on the streets of London. The Liverpool-Manchester railroad is formally opened. The steel slit pen gets a patent.** France captures Algiers; there is revolution in Paris again. Charles X of France abdicates. There is a cholera pandemic which starts in India then spreads to Russia, central Europe, and reaches as far as Scotland within six years. German emigration to America is at 15,000 (in ten years it will be 43,000). The first horse-drawn buses and trolleys show up in New York. *The French Foreign Legion is formed in French colonies in Africa.* Mysore is added to the Raj. Lots of folks gaining and losing thrones and high offices in Europe. **Friction matches are a well established niche of manufacturing in Europe. The Etienne to Adrezieux railroad line in France begins to carry passengers. Two-wheeled, one-horse Hansom cabs arrive in London.** Trevithick, the inventor who could be called "first in steam", dies. Factory inspections begin in Britain. The first penny daily, "The New York Sun" is founded. Amateur rowing clubs begin forming in New York. There is a disastrous fire in the British Houses of Parliament. **One of the first sewing machines is constructed in New York.** P.T. Barnum begins his career exhibiting a woman who claims to be over 160 years old and George Washington's nurse when he was a child. **The burglar-proof safe is patented. Sam Colt takes out an English patent for his single-barreled pistol and rifle.** Melbourne and Adelaide are founded in Australia. "The Lancers" becomes the dance to do in Europe. *Halley's Comet reappears.* **The first Canadian railroad is in operation.** England says "register your baby." There is a financial and economic panic in America. The first "Stenograhic Soundhand" book is published. **The American patent for white phosphorus matches is granted.** William IV, King of Great Britain dies, which means Victoria becomes queen in 1837. There are constitutional revolts in Upper and Lower Canada. J. L. McAdam, the originator of the crushed-stone (macadam) roads dies. **Samuel Morse shows off his electric telegraph in New York.** *The "New York Herald" is the first US newspaper to employ European correspondents.* When it comes to Navies GB has 90 ships, Russia 50, France 49, and the US has a measly 15. Abner Doubleday builds a baseball field and enjoys the first game in Cooperstown, NY. **Samuel Cunard starts a steam packet company.** Prussia restricts juveniles to working a maximum of 10 hours a day. **The Daguerre-Niepce method of photography is presented in**

Paris. William Clark of Lewis and Clark fame dies. ***The parallax measurement for a fixed star is first defined.*** John Stevens, an American steam navigation pioneer dies. **Goodyear makes rubber commercially ready with the discovery of the vulcanization process. Schönbein discovers and names the ozone. Steinheil builds the first electric clock.** Scribblers making a living with their pen are: Balzac, Bulwer-Lytton, Disraeli, Goethe, Irving, Tennyson, Robert Browning, Dickens, Longfellow, George Sand, Hugo (has the best seller of 1834 with "The Hunchback of Notre Dame"), Pushkin, Hans Christian Andersen, Elizabeth Barrett Browning, and Poe. Musically: "Jim Crow" becomes an early popular song in the US, Chopin arrives in Paris and later takes up with George Sand, Bellini, Mendelssohn, and Jenny Lind makes her debut in Stockholm. Fanny Elssler, an Austrian ballerina takes the Paris Opéra by storm. Unfortunately, actress Sarah Siddons dies, as does Sir Walter Scott, Anglo-American actor Edwin Booth, actor Edmund Kean, and William Henry Ireland (a forger of Shakespearian plays). Celtic is identified as part of the Indo-European language family and ***the antiquities of the ancient Maya in Central America are discovered.***

Can you tell that transportation and communication are two things that quickened their pace along with the chug and hiss of engines? We're in the throes of the Industrial Revolution for certain now. So let us proceed.

1840s: Victoria marries Albert. Upper and Lower Canada united by Act of Parliament. Afghan forces surrender to the British and the Afghan War ends. The fundamentals of artificial fertilizer are discovered. Beau Brummell dies. The transportation of criminals from England to New South Wales in Australia ends. The game of ninepins is all the rage in the US. **There are 2,816 miles of railroad in the US and 1,331 in England. Penny postage in GB is established**. In the US the Washington Temperance Society arrives. President William Henry Harrison dies after one month in office (actually from a chill he caught giving a long winded inauguration speech). Victoria gives birth to her first born, Edward. New Zealand starts flying the British flag. The Treaty of Nanking gets Britain Hong Kong as the Opium War with China ends. There are riots and strikes in Britain's industrial north. The Boers set up the Orange Free State in Africa. **Hypnosis is discovered. A photographic portrait lens with a speed of f/3.6** (which perhaps a photographer will understand but I don't) **is developed. Doppler writes "On the colored light of the Binary Stars", which is also known as The Doppler Effect. Ether is used for surgical anesthesia.** The Maori of New Zealand revolt against the British. Future Confederate President Jefferson Davis first enters politics. Frémont crosses the Rocky Mountains en route to California. **Morse' telegraph gets messages through from Baltimore to Washington for the first time. The hydraulic crane is patented. American E.B. Bigelow builds a power loom to manufacture carpets. The English Channel gets the first submarine cable. A machine for combing cotton and wool is patented. The compound steam engine is developed. Elias Howe patents the sewing machine. An Italian chemist stirs up a batch of nitroglycerine.** Andrew Jackson dies. The Anglo-Sikh War begins in India, then after British victories, the First Sikh War ends. The war between the US and Mexico ends with the US getting the future states of New Mexico, Arizona, Nevada, and California out of the deal. Oddly enough, two years later *gold is discovered in California.* Poland is experiencing revolts, as is Paris, Vienna, Venice, Berlin, Milan, Parma, Dresden, Baden, and Rome. **John Deere builds a steel plow. Evaporated milk is now available. The first safety matches are created and the first appendectomy is performed.** Britain annexes the Punjab (India) and settlers begin arriving in New Zealand. *David Livingstone crosses the Kalahari Desert.* Barnum opens his museum in NYC. The Bradshaw Railway Guide comes into being just in time for Thomas Cook, British travel agent, to possibly use it for his first booked excursion. American women are now able to be granted university degrees (1841). The polka comes into fashion. **Victoria gets on her first train, Windsor to Paddington Station in London.** The slave population in Cuba is around 436,000. Shocking conditions in prisons and asylums are revealed by social reformer Dorothea Dix in America. **The first propeller driven ship, the SS "Great Britain", is launched from Bristol. Congress gives Morse $30,000 to build the first telegraph line.** *In Paris, the world's first night club opens, "Le Bal des Anglais".* Sequoya, creator of the Cherokee alphabet dies. Siamese twins Chang and Eng Bunker marry Sarah and Adelaid Yates. Skiing becomes a sport in Norway. **Liverpool gets their first public bath and wash houses.** Important for writers, **wood-pulp paper is invented. Even safer matches are created by incorporating combustion ingredients on the striking surface.** The YMCA is founded in England. The rules of baseball are codified. Annapolis (U.S. Naval Academy) opens. There is famine in Ireland when the potato crop goes bad. But Christmas is perked up by the first painted card. *The Smithsonian Institution is founded in Washington.* Women and children aged 13 to 18 can now only work 10 hours in Britain. Amelia Bloomer tries to sway fashion trends. Writers: James Fenimore Cooper, Robert Browning, Dickens, Hugo, Poe, Bulwer-Lytton, Longfellow, Washington Irving (gets post as ambassador to Spain), Tennyson, Elizabeth Barrett Browning, Disraeli, John Stuart Mill, Noah Webster,

Emerson, Thackeray, Balzac, Dumas pere, Hans Christian Anderson, Dostoevsky, Melville, George Sand, Charlotte Bronte, Emily Bronte, Dumas fils, Jakob Grimm, Henry Ward Beecher, Karl Marx and Macaulay. Poe and Fanny Burney die, while Dostoevsky is sentenced to death then commuted to penal servitude in Siberia. **The first "Who's Who" is published.** Spiritualism is hot stuff in the US. Brigham Young leads the Mormon flock to Utah. Musically: Paganini dies, Schumann gets married, Rossini going strong as is Schumann after the honeymoon. The New York Philharmonic is founded. Wagner is writing in Dresden. Mendelssohn puts Shakespeare to music. Verdi has got a piece or two out. Mendelssohn dies as does Chopin and Johann Strauss I. Richard Wagner gets involved in politics and ends up fleeing Dresden for Zurich. Theatrically: Viennese dancer Fanny Elssler tours the US. Drury Lane puts on "The Bohemian Girl." **Electric arc lighting comes to the Opera in Paris. And the first harmonium is created.**

1850s: The Taiping rebellion takes place in China. The Anglo-Kaffir War breaks out. California becomes a state. Cuba declares independence. Victoria announces that henceforth Australia is a separate colony. The Transvaal is established in South Africa. The second Burmese War begins. The Duke of Wellington dies. Britain annexes Nagpur, a Mahratta state. Britain and France align themselves with Turkey and declare war on Russia, and the siege of Sebastopol begins. Charge of the Light Brigade happens at the Battle of Balaklava. "Bleeding Kansas" is a tug of war place between the abolitionists and the slave states. Czar Nicholas I of Russia dies and is succeeded by Alexander II. Britain and Afghanistan align against Persia. The Taiping Rebellion ends. Victoria creates a military award: the Victoria Cross. Anglo-Chinese War begins; Brits bombard Canton. Tasmania is granted free government, compliments of the British Empire. Unhappy things in India: the Mutiny, siege of Delhi. Czar Alexander begins freeing serfs. Peace in India at last. East India Company transfers control to the Empire. Bismark becomes Prussian ambassador to the Russians in St Petersburg. **The gas burner takes its bow. The speed of the nervous impulse is established. A cast-iron frame building goes up.** Louis Daguerre dies. **Singer comes up with the continuous stitch sewing machine.** *Livingstone explores Zambezi.* **A Dutch army surgeon is the first to combine bandages with plaster (voila! The cast is born!) Sam Colt is turning out small arms. A German watchmaker comes up with the earliest electric light bulb. A patent is taken out for the production of rayon. The printing telegraph is invented, as is tungsten steel, the turret lathe, and a converter in the process for making steel.** *Livingstone discovers*

Victoria Falls. Explorers Richard Burton and John Speke discover Lake Tanganyika. Lister studies the coagulation of blood. The first oil well is drilled in Pennsylvania and the steamroller is invented, and so is the high tension induction coil. Pure cocaine is extracted from cocoa beans (no wonder we love chocolate!). Writers: Sir Richard Burton pens a travel book, "Pilgrimage to Mecca"; Balzac, Wordsworth, Fenimore Cooper, Charlotte Bronte and Washington Irving die; Elizabeth Barrett Browning, Robert Browning, Emerson, Hawthorne, Ibsen, Longfellow, Melville ("Moby Dick" a dud when it came to sales), Dumas fils, Harriet Beecher Stowe ("Uncle Tom's Cabin"), Tennyson ("Charge of the Light Brigade"), Thackeray, Thoreau ("Walden"), Dickens, Whitman ("Leaves of Grass"), Trollope, Flaubert ("Madam Bovary"), Hugo, Ibsen, and George Eliot. Musically: Jenny Lind tours America; Schumann, Wagner, Verdi, and Liszt still churning out the hits. Henry Steinway and sons go into the piano business in New York. Schumann attempts suicide but doesn't actually die until two years later. Wagner is in London to conduct a series of concerts. Bechstein also founds a piano factory. The New York Symphony gives its first performance. Daniel Decatur Emmett composes "Dixie". Adelina Patti makes her New York debut. It's the Era of Neo-Gothic. **William Cubitt builds King's Cross Station in London, while another contractor does Paddington Station. Prince Albert rebuilds Balmoral Castle to his specifications. The National Portrait Gallery and the Victoria and Albert Museum both open in London.** Turner dies. Whistler dabs a bit of paint. There is old-age insurance in France. **The first double-decker bus is introduced.** *Gold is found in Victoria, New South Wales!* The "New York Times" appears in September 1851. The US now has more folks (23 million) than Britain (20.8 million) but really lags behind China which already has 430 million. Maine and Illinois begin to enforce prohibition (long before the infamous 1920s). The US imports sparrows from Germany to snack on caterpillars. Wells Fargo and Company is founded. **You can now travel on a railway through the Alps**. Victoria has a whiff of chloroform for the birth of her seventh child. Vaccination is made compulsory against smallpox in Britain. *The largest tree in the world is discovered growing in California.* Cunard's first iron steamer takes just nine and a half days to cross the Atlantic. The London sewers are modernized after major cholera problems. Florence Nightingale gets persnickety over hygienic standards at her military hospital curing the Crimean War. The Paris World's Fair opens in 1855. **There are 40 tunnels on the newly opened Black Forest railroad.** The longest bare-knuckle boxing fight takes place in Melbourne – 186 rounds lasting 6 hours and 15 minutes. *The really old past catches up when a Neanderthal skull is found in a cave near*

Dusseldorf. **The bell for "Big Ben" is cast.** The "Atlantic Monthly" is first published. *Speculation in US railroad shares leads to a financial and economic crisis in Europe.* **The first safety elevator is installed by American civil engineer E. G. Otis. The Transatlantic cable is laid.** The National Association of Baseball Players is organized. **At 27,000 tons, the S.S. "Great Eastern" is not only launched but is the largest ship – period!** *Frenchman Charles Blondin crosses Niagara Falls on a tightrope (the first daredevil!).* And a fellow named Samuel Smiles pens a manual called "Self-Help" that tells one how to succeed in life.

1860s: Abraham Lincoln is elected President of the US. The American Civil War breaks out in 1861 and ends in the spring of 1865. But not before Confederate spies set fire to Barnum's museum and Astor House hoping to burn down NYC. Lincoln is killed while attending the theatre. In Warsaw demonstrators are fired on and massacred. Prince Consort Albert dies and Victoria goes for an all black wardrobe from then on. The French capture Mexico City. There is a massacre of Cheyenne and Arapahoe in Colorado. Lots of trouble, invasion, and intrigue in the German States, involving Prussia, Austria, Italy, Hanover, and Saxony. Russia sells Alaska to the US. There is revolution in Spain. Ulysses S. Grant goes from hot shot general to President. Canada becomes a Dominion. **Cork linoleum is invented as is a practical internal-combustion engine. The first machine-cooled cold storage unit is built. The speed of light is successfully measured. Earth currents are discovered**. Ebenezer Butterick puts out the first paper dress patterns. **Pasteur invents pasteurization for wine.** The composition billiard ball replaces the ivory one (elephants rejoice!). *Lister starts using carbolic acid on compound wounds in his antiseptic surgery.* **The ice machine is invented.** The Law of Heredity is detailed. **The first oil pipeline – a full six miles long – is run in Pennsylvania. Pasteur saves the French silk industry by curing silkworm disease. Alfred Nobel invents dynamite. The underwater torpedo is also invented.** *Livingstone explores the Congo.* **Pierre Michaux builds a bicycle business. Reinforced concrete is patented.** *A diamond field is discovered in South Africa. The first homo-sapien, Cro-Magnon man's skeleton is found in France.* **Celluloid is invented. The periodic law for element classification is formulated**. San Francisco enjoys its first baseball game; baseball is already a hit in Boston and New York. The first British Open golf tournament is held. Skiing becomes a competitive sport. **Another primitive form of the typewriter appears.** *Weather forecasts are a daily affair in Britain.* Victoria starts awarding the Order of the Star of India. *The US introduces passports.* The International Exhibition opens in

London. **Construction on the London Underground railroad begins.** Travelers Insurance Company opens for business. The US Congress dreams up free city mail delivery. Roller skating hits America. The first stolen base occurs during a baseball game. The first US salmon cannery is in business in California. London tenement dwelling reforms begin. *The Roman catacombs are explored.* "In God We Trust" appears on US coins. There are now 91 baseball clubs. The Salvation Army is created from the Christian Revival Association in London. **The first carpet sweeper comes into use.** Canoeing becomes a sport. The London Metropolitan Fire Service is born. **Pullman designs railroad sleeping cars in US.** The Queensberry Rules are formulated for boxing. The first train holdup occurs not in the Old West but in North Bend, Ohio. Chicago's Union stockyards open. In an explosion on the steam paddlewheel "Sultana" on the Mississippi River 1700 die. *The Matterhorn gets climbed.* The first home for destitute children opens in Stepney, London. 1866 sees a "Black Friday" on the London Stock Exchange. Tom Morris wins his first professional golf championship at St. Andrews – he's probably playing with a niblick and a mashie, by the way. Gold is discovered in Wyoming. Armour opens a meat-packing factory in Chicago. Badminton is invented. *In Paris they are racing bicycles.* The Cincinnati Red Stockings becomes the first professional baseball club and introduces the idea of wearing uniforms and the idea of getting salaries to play. British debtors prisons are discontinued. **The "Cutty Sark" clipper ship is launched**. The first postcards are introduced in Austria. Princeton and Rutgers create the first intercollegiate football game. Writers include Mrs. Beeton who pens the "Book of Household Management", Wilkie Collins (mystery writer), George Eliot, Thackeray, Dickens, Dostoesky, Oliver Wendell Holmes, Flaubert, Hugo, Artemus Ward, Longfellow, Ibsen, Tolstoi, Trollope, Lewis Carroll ("Alice's Adventures in Wonderland"), Mark Twain, Whitman, Louisa May Alcott ("Little Women"), Robert Browning, Bret Harte, Hugo. Elizabeth Barrett Browning, Thoreau, Jakob Grimm, Thackeray, and Hawthorne die. Theatrically: Sarah Bernhardt's debut in Racine's play at the Comedie Francaise. Musically: Stephen Foster and Rossini die, Wagner, Brahms, Verdi, and Johann Strauss II ("The Blue Danube" waltz) continue to compose. Painters: Degas, Manet, Dore, Whistler, Winslow Homer, and Cezanne all getting paint on their hands. Sandringham House is built as Victoria's country residence in Norfolk. Yale opens the first Department of Fine Arts in the US. **And line geometry is invented**.

1870s: Standard Oil Company is founded by John D. Rockefeller. Bank holidays occur in England and Wales. Barnum's circus "The

WRITING STEAMPUNK

Greatest Show on Earth" opens in Brooklyn. The Great Fire of Chicago seems to demand a building boom. *Stanley supposedly says "Dr. Livingstone, I presume?" in Africa.* **The first of the modern luxury liners is launched by the White Star Line.** *Heinrich Schliemann begins his Troy excavations.* Bank holidays show up in England and Wales. **The pneumatic rock drill is invented.** *Charles Darwin gets people riled up with "The Descent of Man."* The Albert Hall in London opens. There is a civil war in Spain. The Ballot Act in Britain now makes how a man (no women need apply) votes secret. There is famine in Bengal. Disraeli becomes prime minister. For those of you who watched the World Cup, the first international soccer game is held: England vs Scotland. Following in the footsteps of the baseball clubs, the American Football clubs (not soccer ones) decide to have uniforms, too. Germany adopts the mark as its unit of currency. The Vienna World Exhibition opens. The modern game of lawn tennis is introduced as Sphairistike – badmittion to the rest of us? Oddly enough, after watching English officers play tennis, a visiting American miss returns from her vacation to introduce the game to America. Civil marriage is now compulsory in Germany. In Philadelphia the first American zoo opens. There is rebellion in Cuba. The Prince of Wales takes a trip to India. Britain buys a lot (176,602) of shares in the Suez Canal. In the Far East, Korea is now an independent country. Ethiopians defeat the Egyptian forces in a battle at Gura. There is a massacre of Bulgarians by Turkish soldiers. Serbia declares war on Turkey, probably with good reason. Then Russia declares war on the Turks, too. In a "I don't already have enough titles" coup, Victoria becomes Empress of India. The first Kaffir War begins. The courts in Japan are reformed but two years later there is a revolt in Japan that needs to be put down. **In London, not only is the sewerage system finished but a roller-skating rink opens in 1875.** Capt. Matthew Webb takes a long swim from Dover to Cap Griz Nez on the other side of the English Channel (21 hours and 45 minutes), making him the first fool to do so. The Deutsche Reichsbank opens (in the event you need some cash). The World Exhibition opens in Philadelphia in 1876. More famine in Bengal. **Alexander Graham Bell invents the telephone and the next year the first public telephones appear in the US. Frozen meet is shipped from Argentina to Europe for the first time. Thomas Edison and his team invent the phonograph and improve the telegraph. Saccharin is discovered. The first London telephone exchange arrives.** Besides Darwin, writers busy with their pens are: Disraeli, Jules Verne, Lewis Carroll, George Eliot, Thomas Hardy, Tolstoi, Flaubert, Victor Hugo, Mark Twain, Henry James, Ibsen, and Robert Louis Stevenson. A number of authors pass away though: Dickens, Bulwer-Lytton, Hans Christian

Andersen, and George Sand. Among our working painters are Cezanne, Pissarro, Whistler, Manet, Renoir, Winslow Homer, and William Morris. Rodin is busy with sculptures. The first impressionist exhibition is held in Paris. In the music world our composers are: Tchaikovsky, Wagner, Verdi, Rimsky-Korsakov, Brahms, Johann Strauss II, and Gilbert and Sullivan join the group with "H.M.S. Pinafore."

1880s: Knowing a future vacation spot if they ever saw one, France annexes Tahiti. There is war in the Pacific: Chili vs Bolivia and Peru. **Bingo, the game, is developed. New York is one of the first cities to have its streets lit by electricity. Canned fruits and meats begin appearing in stores** (canned vegetables have been around since before the American Civil War). There is now a parcel post system in England. The World Exhibition moves to Melbourne. The Transvaal Boers try to push the British out and succeed. A French protectorate is welcomed, or at least accepted, by the Bey of Tunis. Political parties make an appearance in Japan. The US bans Chinese immigration for ten years. Cairo is occupied by the British. A reform of American civil service positions begins. In North Africa, the French snap up Tunis. Britain says, let's get everyone out of the Sudan, what? Flogging is no longer cricket in the British Army or Navy in 1881. The World Exhibition moves to Moscow. Without bothering to wrap it up, Victoria gives Epping Forest to the nation. John L. Sullivan wins the heavyweight boxing crown. Bismarck introduces sickness insurance, probably without a goose to help him, in Germany. **The first skyscraper goes up in Chicago – 10 stories!** Whew! **The famed Orient Express makes its first run along the rails from Paris to Istanbul.** Bill Cody organizes a wild west show. **The Brooklyn Bridge is opened to traffic in New York.** The World Exhibition moves to Amsterdam. The Germans decide to diversify and occupy South-West Africa, then annex Tanganyika and Zanzibar. As if it were a jewel, the Congo becomes the personal possession of Leopold II of Belgium. When General Gordon is killed in the fighting at Khartoum, the British leave the Sudan. A protectorate is organized by Great Britain over North Bechuanaland, the Niger River region, and South New Guinea. They occupy a niche of Korea. Ulysses S. Grant dies. Gladstone is now Prime Minister and introduces the idea of Home Rule for Ireland. To make it even more tempting, **gold is discovered in the Transvaal**. Golf is introduced to America. **The Canadian Pacific Railway and the Northern Pacific Line are both completed**. *The British School of Archeology opens in Athens*. The first amateur gold championship is played. Jack the Ripper murders six women in London. *The Kimberley diamond companies are in existence.* There is an aeronautical Exhibition in Vienna and the first beauty contests ever are held in Spain and Belgium. *Greenland is being explored by adventurers on snowshoes.* Victoria's Golden Jubilee is celebrated. Oklahoma is opened to non-Indian settlement (previously it had been where a number of tribes were sent to live). There is a London dock strike and Brazil starts calling itself a republic. Barnum and Bailey's Circus comes to London. Among our writers: Disraeli, Dostoevsky, Longfellow, Flaubert, Anatole France, Henry James, Maupassant, Stevenson, Ibsen, George Bernard Shaw, Mark Twain, Sir Richard Burton (the explorer, not the actor), Tolstoi, Rider Haggard, Nietzche, Arthur Conan Doyle ("A Study in Scarlet", the first Sherlock Holmes tale), Kipling, Quiller-Couch, Oscar Wilde, J. M Barrie, and Yeats. Those who died: Flaubert, George Eliot, Dostoevsky, Anthony Trollope, and Robert Browning. Painters: Cezanne, Pissarro, Renoir, Monet, Van Gogh, Sargent, Toulouse-Lautrec. Rodin is still sculpting. Painters who left the mortal coil: Dore and Manet. The Statue of Liberty goes up in NY waters and the Eiffel Tower is designed. Musically: Gilbert and Sullivan, Brahms, Offenbach, Tchaikovsky ("1812 Overture"), Rimsky-Korsakov, Wagner, Debussy, Strauss, and Verdi. Both Richard Wagner and Franz Liszt die.

1890s: The Gay (as in the connotation of "happy") Nineties. Bismarck is dismissed from office in Germany by William II. The Swiss begin governmental social insurance. **Britain, France, Germany, Italy, Russia, Japan and the US are all involved in the expansion business (in Africa, the South Seas and in neighboring areas in the Far East) and many end up at war in their newly grabbed provinces.** The first general election is held in Japan. A Marxist program is adopted by German Social Democrats. The Triple Alliance of Germany, Austria and Italy is renewed for another 12 years. Gladstone becomes prime minister. The Independent Labour Party is founded in England. **Hawaii is proclaimed a republic**. There is a trial in Paris over corruption in the building of the Panama Canal. French officer Captain Dreyfus is arrested for treason and sent to Devil's Island in French Guiana; turns out he was innocent. Czar Alexander III is succeeded by his son Nicholas II (who becomes the last czar). Armenians are massacred in Turkey, then more are killed in Constantinople. Cuba is struggling with Spain for independence yet. Bismark and Gladstone both die and Empress Elizabeth of Austria is murdered. "The Boxers" are formed in China. The Boer War starts rolling in Africa (Britain vs the Boers). **Germany snags a contract to build the Baghdad Railroad**. And the Spanish-American War has more casualties from influenza than bullets but gives us a couple iconic things: "Remember the 'Maine'" and Teddy Roosevelt shouting "Charge!" In other news: there are global influenza epidemics, widespread famine has hit Russia and India, and an earthquake in Japan whittles 10,000 from the population. But on the upside, **the first English electrical power station opens in England, the first entirely steel-framed building goes up in Chicago,** *Pithecanthropus erectus is discovered in Java* and **the clothing zipper is invented (though not put to use until 1919).** "Gentleman Jim" Corbett takes the heavyweight boxing title away from John L. Sullivan. The longest recorded boxing fight takes place in New Orleans, running 7 hours 4 minutes and going 110 rounds (heroes like that sort of thing usually). **You can get pineapple in cans.** Death duties are introduced in Britain. *Baron de Coubertin decides to organize the modern Olympics; the first new set of games is held in 1896 in Athens.* Lady Margaret Scott dazzles everyone with her swing as she takes the first British golf championship for women. **Gillette invents the safety razor.** Oscar Wilde has an unsuccessful libel action against the Marquis of Queensberry. The American Bowling Congress is formed to govern the game. The first professional football game is played in the US and so is the first US. Open Golf Championship. The Prince of Wales' horse Persimmon wins the Derby in England. The Royal Victorian Order comes into being. Gold is discovered in the Klondike. The World Exhibition is in Brussels. The Royal Automobile Club is founded in London in 1897. Victoria's Diamond Jubilee is celebrated. **The Paris Metro is opened. Scientifically: rubber gloves are used for the first time in surgery, antitoxins are discovered. The first automatic telephone switchboard is introduced. Diesel takes out a patent on his internal combustion engine. Karl Benz puts together his four-wheel car and Henry Ford builds his first car (both in '93). The cinematograph is invented and a horizontal gramophone disc begins replacing the original cylinders for recording sound. Marconi invents a little thing he calls radio telegraphy while the Lumieres invent a camera that takes moving pictures. The principle of rock reaction propulsion is formulated. Helium, xenon, crypton and neon are discovered. An hydroelectric plant opens at Niagara Falls. Radioactivity is discovered as is the malaria and dysentery bacilli and the electron. Zeppelin builds his airship (1898). The first magnetic recording of sound is accomplished**. The future is catching us up quickly now. Writers: Shaw, Kipling, Wild, Ibsen, Conrad, James, Wells, Yeats, Chekhov, Thomas Hardy, and Tolstoi are working. Whitman, Tennyson, Maupassant, Oliver Wendell Holmes, Stevenson, Harriet Beecher Stowe, and Lewis Carroll die. Cinemagraphically: **Edison's Kinetoscope Parlor opens in New York.** Musically: Lottie Collins, an English music-hall star, sings "Ta-ra-ra-boom-de-ay"! Richard Strauss, Tchaikowsky, Rachmaninoff, Puccini,

Verdi, Dubussy are working, and the last Gilbert and Sullivan comic operetta is written. Tchaikovsky dies. In the art world: Gauguin moved to Tahiti, Toulouse-Lautrec does his first music hall posters, and Cezanne, Monet, Aubrey Beardsley, Degas, Matisse, and Rodin are working. Van Gogh dies. Art Nouveau style is THE style.

APPENDIX II
19th CENTURY TECHNOLOGY

Got some ideas percolating? Then let's add some "just tech" stuff to the things you can work with.
So let's see what was tumbling from inventors' minds and onto patent paperwork in the first half of the 19th century. This time I'll stick only with what might tickle your Steampunk imaginings.

1804 has Freidrich Winzer or Winsor patenting gas lighting (which had been invented by someone else 12 years before – industrial espionage!) But more importantly, Richard Trevithick developed the first steam-powered locomotive, which was so heavy it broke the rails – back to the drawing board for Trev.

1809 The first electric light – the arc lamp – is invented by Humphry Davy; 1810 the printing press is improved by Frederick Koenig, and the tin can is invented by Peter Durand.

1814 sees George Stephenson pushing Trevithick aside and designing a steam locomotive, which is also noted as being the first invented – don't know who proofed the list at About.com. They need to make up their minds before George and Dick resort to fisticuffs.

Also in 1814 the first plastic surgery is performed in England (handy for those of you designing cyborgs or Frankensteinian hunks) and von Fraunhofer invents the spectroscope for chemical analysis of glowing objects. Ooh! Joseph Nicephore Niepce (don't ask me to spell that again) takes the first photograph with a camera obscura set in the window of his home – it took eight hours for the camera to take the picture.

1815 If there is spelunking in your character's future they might want to use the miner's lamp Humphrey Davy invented. Improvement on his arc lamp, perchance?

1819 The soda fountain is patented by Samuel Fahnestock – doubt this is the counter with stools to share a drink with your main squeeze; but Rene Laennec wanted to listen to his sweetie's heart and invented the stethoscope. Okay, so I'm 100% sure that's why he made one.

1823 was a great day for spies, future private detectives and news anchors – Charles Mackintosh invented the Mackintosh (a raincoat). While I picture a trenchcoat, it probably was a version of a great coat – far more in sync with the fashion of the day.

1824 Portland cement is patented by Joseph Aspdin. Why add this? Bad guys. Early Steampunk mafia bad guys who need to get rid of squealers, capish?

1825 The electromagnet is invented by William Sturgeon.

1827 makes carrying flint with you to light a lamp, a smoke, or whatever no longer necessary for the modern match is invented by John Walker (so why did they get named Lucifers? Probably, don't quote me on this, a brand name). Charles Wheatstone coined the word microphone – why, I've no idea.

1829 William Austin Burt invents AND patents a typographer, the forerunner of the typewriter while Louis Braille invents Braille printing to enable the blind to read.

1830 Barthelemy Thimonnier did seamstresses a favor, he invented the sewing machine.

Back in 1824 Michael Faraday invented the first toy balloon but he got much more serious after that and in **1831** invents the electric dynamo (which actually sounds like a larger toy, possibly a T-Rex with remote control, but is really a generator).

1832 the first stereoscope is invented by Charles Wheatstone but doesn't get patented until 1838.

1834 Henry Blair becomes the second black person to receive a U.S. patent – his is for a corn planter, no idea what the other fellow did (this is tossed in to illustrate that it isn't just Europeans or those of European descent inventing things). This is also the year the earliest refrigerator type of thing is invented, an ether ice machine, dreamed up by Jacob Perkins.

1835 sees improvements in photography, when Henry Talbot invents the calotype; in mechanical tools when Solymon Merrick patents the wrench; in what will aid transportation with Francis Pettit Smith's propeller, AND Charles Babbage invents a mechanical calculator, deemed the first computer.

1836 Samuel Colt invents the very first revolver...which is different from a pistol (which could be a flintlock or a matchlock).

1837 Samuel Morse invents the telegraph then in 1838 invents Morse Code to use in conjunction with the telegraph.

1839 has Goodyear (Charles by name) inventing rubber vulcanization; Louis Daguerre and his buddy Niepce co-inventing Daguerreotype photography; Kirkpatrick Macmillan either inventing or re-inventing (if you listened to those Scotsmen) the bicycle, and Sir William Robert Grove comes up with the idea for (doesn't invent or patent) the first hydrogen fuel cell.

1840 is when John Herschell invented the blueprint. How did anything get built before this?

Handy for the researcher who prints tons of stuff via the Net or copy machine, in 1841 the stapler was patented by Samuel Slocum.

1843 is when Alexander Bain invented the facsimile (he no doubt heard about the stapler), using photographic equipment, I believe.

1844 mercerized cotton is invented by, astoundingly enough, John Mercer. While in 1845 Elias Howe invents a sewing machine (perhaps he hadn't heard of the one Thimonnier created back in 1830); and Robert William Thomson patented the vulcanized rubber pneumatic tire. Quite a mouthful so I don't recommend attempting to say it quickly.

1846 saw Dr. William Morton using anesthesia for tooth extraction in Massachusetts. (Didn't mention this in the 19th century section (aka Appendix I), but there was such as thing as "Waterloo teeth" which were false teeth made from a) animal bone or teeth, b) cadaver teeth – actually got their name from the extractions that occurred on the battlefield among the dead, and/or c) teeth the poor donated in exchange for cash – they were the ones I'll bet who would have appreciated the anesthesia and probably weren't given it.)

1847 Antiseptics are invented by Ignaz Semmelweis of Hungary.

1848 With all the teeth being pulled, or so I surmise, Waldo Hanchette decided to patent the dental chair.

1849 closes the first part of the century with the invention of the safety pin by Walter Hunt.

One never knows what might come in handy. I mean, you might be able to fix a machine using a safety pin!

What 1850 marks is the beginning of what historians call the Second Industrial Age. Sometimes even called "The Age of Synergy" (1867-1914). Things begin being turned out lickety-split now and they are frequently based on science rather than mechanics. Odd, huh, considering we think clockwork movements, gears, and such in terms of Steampunk usually. This is also the era that the majority of the Victorian and Weird West Steampunk tales are set though. To save time I'm not giving specific years or inventors names, just what was invented in the order it was invented. Okay, I'll at least break it down into decades.

1850s: patent for a dishwasher; the Singer sewing machine; the gyroscope; first airship powered by first aircraft engine—didn't work well together; the manned glider; the principles of fiber optics demonstrated; the sewing machine motor; rayon; pasteurization; Pullman Sleeping Car;

rotary washing machine; internal combustion engine.

1860s: elevator safety brakes; another bicycle invented; the Yale lock or cylinder lock; the machine gun/Gatling gun; first man-made plastic; dynamite; tin can with a key opener; the torpedo; the first practical and modern typewriter; air brakes for trains; tungsten steel; traffic lights.

1870s: the metal windmill; first mail-order catalog (Montgomery-Wards); barbed wire; shoe welt stitcher; the telephone, first practical four-stroke internal combustion engine; the carpet sweeper; the cylinder phonograph, the first moving pictures; a practical and longer-lasting electric lightbulb.

1880s: toilet paper!!!; the modern seismograph; first crude metal detector; roll film for cameras, automatic player piano; paper-strip photographic film, first practical fountain pen, first working, mechanical cash register, the steam turbine; the machine gun (Maxim's is apparently different than Gatling's); first practical automobile powered by internal-combustion engine; first gas-engined motorcycle; the dishwasher (by Josephine Cochrane – yes, a female! It was used in restaurants, not the home, and she sold the patent to Kitchenaid); world's first four-wheeled motor vehicle (Daimler); Coca Cola; radar; barbed wire; gramophone; first wearable contact lenses; first paper drinking straws; first commercially successful pneumatic tire (Dunlop), the AC motor and transformer (Tesla); the matchbook; Cordite, a smokeless gunpower.

1890s: the escalator; the diesel-fueled internal combustion engine (Diesel); the Dewar flask or vacuum flask; the zipper; carborundum (no idea what it is); portable motion-picture camera, film processing unit and projector called the Cinematographe (the Lumiere Brothers who were then able to present a projected motion picture to an audience of more than one person – going to the movies was born in 1895!); the rubber heel (might keep you from getting electrocuted, eh?); the roller coaster; the bicycle frame; and the motor-driven vacuum.

APPENDIX III
EARLY 20th CENTURY: WHAT'S HAPPENING

1900s: Boxer risings in China occur. Umberto I of Italy is killed by an anarchist; Victoria dies of natural causes, President McKinley is gunned down by an anarchist (Theodore Roosevelt, VP, becomes President) and the king and queen of Serbia are murdered. The Boers are using guerilla warfare in South Africa; casualties counts are 5,774 British and 4,000 Boers. Cuba comes under US protection. The US takes over the Panama Canal project. There is a coal strike in the US. Portugal is bankrupt. Trotsky escapes prison in Siberia and settles in London. The Alaskan frontier is settled. The Russo-Japanese War breaks out, there is a dictatorship in Columbia, revolts in German South-West Africa, and Bolivia and Chile come to terms. The Greeks revolt against the Turks and things aren't too happy in Russia where Rasputin is gaining influence at court. The Panic of 1907 causes a run on banks in the US. Britain's Edward VII is visiting various foreign courts (he is known as Europe's Uncle because so many of his sisters and nieces married into regal families – his sister, I believe, is the Czarina of all the Russias.) In lighter news, the Cake Walk is the dance fad, the Davis cup comes into being, the World Exhibition is in Paris. Oil drilling begins in Persia. Boxing becomes a legal sport in England. **The first British submarine is launched** and Edward VII creates the Order of Merit. Chicago hosts the first American Bowling Club tournament. The town of St. Pierre on Martinique is destroyed by a volcano. **Motor-cars are restricted to 20 mph speed limits in Britain. The first motor taxis appear in London. Henry Ford spends $100,000 to open the Ford Motor Company. You can cross the US in 65 days by motor-car.** The first teddy bears are designed. The first Tour de France is peddled. The World Series is called off due to a dispute – sorry Giants and Boston clubs. The 10-hour work day is official in France. There is a Paris Conference on the white slave trade (sort of shades of *Thoroughly Modern Millie*!). In New York, a woman is arrested for smoking in public. **The Broadway subway is now open**. Both the World Exhibition and the Olympics are held in St. Louis (reasons to "Meet Me In St. Louis, Louie"). **The first trenches are used in warfare in the Russo-Japanese War. In Berlin the Lindstrom**

Company is turning out both phonographs and records to play on them. Steerage rates are cut to $10 by foreign lines for immigrants to the US. Not all that long after, immigration to the US is restricted by law. Ty Cobb begins his baseball career. **The Astin Motor Company forms up in England where the first motor buses are being used in London and the Piccadilly and Bakerloo underground line has opened. Neon signs are appearing.** *The Cullinan diamond is found (over 3,000 carats).* The Rotary Club is founded. London beats out NYC yet in population, 4.5 million to 4 million (Paris and others left in the dust). The night-shift is internationally forbidden for women. The US Pure Food and Drugs Act is formed in reaction to conditions in the Chicago stockyards. The first Grand Prix race is held. An earthquake in San Francisco kills 700 and has $400 million in damage and property loss. In what sounds like an odd World Series, Chicago beats Chicago (two different leagues though). The Boy Scouts are founded. In the scandal sheets: divorced for adultery, Crown Princess Louis of Sachsen marries an Italian violinist. Mother's Day is established in the US. The first daily comic strip appears (in *San Francisco Chronicle*). A more determined earthquake in Sicily and southern Calabria kills 150,000. London hosts the Olympic Games and the US takes 15 firsts out of 28 in track and field. **The first trial flight of a zeppelin occurs and a nasty zeppelin disaster happens near Echterdingen a few years later.** The spitball is made illegal in baseball. Fountain pens become popular. The first Model "T" rolls from the Ford factory. The Girl Guides are founded in England. The first permanent waves are available from hairdressers in London. And attention shoppers: Selfridge opens his department store on Oxford Street, London. In Science and Manufacturing: **the first Browning revolvers are manufactured, human speech is transmitted by radio waves,** *excavations in Crete result in the discovery of the Minoan culture,* **radon is discovered and Max Planck formulates quantum theory. The age of steam is replaced by the age of electricity. The hormone adrenalin is isolated. Marconi transmits telegraphic radio messages. The first motor-driven bicycles (motor cycles) appear. The first Mercedes rolls off the Daimler production line. The third law of thermodynamics is postulated. In '02 the Irish Channel is crossed by a fellow in a balloon. Orville and Wilbur Wright get their manned, motorized plane in the air in '03 then improve it to fly 30 miles in 40 minutes by '08. The electrocardiograph is invented. The theory of radioactivity is postulated and the first practical photoelectric cell is devised.** Yellow fever is wiped out in Panama where works continues on the canal. **Rolls-Royce is founded. Photographs are first transmitted telegraphically. Silicone is discovered. Einstein comes up with $E=mc^2$. Rayon yarn is**

manufactured now. The term "allergy to medicine" is first used. *The magnetic North Pole is determined.* China and Britain agree to cut back on opium production. "Typhoid Mary" is identified and incarcerated. **The first radio program is broadcast in the US in '06 – has both voice and music.** Tissue cultures are developed and the gyrocompass is improved. Lumiere develops color photography! Bakelite is invented and the age of plastics begins. Research into genetics begins. *A Frenchman crosses the English Channel in a plane in 37 minutes. Peary reaches the North Pole.* When it comes to writers, we have Colette, Conrad, Gorki, Tolstoi, Chekhov, Freud, Kipling, Barri, Conan Doyle, Beatrix Potter, Shaw, James, Jack London, G. K. Chesterton, Hermann Hesse, O'Henry, Wells, Wharton, Verne, E. M. Forster, John Galsworth, Upton Sinclair, Anatole France, Mary Roberts Rinehart, Gertrude Stein, Baroness Orczy ("The Scarlet Pimpernel"), Kenneth Grahame ("The Wind In the Willows") and Ezra Round. Stephen Crane and Oscar Wilde die, as do Anton Chekhov, Jules Verne, Lew Wallace (of "Ben Hurr" fame) and Henrik Ibsen. When it comes to composers: Sullivan of Gilbert and Sullivan fame dies as does Verdi, Rimsky Kosakov and Dvorak. Puccini, Richard Strauss, Ravel, Rachmaninoff, Debussy, Victor Herbert, and Bartok continue to write high brow stuff. Ragtime jazz is hot in the US and **Enrico Caruso steps up to the mic in the studio to make his first phonograph recording**. Oscar Hammerstein builds the Manhattan Opera House. The first recording of a Verdi opera is made. In the art galleries you'll find Picasso, Gauguin, Cezanne, Renoir, Sargent, Toulouse-Lautrec, Edvard Munch, Rodin, Max Klinger, Gustav Klimt, Marc Chagall, and Vassily Kandinsky all have things. Matisse dreams up the term "Cubism." Frank Lloyd Wright builds the Robie House. Henri Toulouse-Laurec, Whistler, Gauguin, Pissaro, Frederick Remington and Cezanne all die. Theatrically: The police censor closes the theatre in New York after one performance of Bernard Shaw's "Mrs. Warren's Profession." George M. Cohan produces a show on Broadway. In New York the first Ziegfeld Follies lightens things up. Isadora Duncan is popular for her dance interpretation. **And silent movies are being made ("The Great Train Robbery" in '03 is the longest film to this point, running 12 minutes!) and the first "slow motion" effect is seen. The first newsreels become a fixture in the theatres and the first movie star, Mary Pickford, is featured on the big screen.**

1910s: **Halley's comet shows up again and in the US the "week-end" becomes popular.** There is revolt in Albania and Portugal; Japan annexes Korea; the Egyptian premier is assassinated. Edward VII dies and George V takes over in Britain. China abolishes slavery while in the US the Mann

Act makes it illegal to transport "women across state lines for immoral purposes"! There's been a civil war in Mexico, but it now ends. The German gunboat "Panther" creates an international crisis when it docks in Agadir. The Kaiser is going on about Germany's "place in the sun", which can't be good. There is war between Turkey and Italy and revolution in central China. The National Chinese Party is founded. In GB there is a coal strike, a dock strike in London and a transport workers' strike. Turkey closes the Dardanelles to shipping. The German, Austrian, Italian alliance is renewed. Lenin and Stalin get their heads together. After suffragette demonstrations in London, Mrs. Pankhurst is jailed in connection with explosives showing up at Lloyd George's home. Woodrow Wilson becomes President in the US; George I of Greece is assassinated. A Balkan war is on. Mahatma Gandhi is arrested. The US. Federal Reserve System comes into being. There's scandal in France over Mme Caillaux killing Gaston Calmette but **the outbreak of World War in 1914** soon trumps that sort of thing. Archduke Francis Ferdinand of Austria and his wife are assassinated and war is declared on Serbia, then Germany declares war on Russia and France invades Belgium so Britain declares war on Germany, then Austria declares war on Russia and...well you get the idea. It isn't until 1917 that the US declares war on Germany (they were busy subduing folks in the Dominican Republic before this) and the war ends in 1918. *There are tetanus epidemics in the trenches.* The Peace Conference is held in Paris. But that doesn't mean there aren't still other wars going on: the Brits, Afghans and Indians (of India) are at it, as is Finland and Russia (now the U.S.S.R), and strikes in Canada and the US, race riots in Chicago, and the US Congress shoots down the idea of joining the League of Nations. T.E. Lawrence (aka Lawrence of Arabia) becomes liaison officer to Faisal's army. Pancho Villa has General Pershing after him down on the US-Mexican border. Food rationing begins in 1916 in Germany where 1917 turns into a "year of starvation". Mata Hari is executed for spy stuff. The US buys the Dutch West Indies. There's now a literacy requirement to become a US citizen. Czar Nicholas II and his family are executed in Russia. Women over 30 get the vote in England in 1918, too. Teddy Roosevelt, Florence Nightingale, and Buffalo Bill Cody all die late in the decade, but Rasputin gets his in '16. And Lady Astor becomes the first female member of Parliament. **There are now 122,000 telephones in use in GB.** In the US the Postal Savings program is established. **The Manhattan Bridge is completed. Barney Oldfield drives his Benz going 133 mph. in Florida.** Father's Day is first celebrated. In England the Official Secrets Act becomes law. **The first flight at a height of 12,800 ft is recorded in Germany.** Worth knowing: on August 9th, 1911, the temperature is 100 degrees Fahrenheit in London! Woolworths is founded. **The first successful parachute jump is recorded**. Jim Thorpe loses all his gold medals and trophies at the Olympic Games in Stockholm when they find out he played semi-professional baseball the year before and the Olympics is an amateur competition yet. Thorpe goes back to playing professional baseball. The Titanic sinks with 1513 drowned. The foxtrot comes into fashion in '13. **Zippers finally become popular**. Grand Central Terminal in NYC opens. The Panama Canal opens in '14. Margaret Sanger is jailed for writing a book about birth control. When she gets out she opens a birth control clinic. Attention fashionistas: bobbed hair for ladies sweeps the US and Britain. The US Senate rejects the suffrage bill in '17 and four women get six months in jail for picketing the White House in behalf of suffage. **Regular airmail service is a done deal between NYC and Washington D.C., and Chicago to New York. Daylight savings time is introduced in the US**. A new 8-hour work day is established in Germany. In Hong Kong the Jockey Club racetrack grandstand topples and 600 die. A world-wide influenza epidemic is in progress (close to 22 million will die by 1920). Heavyweight boxing champion John L. Sullivan dies as does H.H. Bancroft, historian of the American West. War statistics show 8.5 million were killed, 21 million wounded, 7.5 million were prisoners or missing in action. Mobilized forces had been 63 million at a cost of $232,058 million. There are 103.5 million people in the US in 1918. Jack Dempsey gains the US heavyweight boxing championship in 14 seconds, then takes the world championship as well. The first nonstop flight from Newfoundland to Ireland is made. Austria abolishes the death penalty. **The Radio Corporation of America (RCA) opens for business**. Babe Ruth hits a 587 foot home run. The baseball world is rocked by the Black Sox bribery scandal. The American Legion is formed. Sir Barton is the horse that is hard to beat, as the four legged knight is the first horse to win the triple crown of Kentucky Derby, Preakness and Belmont Stakes. Matador Juan Belmonte of Spain does in 200 bulls in 109 corridas, and **the development of the mechanical rabbit gets modern greyhound racing off in a flash.** In the book world: E. M. Forster, H.G. Well, John Galsworthy, D.H. Lawrence, Edith Wharton, G. K. Chesteron, Ezra Pound, Somerset Maugham, C.G. Jung, Willa Cather, Marcel Proust, Shaw, Jack London, Robert Frost, Conrad, James Joyce, Bertrand Russell, Freud, Hermann Hesse, Carl Sandburg, Theodore Dreiser, Edna Ferber, T.S. Eliot, Barrie, Upton Sinclair, Anatole France, Aldous Huxley, Booth Tarkington, Sherwood Anderson, and Ring Lardner are all writing. Twain, Henry James and Tolstoi die. James Joyce's "Ulysses" goes up in flames as the US Post Office burns installments published in the *Little Review* magazine. Theatrically: 72 year old Sarah Bernhardt begins her last tour of America in '17; **Mary Pickford is still a film darling while Charlie Chaplin is making $1 million a year. London has 400 cinemas but they can't beat the 5 million people who go to the movies daily in the US.** In spite of daily bombardment of the city during the war, the Paris Opera says "the show must go on". Gilbert (of Gilbert and Sullivan fame) dies. The tango gains immense popularity in the US and Europe. Musically: Jazz arrives in Europe. Irving Berlin, George M. Cohan and Jerome Kern have some snappy tunes out. New Orleans jazz, and really just any kind of jazz, is all young America wants to hear. The old schoolers Strauss, Rimsky-Korsakov, Puccini, Stravinsky, Victor Herbert, Gustav Mahler, Ravel, Debussy, and Bartok continue to do their thing. **The first jazz recordings are made** and a Dixieland jazz band is booked into Reisenweber's Restaurant in New York. In regards to art: There is a Post-Impressionist Exhibition in London and Frank Lloyd Wright is not only well known for domestic architecture, he's influential. Da Vinci's "Mona Lisa" is stolen from the Louvre in '11 and found in Italy in '13. The Peter Pan statue goes up in Kensington Gardens. Busy at their canvases or sculpting are Renoir, Matisse, Klee, Chagall, Picasso, Modigliani, Sargent, Munch, Nash, and Kandinsky. Bauhaus is founded. Winslow Homer, Degas, Rodin, Renoir, and Rossetti die. Scientifically: *The excavation of Cnossus on Crete is completed, the first deep-sea research expedition head out, the South Pole is reached*, **the theory of atomic structure is formulated, and the first practical electric self-starter for automobiles is developed. The process for making cellophane is invented.** Lister dies. **The theory of stellar evolution is formulated and the basic ideas of jet propulsion are laid out. Rocketry experiments begin. The first successful heart surgery is performed—on a dog. Coal dust is turned into oil. The first fighter plane is built in '15. Ford develops a farm tractor and his factory produces its one millionth car. The first transcontinental phone call is placed by Alexander Graham Bell in New York to his friend and colleague Tom Watson in San Francisco. Blood for transfusions is now refrigerated**. Astronomer Percival Lowell dies. The theory of shell shock is first suggested. **Ultrasonic detection of submarines is built** (funny how war makes these things progress more quickly, isn't it?). Ferdinand Zeppelin dies. *Excavations at Babylon begin.* **The true dimensions of the Milky Way (galaxy, not candy bar) are discovered.** In weather news there was some brow slapping over **the idea that cyclones originate as waves which separate in different air masses. There is a total eclipse of the sun which in some way was considered to prove Einstein's theory of relativity. Word came that the atom is not the final bit of universe building material. The first experiments** with shortwave radio occur. A two man team flies from London to Australia in 135 hours (and a lot of stops for petrol). And experiments are on the ground and running to create a film with sound.

APPENDIX IV
EARLY 20th CENTURY TECHNOLOGY

1900s: the zeppelin; the modern escalator; the double-edged safety razor; **the radio receiver which successfully received a radio transmission**; the compact, modern vacuum cleaner; the air conditioner; the lie detector or polygraph machine; **the neon light**; crayons; bottle-making machinery; **the first gas motored and manned airplane** (the Wright Flyer); windshield wipers (invented by Mary Anderson); ductile tungsten used in lightbulbs; teabags!!; the tractor; the vacuum diode or Fleming valve; $E=mc^2$; Cornflakes; first sonar like device; **the triode (electronic amplifying tube)**; Bakelite; **color photography** (the Lumiere Brothers again); the **first piloted helicopter**; **the gyrocompass**; cellophane; first Model T sold (1908); Geiger counter; and instant coffee.

1910s: first talking motion picture (demonstrated by Edison); **automobile electrical ignition system**; motorized movie cameras replace hand-cranked ones; **the first tank**; Life Savers candy (1912); the crossword puzzle (1913 though it was a real fad in the 1920s); Merch Chemical Company patented what is known today as ecstasy; the bra, the modern zipper; **the Morgan gas mask (in 1914, just in time for the trenches of WW I)**; Pyrex; **radio tuners that received different stations**; stainless steel; **the superheterodyne radio circuit invented** (still used in radios and TV sets today, as I understand it); fortune cookies (1918); the pop-up toaster; **short-wave radio**; **flip-flop circuit**; and the arc welder.

This is by no means a complete listing of all the things that were invented or improved upon during the Industrial Revolution or its brother, the Second Industrial Revolution. And a lot of inventors got left out once I went into the longer lists of things. It is simply a start, and idea generator for your Steampunk dreaming.

APPENDIX V
THE COMPETITION
TITLES and AUTHORS
CURRENTLY AVAILABLE AT BOOKSELLERS

Whether you are writing Steampunk or a story that better fits one of the other popular genre niches, the one thing a writer can not skip doing is READ, READ, READ in the genre they intend to target. This is not just to familiarize yourself with what is being written, but to evaluate the effectiveness of what someone else has written. It is certainly how I came up with some of the choices I offered you early on here. And I have not read every Steampunk novel available – not only are new titles being released constantly but not every writing style or storyline catches my interest. The more you read, the more you find yourself gravitating to particular types of tales, and that will help when it comes to spinning your own Steampunk adventure.

Let's look at the statistics for they surely show the leaps in Steampunk interest, if not in readership, at least at the publishing houses.

From 1967 to 2000 there were 15 titles with Steampunk elements and over half of those came off the presses from 1990 to the close of the century.

From 2001 to the close of 2010, 51 adult novels, 3 erotica, 5 anthologies, 10 YA and 19 middle grade Steampunk titles were released – a total of 88 books. 33 of them are spread out from 2001 through 2008. The pack begins to swell in 2009.

That year saw 17 Steampunk titles hit the bookshelves: 12 adult, 2 erotica, 2 YA and 1 middle grade.

It multiplied in 2010 with a total of 23 adult novels, 3 anthologies and 12 YA/MG books. That's 38 books, a jump of 123%, the majority of these released in the second half of the year.

These tallies don't even take into consideration the graphic novels or the independently published e-books or titles from e-book publishers that aren't released through Amazon's Kindle or Barnes and Noble's Nook.

Early in March 2011, another 13 new titles were showing on Amazon as either already published or scheduled for publication, which seems to indicate that even more Steampunk titles will be released by year's end. Partly because a number of those 2010 books were the starts or second books in a series.

That's where the market stands now, poised for more growth. And you're on the edge of the diving board, staring down into the pool of possibilities.

It will help to know what your competition is writing, what those who read Steampunk and watch flixs with Steampunk elements are being exposed to already.

WHAT HAS PROCEEDED YOUR STEAMPUNK TALE

It may appear odd to have the lists of authors and titles at the conclusion of the book. I'm treating it here as more of a bibliography from which you can choose. These are the titles available into March of 2011, or those available in the coming months. I won't say this is all there is out there. This is merely what I turned up in various online searches. Additions to the list will appear on my website
www.RomanceAndMystery.com
on the Steampunk page. If you come up with something I've missed, send a message along to
beth@RomanceAndMystery.com
with STEAMPUNK BOOKS in the subject line and I'll add it to the tally.

I may not have included something you consider Steampunk or included something you don't consider as Steampunk in these tallies. What I have done is included what I felt had at least a chance of rubbing shoulders with Steampunk or shared some Steampunk elements.

EARLY SCIENCE FICTION
(the Grandfathers of all
20th and 21st Century Steampunk tales)

JULES VERNE (not all of Verne's 54 novels have been given, just those most familiar to most of us)
A JOURNEY TO THE CENTER OF THE EARTH 1864, *FROM EARTH TO THE MOON* 1865, *TWENTY-THOUSAND LEAGUES UNDER THE SEA* 1870, *AROUND THE WORLD IN EIGHTY DAYS* 1873, *THE MYSTERIOUS ISLAND* 1875,

H. G. WELLS (while Wells wrote into the 1940s he shifted focus so that only these early titles apply to our Steampunk themes well)
THE TIME MACHINE 1895, *ISLAND OF DR. MOREAU* 1896, *THE INVISIBLE MAN* 1897, *THE WAR OF THE WORLDS* 1898, *THE FIRST MEN IN THE MOON* 1901

ARTHUR CONAN DOYLE
THE LOST WORLD 1912

H. RIDER HAGGARD
KING SOLOMON'S MINE'S 1885, *ALLAN QUATERMAIN* 1887, *SHE* 1887, *ALLAN'S WIFE* 1889, *PEOPLE OF THE MIST* 1894, *AYESHA* 1905, *QUEEN SHEBA'S RING* 1910, *ALLAN AND THE HOLY FLOWER* 1915, *WHEN THE WORLD SHOOK* 1919, *WISDOM'S DAUGHTER* 1923, *HEU-HEU* 1924, *TREASURE OF THE LAKE* 1926

BRAM STOKER
DRACULA 1897, *LADY OF THE SHROUD* 1909, *THE LAIR OF THE WHITE WORM* 1911, *DRACULA'S GUEST AND OTHER WEIRD TALES* 1914 (published posthumously by Stoker's widow)

OSCAR WILDE
THE PICTURE OF DORIAN GRAY 1890

ROBERT LOUIS STEVENSON
THE STRANGE CASE OF DR. JEKYLL AND MR. HYDE 1886

EDGAR RICE BURROUGHS (I've cut Burroughs' list off at 1940 – there are still a few titles after that date with none appearing in the 1950s but resurfacing in the 1960s again)
A PRINCESS OF MARS 1912, *TARZAN OF THE APES* 1912, *THE RETURN OF TARZAN* 1913, *THE BEASTS OF TARZAN* 1914, *THE SON OF TARZAN* 1914, *THE GODS OF MARS* 1914, *THE MAN-EATER* 1915, *THE LOST CONTINENT* 1916, *TARZAN AND THE JEWELS OR OPAR* 1916, *THE WARLORD OF MARS* 1918, *THE LAND THAT TIME FORGOT* 1918, *THE PEOPLE THAT TIME FORGOT* 1918, *OUT OF TIME'S ABYSS* 1918, *TARZAN THE UNTAMED* 1919, *THUVIA, MAID OF MARS* 1920, *TARZAN THE TERRIBLE* 1921, *THE CHESSMEN OF MARS* 1922, *TARZAN AND THE GOLDEN LION* 1922, *TARZAN AND THE ANT MEN* 1924, *THE CAVE GIRL* 1925, *THE ETERNAL LOVER* 1925, *THE MOON MAID* 1926, *TARZAN, LORD OF THE JUNGLE* 1927, *THE MASTER MIND OF MARS* 1928, *TARZAN AND THE LOST EMPIRE* 1928, *TARZAN AT THE EARTH'S CORE* 1929, *THE MONSTER MEN* 1929, *TARZAN THE INVINCIBLE* 1930, *TARZAN TRIUMPHANT* 1931, *A FIGHTING MAN OF MARS* 1931, *TARZAN AND THE CITY OF GOLD* 1932, *JUNGLE GIRL* 1932, *TARZAN AND THE LION MAN* 1933, *PIRATES OF VENUS* 1934, *LOST ON VENUS* 1935, *TARZAN AND THE LEOPARD MEN* 1935, *TARZAN'S QUEST* 1935, *SWORDS OF MARS*

1936, *TARZAN THE MAGNIFICENT* 1936, *THE RESURRECTION OF JIMBER-JAW* 1937, *TARZAN AND THE FORBIDDEN CITY* 1938, *THE LAD AND THE LION* 1938, *CARSON OF VENUS* 1939, *SYNTHETIC MEN OF MARS* 1940

LATE 20TH CENTURY
(the first Steampunk titles)
Alphabetical order by author's surname

STEPHEN BAXTER
ANTI-ICE 1993
JAMES BLAYLOCK
HOMUNCULUS 1986; *LORD KELVIN'S MACHINE* 1992
RONALD W. CLARK
QUEEN VICTORIA'S BOMB 1967
PAUL DI FILIPPO
THE STEAMPUNK TRILOGY 1995
WILLIAM GIBSON and BRUCE STERLING
THE DIFFERENCE ENGINE 1990
K.W. JETER
MORLOCK NIGHT 1979; *INFERNAL DEVICES* 1986/7
MERCEDES LACKEY
THE FIRE ROSE 1996
CHINA MIÉVILLE
PERDIDO STREET STATION 2000
MICHAEL MOORCOCK
WARLORD OF THE AIR 1971; *THE LAND LEVIATHAN* 1974; *THE STEEL TSAR* 1981
KIM NEWMAN
ANNO DRACULA 1992
TIM POWERS
THE ANUBIS GATES 1997
NEAL STEPHENSON
THE DIAMOND AGE 1995

21ST CENTURY STEAMPUNK
(the Tidal Wave)
Alphabetical order by author's surname
ADULT MARKET

TIM AKERS
HEART OF VERIDON 2009, *THE HORNS OF RUIN* 2010

PAOLO BACIGALUPI
THE WINDUP GIRL 2010
JONATHAN BARNES
THE SOMNAMBULIST 2009
ELIZABETH BEAR
NEW AMSTERDAM 2008
JEDEDIAH BERRY
THE MANUAL OF DETECTION 2009
MELJEAN BROOK
HERE THERE BE MONSTERS (novella in *Burning Up* with other writers 2010); *THE IRON DUKE* 2010
GAIL CARRIGER
SOULLESS 2009, *CHANGELESS* 2010, *BLAMELESS* 2010, *HEARTLESS* 2011
CIAR CULLEN
STEAMSIDE CHRONICLES 2010
GORDON DAHLQUIST
THE GLASS BOOKS OF THE DREAM EATERS 2006
WARREN ELLIS and PAUL DUFFIELD
FREAKANGLES: VOLUME 1 2008, *VOLUME II* 2009, *VOLUME III* 2009, *VOLUME IV* 2010, *VOLUME V* 2011 (each collected issues of graphic novel series in book form)
FELIX GILMAN
THE HALF-MADE WORLD 2010
NATHALIE GRAY
FULL STEAM AHEAD 2010
JONATHAN GREEN
PAX BRITANNIA 2007
PAUL GUINAN and ANINA BENNETT
BOILERPLATE 2009 (appears to be part graphic novel and part not)
GINN HALE
WICKED GENTLEMEN 2007
MARK HODDER
THE STRANGE AFFAIR OF SPRING HEELED JACK 2010, *THE CURIOUS CASE OF THE CLOCKWORK MAN* 2011
JONATHAN L. HOWARD
JOHANNES CABAL, THE NECROMANCER 2010, *JOHANNES CABAL, THE DETECTIVE* 2010
STEPHEN HUNT
THE COURT OF THE AIR 2009, *THE RISE OF THE IRON MOON* 2009, *KINGDOM BEYOND THE WAVES* 2010, *SECRETS OF THE FIRE SEA* 2010, *JACK CLOUDIE* 2011

ANTHONY HUSO
THE LAST PAGE 2011
WILLIAM JABLONSKY
THE CLOCKWORK MAN 2010
THEODORE JUDSON
FITZPATRICK'S WAR 2004
MERCEDES LACKEY
ELEMENTAL MASTERS series: *THE SERPENT'S SHADOW* 2002, *THE GATES OF SLEEP* 2003, *PHOENIX AND ASHES* 2004, *THE WIZARD OF LONDON* 2006, *RESERVED FOR THE CAT* 2008, *UNNATURAL ISSUE* 2011
JAY TOBIAS LAKE
MAINSPRING 2007, *ESCAPEMENT* 2009
JOE R. LANSDALE
ZEPPELINS WEST 2001, *FLAMING LONDON* 2006
KATIE MACALISTER
STEAMED 2010
GEORGE MANN (Newberry and Hobbs series)
THE AFFINITY BRIDGE 2008, *THE OSIRUS RITUAL* 2010, *THE IMMORTALITY ENGINE* 2011
LIZ MAVERICK
CRIMSON AND STEAM
JASON MURK
THE DREAMBOOK OF SKYLER DREAD 2009
CINDY SPENCER PAGE
STEAM AND SORCERY 2011
S.M. PETERS
WHITECHAPEL GODS 2008
CHERIE PRIEST
BONESHAKER 2009; *DREADNOUGHT* 2010; "Clementine" a novella 2010
JOE RABANSDALE
FLAMING ZEPPELINS: THE ADVENTURES OF NED THE SEAL
MIKE RESNICK
THE BUNTLINE SPECIAL 2010
ADAM ROBERTS
SWIFTLY 2010
S. M. STIRLING
THE PESHAWAR LANCERS 2001
JEAN-CHRISTOPHE VALTAT
AURORARAMA 2010

WRITING STEAMPUNK

STEAMPUNK EROTICA
(Could be collections of
short stories by various authors)

LIKE CLOCKWORK 2009
LIKE A WISP OF STEAM 2008
LIKE A CORSET UNBOUND 2009
D.L. KING
CARNAL MACHINES 2011
ORA LE BROCQ
STEAMPUNK EROTICA 2010, *STEAMPUNK EROTICA II* 2011

ANTHOLOGIES

MIKE ASHLEY and PAUL DI FILIPPO
STEAMPUNK PRIME: A VINTAGE STEAMPUNK READER 2010
JONATHAN D. BAIRD, ET AL
MONSTERS, MAGIC AND MACHINES: A STEAMGOTH ANTHOLOGY 2011
NICK GEVERS, Editor
EXTRAORDINARY ENGINES 2008
JEAN RABE and MARTIN H. GREENBERG
STEAMPUNK'D 2010
ANN VANDEERMEER and JEFF VANDERMEER
STEAMPUNK 2008, *STEAMPUNK II: STEAMPUNK RELOADED* 2010

NOVELS WITH STEAMPUNK ELEMENTS

SUSANNA CLARKE
JONATHAN STRANGE AND MR. NORRELL 2004
SETH GRAHAME-SMITH
ABRAHAM LINCOLN: VAMPIRE HUNTER 2010
A.E. MOORAT
QUEEN VICTORIA: DEMON HUNTER 2009

YOUNG ADULT MARKET

CASSANDRA CLARE
CLOCK WORK ANGEL 2010
CATHERINE FISHER
INCARCERON 2010, *SAPPHIQUE* 2010
DRU PAGLIASSOTTI

CLOCKWORK HEART 2008
PHILIP PULLMAN
HIS DARK MATERIALS (trilogy comprising *THE GOLDEN COMPASS* 2006, *SUBTLE KNIFE* 2007, and *AMBER SPYGLASS* 2007
SCOTT WESTERFELD
LEVIATHAN 2009, *BEMOUTH* 2010, *GOLIATH* 2011
NICK VALENTINO
THOMAS RILEY 2009

MIDDLE GRADE MARKET

D BENZ AND J.S. LEWIS
GREY GRIFFINS: THE CLOCKWORK CHRONICALS (*THE BRIMSTONE KEY* 2010, *THE RELIC HUNTERS* 2011)
L. BUCKLEY-ARCHER
THE GIDEON TRILOGY: THE TIME TRAVELERS 2007, *TIME THIEF* 2008, *TIME QUAKE* 2010
DAVID BURTON
SCOURGE: A GRIM DOYLE ADVENTURE 2010
JEREMY DE QUIDT and GARY BLYTHE
THE TOYMAKER 2008
MATTHEW KIRBY
CLOCKWORK THREE 2010
JOHN MCNICHOL
THE TRIPODS ATTACK! THE YOUNG CHESTERTON CHRONICLES 2008
KATE MILFORD and ANDREA OFFERMANN
THE BONESHAKER 2010
KENNETH. OPPEL
AIRBORN 2004
PHILIP REEVE
HUNGRY CITY CHRONICLES: MORTAL ENGINES QUARTET 2001 (4 in the series *Mortal Engines* 2004, *Predator's Gold* 2004, *Infernal Devices* 2005, *A Darkling Plain* 2007), *LARK LIGHT* 2006, *FEVER CRUMB* 2011
MARIE RUKOSKI
THE CABINET OF WONDERS: THE KRONOS CHRONICLES 2010, *THE CELESTIAL GLOBE* 2010, *THE JEWEL OF KALDERASH* 2011
ARTHUR SLADE
THE DARK DEEPS: THE HUNCHBACK ASSIGNMENTS 2009, *THE DARK DEEPS* 2010, *THE EMPIRE OF RUINS* 2011
LEMONY SNICKET

WRITING STEAMPUNK

A SERIES OF UNFORTUNATE EVENTS (some Steampunk elements) 1999-2006

THE GRAPHIC NOVELS
Year denotes start of series,
some still active, some discontinued

HIROMU ARAKAWA
FULLMETAL ALCHEMIST 2001
KIA ASAMIYA
STEAM DETECTIVES 1998
PHIL FOGLIO and KAJA FOGLIO
GIRL GENIUS 2001
MATT FRACTION and STEVEN SANDERS
THE FIVE FISTS OF SCIENCE 2006
LEA HERNANDEZ
CATHEDRAL CHILD (part of the *TEXAS STEAMPUNK* SERIES) 1998
JOE KELLY and CHRIS BACHALO
STEAMPUNK 2000
MIKE MIGNOLA
THE AMAZING SCREW-ON HEAD AND OTHER CURIOUS OBJECTS 2011
ALAN MOORE and KEVIN O'NEILL
THE LEAGUE OF EXTRAORDINARY GENTLEMEN 1999
ALEX SHEIKMAN
ROBOTIKA 2009, *ROBOTIKA II: FOR A FEW RUBLES MORE* 2009
BRYAN TALBOT
GRANDVILLE 2009
BRYAN TALBOT and MICHAEL MOORCOCK
THE ADVENTURES OF LUTHER ARKWRIGHT (first 1978-1982; 1987, 1989, 1999, webcomic 2006)
DOUG TENNAPEL
IRON WEST 2006

THE MOVIES

TIME AFTER TIME 1979
THE WILD, WILD WEST 1999
AROUND THE WORLD IN 80 DAYS various versions
JOURNEY TO THE CENTER OF THE EARTH various versions
20,000 LEAGUES BENEATH THE SEA various versions
THE LEAGUE OF EXTRAORDINARY GENTLEMEN 2003

VAN HELSING 2004
THE PRESTIGE 2006
SHERLOCK HOLMES 2009
SHERLOCK HOLMES II 2011

Movies with Steampunk Elements

SKY CAPTAIN AND THE WORLD OF TOMORROW 2004
THE ILLUSIONIST 2006
SERENITY 2005

ANIME and ANIMATED

ATLANTIS: THE LOST EMPIRE 2001
METROPOLIS 2001
HOWLS MOVING CASTLE 2004
STEAMBOY 2004

THE TV SHOWS
Year first episode aired given

THE WILD, WILD WEST 1965
BRISCO COUNTY JR 1993
THE SECRET ADVENTURES OF JULES VERNE 2000
FIREFLY 2002

ACKNOWLEDGEMENTS

As many writers have said before me, I would be remiss in not acknowledging the encouragement, aid (sometimes unconsciously given), and flurry of questions that led to the creation of *Writing Steampunk*.

Lea Nolan's list of YA and Middle Grade titles far surpassed those I'd found. Students in my various Steampunk online workshops inadvertently supplied me with more and more titles as they reported in on what they'd read and thus added to the lists given.

I accessed so many different websites, I lost track of where I found what, but I am indebted to all those who posted titles on those websites and in those blogs. Without those mentions, many a story would have eluded inclusion here.

Can't claim to have read every title, but have indulged in many of them. Each has done its part to cement the elements that make up 21st century Steampunk.

Beth Daniels

AUTHOR

Beth Daniels writes fiction as Beth Henderson, J.B. Dane, Lisa Dane, Beth Cruise and Nied Darnell. She is the author of over twenty-five published novels, with titles translated into over a dozen languages and available in over twenty countries. She has worked with editors at Berkley, Harlequin, Kensington/Zebra, Dorchester/Leisure, M. Evans, Simon and Schuster/Aladdin Paperbacks, and with a now defunct e-book publisher. She has also had short stories published as J.B. Dane, a number of non-fiction articles on writing popular fiction in e-zines as Beth Daniels, and is the creator and presenter of over fifty online workshops related to writing fiction, seven of them dealing with Steampunk. She is currently at work on her second and third Steampunk manuscripts.

For information on available/forthcoming titles or workshops, visit

www.RomanceAndMystery.com.

Contact her via email at
Beth@RomanceAndMystery.com.
Put STEAMPUNK in the subject line.

Made in the USA
Lexington, KY
28 May 2012